Jonathan could do nothing to stop his wife's losing battle with cancer. With twenty years into the ministry, he can't believe the Lord would leave him with both an empty nest and empty spot on the other side of the bed.

Kat, music teacher and mother of grown twins, feels settled in small-town Texas. Life may be dull, but it's predictable, unlike her life with her late husband. Kat concludes a happy, committed relationship with a male is impossible, so she makes peace with herself. If nuns can live celibate, why can't she?

One Sunday, Jonathan spies a golden beam of light descending upon Kat while she's directing the choir. Why hasn't he noticed how beautiful she was before? From here on out, Jonathan knows he'll be preachin' to the choir, but will Kat — and his congregation and their children — let him?

Preachin' to the Choir
Copyright © 2019 Cynthianna
ISBN: 978-1-4874-1593-8
Cover art by Carol Fiorillo

Published by eXtasy Books Inc or
Devine Destinies, an imprint of eXtasy Books Inc

Look for us online at:
www.eXtasybooks.com or www.devinedestinies.com

PREACHIN' TO THE CHOIR

BY

CYNTHIANNA

DEDICATION

To all who thought love passed them by but never gave up until it found them. You are the true romantics.

PROLOGUE

A powerful swell of organ music cloaked Jonathan Rawlins in an invisible curtain of solitude as he stepped into the pulpit. These past few Sundays felt different. In his over twenty years in the ministry, he couldn't once remember experiencing such an unsettling awareness while conducting a worship service, including his first faltering attempts fresh out of the seminary. Here it was again, that odd feeling of restlessness permeating his soul. He tried to shake it off, but it clung to him like grit on a screen window after a dust storm.

The members of his flock lifted their encouraging faces and fixed their gazes upon his, waiting with polite expectation for his sermon to commence. He had been blessed today, as the lessons were relatively straightforward. He began by re-reading a part of the Old Testament passage:

"From Ecclesiastes, fourth chapter: Two are better than one, because they have a good return for their work: if one falls down, his friend can help him up. But pity the man who falls and has no one to help him up! Also, if two lie down together, they will keep warm. But how can one keep warm alone? Though one may be overpowered, two can defend themselves. A cord of three strands is not quickly broken . . ."

Jonathan's voice faded away. He cleared his throat once, twice, but still the words were trapped. His vocal battery had died and needed a jump. He reached under the pulpit and found the small glass of ice water one of the altar guild ladies always placed on the hidden shelf for just such an occasion and took a long, cool sip.

The tension in his throat immediately relaxed, but the mental roadblock remained—anxious seconds ticked by slowly. Jonathan put the glass away and glanced over his page of notes, desperate to push his stalled vehicle of a sermon back on the open road.

What was he going to talk about this morning? Oh, yes, the significance of the three strands. What did the three strands represent? The first stood for the Lord, the second for himself, and the third strand? The third strand of his own cord had been cut this past winter. Jonathan's cord had unraveled as he'd laid to rest his wife of twenty-five years in the cold, rocky earth of the Texas Hill County.

A dull, familiar ache pierced his heart. Jonathan turned to the front left pew for strength. It had been Ruth's favorite spot. Recently dear Aunt Mabel, as everyone called his biggest cheerleader in the congregation, had occupied the seat, but this week Aunt Mabel was in the hospital mending from a hip operation. The empty spot taunted him.

Jonathan curled his fingers into tight fists at his sides. Frustration blossomed faster than bluebonnets beside the highway after a spring shower. What could he say? Where could he go? Who could he turn to?

He took a deep breath and cleared his throat again, praying for inspiration. Just when all seemed lost, something in the corner of his eye caught Jonathan's attention. His gaze wandered from the left side of the sanctuary to the right and rested on the choir loft. A sense of peace and strength flooded his frame as he focused on the familiar figure seated front row center—St. Luke's new choir director, Kat Dubcek.

Kat raised both her hands in a thumbs-up motion. Her radiant blue-gray eyes and infectious grin lightened the burden Jonathan had been carrying for the past five months. His confidence soared. Smiling his approval, he returned to his sermon notes.

The next fifteen minutes sped by in a glorious blur. With the last "Amen" Jonathan knew he had done it. He had preached his sermon and had been graced with many thoughtful smiles in return. Both relief and anticipation surged through his veins. He could do this. He could still be a pastor to his flock—

And all because Kat Dubcek had indicated he could.

Returning to his chair, Jonathan raised his hymnal high, observing Kat as she took her place to direct the choir's offertory selection. Raising her arms wide in a welcoming gesture, the choir members rose to their feet. She prompted Gayle at the organ to begin with a discreet nod, then turned her full attention to their performance.

At first it seemed an ordinary enough beginning to an ordinary song, but then the miraculous happened. A sudden burst of sunlight filtered through the narrow, jewel-toned stained-glass windows above the choir loft, bathing Kat in a heavenly glow.

Jonathan shivered. He scanned the sanctuary to see how his congregation was reacting to such a miraculous display of light and color, but no one appeared to notice this extraordinary phenomenon.

Doesn't anyone else see it?

He contemplated the glorious halo of light that encompassed Kat's ash-blonde hair, streaking it with iridescent flashes of spun silver. The creamy white of her choir robe had taken on a stunning brightness, the like of which hadn't been seen since Christ's appearance on the Mount of Transfiguration. There could be no other explanation for it—an angel had lighted upon the earth and taken up residence in St. Luke's choir loft.

Kat's strong alto floated above the organ in distinct counter to the melody, its harmony blending beautifully with the handful of other voices. Her mellow tone resonated with a rich and sensual quality, enrapturing him. He sat transfixed, captivated. Her misty-blue eyes were sparkling sapphires. Her full lips burned red as if kissed by the same purifying coal that had touched the prophet Isaiah's. Her skin glowed alabaster, as smooth and soft as a dove's breast.

Beneath the gleaming radiance, Jonathan sensed the real Kat, both ethereal and earthy. He knew she wasn't some sort of celestial being, although undoubtedly she was one of God's better creations. He continued adoring her from across the room, stealing glances over the edge of his hymn book. It was as if Kat had become translucent, and only he could sense the honesty of her soul and the true depths of her compassion. To Jonathan, Kat Dubcek exemplified the very essence of an angel wrapped up in a beautiful woman's body.

Jonathan's voice rose strong and assured, joining the congregation in the singing of the doxology. No longer did he entertain the overwhelming notion of *going it alone* as he had tried so valiantly to do these past months since Ruth passed away. No longer did his heart feel lost and lonely because no one sat in the first pew, left side. No longer would he worry about whom to preach to —

Because from here on out, he was preaching to the choir.

CHAPTER ONE

Three months earlier

"Why do people think playing the Good Samaritan is so easy?"

Kat bit her tongue—hard. It wouldn't do if she let loose with a string of swear words while she was doing her good deed for the day, particularly considering the locale.

She refocused her attention on removing the folded clothes from the dresser drawers and packing them into boxes. Why she had bothered to dress up for this assignment she had no earthly idea, other than Darla had said on the phone it was Pastor Jon who needed a helping hand. A *female* helping hand, Darla had stressed. Kat, who hated to make a poor impression on anybody, especially the man who had welcomed her into the church, had decided jeans and a t-shirt somehow would not be appropriate attire. Lucky for her, she had picked out dress flats over high heels.

Kat frowned. Darla, Pastor's Gal Friday, could have easily taken a few hours away from typing the Sunday bulletin to help with this onerous chore. Pastor Jon's daughter, Elizabeth, had a legitimate exemption from helping, as her doctor had consigned her to bed rest for the remainder of her pregnancy, but constantly dieting Darla definitely could use the exercise. Any excuse to pry Darla from her desk chair was a good one.

The soft touch of a plaid flannel nightgown against Kat's fingertips felt warm and comforting like a grandmother's hug. Then it struck her—just how many women in her age group actually wore such an enticing garment to bed on a regular basis. Before her mind could wander too far down that path, a squeak of the floorboards alerted her to her employer's presence.

"I suspect you'll find a lot of *like new* items in the bureau."

Jonathan Rawlins's voice was flat, emotionless, tired. A stab of pity pierced Kat's heart. Jonathan's six-feet-plus height seemed halved as he stood, shoulders slumped, in the bedroom doorway. Had it really been only six weeks since Ruth's funeral? Here she was rummaging like a common thief through his late wife's intimate apparel.

Not to say Ruth's lingerie drawer was altogether very exciting, Kat had to admit. Its contents were very functional, very basic, bleached white cotton with little color or satin to liven things up. A sudden pang of guilt stabbed at her heart when Kat considered all the pairs of silky, leopard-spotted, black lace-edged undergarments she owned.

Wiping damp palms against her cotton twill dress pants, Kat rose from her kneeling position.

"You're right about *like new*." Kat held up a pair of brand-new half slips. "She never took the tags off these. See?"

Jonathan turned away. "I don't have to. I know. She even told me to keep the receipt so I could take them back to the store after . . ."

His words faded away unspoken but understood. Kat swallowed the jagged lump building in her throat. She crossed to him and placed a gentle hand on his shoulder.

"If you like, I could return them for you and get a refund."

"No, it's not necessary." He patted the fingers she rested on his shoulders and cracked a wane smile. "I'm sure the women's shelter could make good use of them."

Awareness surged from their point of contact. A curious

tingle traveled the length of Kat's arm and along her spine. It was a pleasurable sensation but totally inappropriate to the current situation. Somehow the touch felt a bit too comfortable, too familiar. Kat quickly retracted her hand.

"The women's shelter can always use donations of new clothes," she rattled on. "They'll be glad to give you a statement for your taxes. I know the shelter was one of . . . one of Ruth's favorite charities."

"Yes. Yes, it was."

One of mine, too.

She could never thank the shelter folks enough for their support of her and the twins during that frightful transition in her life oh-so-many years ago. She and the twins might not even be alive today if it hadn't been for the shelter.

"Kat? You okay?" Jonathan's concerned expression cut into her reverie. "You looked far away for a moment."

"Did I?" Kat forced herself to return to clothes sorting, tendering a curt laugh to cover her embarrassment at being caught reveling in a memory she rarely dragged out of the closet anymore. "After I finish clearing out the drawers, is there anything else you can think of that you want me to help you with?"

"Not really, but I know there are hundreds of things around here that should be . . . that should be . . ." He shrugged, at a loss for words.

"Donated?" Kat suggested.

"Yes, donated. It's been a long time since we did any real weeding out around here. If I took you on a tour of the house, could you point things out to me?"

A tour of the Rawlins's tastefully decorated home? Kat tried not to cringe at the suggestion. She always felt like a Martha Stewart-reject whenever she compared her own hodgepodge home-decorating skills to others. It brought on an inferiority complex of the first degree. Ruth had been a good friend to her, patiently wooing her to become an active member of St. Luke's. Ruth's gentle support had helped her to heal both emotionally and spiritually. It was only fitting Kat return the kindness to Ruth's family now she was gone.

"Sure, Pastor." Kat grinned—like Ruth had grinned at her whenever she'd needed encouraging. "It's why I came here today, to help you make a clean break—um, sweep, I mean."

"Great." Jonathan exited the bedroom, motioning for Kat to follow. "Let's start with the front hall closet. There's so much junk crammed in there. I apologize in advance if it comes crashing down when I open the door."

Those ratty old sweaters could go.

Jonathan shook his head at the thought. Kat had said it only this afternoon as they'd perused the crowded contents of the hall closet. How could he tell her the tattered and torn relics were more precious to him than gold since they were gifts from Ruth?

He knew Kat was right. His life needed to be cleared of the past along with the clutter in his closets. Even Ruth had threatened to pitch his cherished articles of clothing last spring before she'd received her diagnosis.

Jonathan gently replaced the old ruby glass paperweight he had been contemplating on the scratched oak surface of his desk and switched off the lamp. Had it only been a year ago Ruth had received the news about her cancer? How quickly it had spread from her ovaries—she had been only forty-eight years old. Why did God want to have her all to Himself so soon?

Jonathan rose from his desk chair and entered the long hallway to begin his evening walk down memory lane. A colorful tapestry of photos smiled at him from the walls—smiles of hope, smiles of joy, smiles of love and promise. They had been blessed with two healthy children—a strong son and a loving daughter. Eli seemed so determined in his senior photo, ready to take on the world. Eli, proud and brave, in his Marines dress uniform. Elizabeth in her prom dress with Joshua in a tux at her side. Elizabeth in another long gown and Joshua in yet another tuxedo marching down the aisle together as man and wife five years later. Soon, their offspring's photos would decorate the photo gallery as well.

At the end of his nightly journey, just as Jonathan's steps veered toward the right to enter their bedroom, smiled Ruth. Ruth, dressed in her powder-blue Easter dress, her only solo portrait on the family's walk of fame. She had been ashamed of buying it all those years ago when the photographer had shown her how well it had turned out, but she had purchased it all the same along with the family's group portrait. It was a waste of money she had berated herself later, but Jonathan had framed it before she could even think of returning it to the studio for a refund. It was the best decision he had ever made. Now Ruth kept silent watch over him as he lay upon the mattress which permanently carried her shallow dent next to his own deeper one.

Sleep never came easy in a lonely bed. Jonathan closed his devotional booklet an hour later, placing it on the nightstand before chucking his tortoiseshell-rimmed glasses beside his Bible and switching off the bedside lamp. He closed his eyes, and an image of Kat Dubcek centered in his brain.

He could see Kat's smiling face as clearly as he could see Ruth's portrait, but whereas Ruth smiled shyly through tightly compressed lips lightly accented in pale pink, her round face framed by a curtain of auburn curls, Kat flashed white teeth boldly surrounded by full, reddish-purple lips, topped by silvery-blonde, bobbed hair. There was no way to confuse the two women. The differences between them were like night and day.

For one thing, there was little shy or retiring about Kat. In the last three months since she had assumed Ruth's duties as choir director, Kat had proven herself a worthy successor. Whenever he picked a real clunker of a hymn, she never hesitated to point out how impossible it would be for the congregation to sing and that he should leave the musical decisions to the professionals. She had saved his bacon more than once from making some potentially disastrous choices that could have alienated church members. For her decisiveness, he would be eternally grateful.

Jonathan didn't hold Kat's directness, her blunt style of stating things against her, either. Not at all. You always knew where you stood with Kat. He could tell how difficult it had been going through Ruth's things to pack them up to send to the women's shelter, but she had buckled down and done the job without voicing a complaint. Kat was both dependable and talented, an effective combination indeed.

What puzzled Jonathan most about St. Luke's new choir mistress was that Kat had been without a husband for some years now. He found it odd that a woman with such a remarkable personality and pleasing appearance would choose to remain single, but he admired her all the same. It took a strong woman to raise two children without a father's help. Jonathan had made a mental note on several occasions that, when faced with difficulties, Kat didn't bemoan her lot in life. On the contrary, she always displayed a cheerful face and performed her job to the best of her abilities.

Jonathan frowned. He really couldn't see himself living as a *loner* like Kat. He had always had Ruth beside him as he tackled the challenges of the ministry. They had married their senior year in college, and Ruth had worked hard to help support their growing family while he'd attended seminary. She had always been there for him, through both the happy and the sad, the challenging and the frustrating, the good and the bad. Now here it was, the worst time of his life, and she was gone.

"If people like Kat Dubcek can go it alone, make a contribution and not fall apart, I can, too," Jonathan said to the empty room.

He sat up and glanced at his bedside clock—one in the morning. He was really losing it. He needed someone beside him to talk to, to share his problems with, to keep the other side of the bed warm.

He sighed. "Let's face it. It's time for me to get a dog."

"Kat, pick up if you're there. It's BB. Aw, c'mon, Kat. Be a good sport and pick up. I'll make it worth your while. You know how much I can make it worth your while . . ."

Kat grabbed her pillow and crammed it over her head, hoping beyond hope to block out the lecherous laughter and heavy breathing on the phone. She could kill that man! Couldn't he take *no* for an answer? You'd think a man who fit the dictionary definition of a *player* could remember that he had played one too many cards as far as she was concerned.

It had been over three months since Kat last went on what jokingly could be called a date, and the last time she'd had actual sex? Sometime back in the Stone Age. But that was neither here nor there. She had promised Ruth right before she'd passed away that she wouldn't get herself mixed up with any more *losers* like BB. She deserved better.

It wasn't easy being celibate. Night after night she wondered did she, Katrina Dubcek, forty-five, mother of college-age twins, music teacher to the mindless masses of the middle school, still qualify as a woman. She had her doubts.

"Kat? You there, my little pussy willow?"

That was it. She was going to disconnect her answering machine tomorrow. Kat glanced over at the alarm clock. One o'clock in the morning. BB was drunk, definitely drunk. If there was one thing she didn't need in her life again, it was another stinking drunk — no matter how handsome or well-to-do he was.

The painful memories she had quickly squelched earlier in the day came flooding back in all their hideous intensity. Thank heavens for the women's shelter. Not many small communities were blessed with such a resource. Thank heavens Germantown, Texas, was one of them.

The last fateful image she held of her late ex-husband sprang unbidden before her eyes. Dirk had come home very drunk and angry that night after gambling away their meager savings in a dirty poker game. It had been a blessing the twins had slept soundly and hadn't heard their raised voices or the sounds of shattering objects as their argument had grown more and more heated.

But somehow she had found the courage and the presence of mind to call the cops and have Dirk hauled off to jail. With the authorities involved in their ugly sham of a marriage at last, it wasn't long before charges of theft and embezzlement were being leveled against Dirk from his past and current employers.

Kat hadn't held her breath that a lengthy prison sentence could make a new man out of her gambling addict of a husband. She had been hard pressed to shed a tear when she'd learned a few months later that Dirk had been murdered in prison by a fellow inmate he'd cheated in cards.

"Kat, c'mon, I said I was sorry about that other woman you talked to on the phone that night," BB pleaded across the telephone wires, bringing Kat back to the present. "Please talk to me. Aw, c'mon on Alley Kat. Do a little howlin' for me—"

Click. Brrrrr . . .

"Hallelujah, he's passed out." Kat sat up in bed and sighed, grateful BB's lewd whining had ceased. "What goes around comes around."

She slipped from the covers and padded to the kitchen for a long drink of cold water. Maybe BB's harassment was God's way of getting her attention. He was probably telling her she needed to forgive and forget Dirk for the multitude of sins he'd committed against her and the kids all those years ago. Lord, she was trying to give up her grudge, honest she was, but after fourteen years it was still difficult.

About the only thing Kat really felt sorry about was lying to her children whenever they asked whatever became of their sometimes-doting father. It was better if they thought Dirk had gone off to Mexico and been killed fighting as a toreador in a bullring, she reasoned, than for them to discover it had been a stolen butter knife from the prison kitchen slipped under the ribs which had done him in.

Kat retrieved a juice glass from the cabinet and flipped the reverse osmosis filter spigot open. Yuck. Warm water. It was the hundred-degree highs of late May that did that. Why anyone wanted to live in a part of the world where people made snowmen from white spray-painted tumbleweeds and drank mineral-laden tap water at body temperature, she'd never been too sure. Here she had landed in the Texas Hill Country and here she was likely to stay put until she, too, was as dry as one of those comically decorated tumbleweeds.

Kat strolled through the kitchen and into the moonlit living room. She put her tepid drink on a coaster and took a seat at her spinet piano, softly playing Beethoven's *Fur Elise* from memory.

Why she was playing using the damper pedal made no sense. She was alone. Kevin and Keely lived off campus a hundred miles away while attending summer classes at UT, Austin. Mister Friskies had made a premature exit from this earthly existence six months ago due to feline leukemia. The overdose of drugs the vet had injected him with had acted quickly and painlessly.

"What a way to go."

Kat's fingers stumbled over the keys. She was growing maudlin in her old age. She sighed and started over again.

"Face it," she lectured herself. "If your current life is a little on the boring side, except when BB feels like making an obscene phone call, well, that's to be expected. A safe and predictable existence is preferable to the sheer chaos that reigned when Dirk lived here. Remember that next time you're tempted to pick up the phone on Mister District Attorney Heavy Breather."

Kat continued playing, letting her conscious mind go and her muscle memory take control. What she would do without the release of music in her life, she couldn't say, but she was thankful for it. Poor Pastor Jon—all he had were his shelves and shelves of books and ratty, old cardigans for comfort, and old sweaters with gaping holes in the elbows. The mice must be having a field day in his closets.

"Maybe he ought to adopt a cat like I'm thinking of doing?" Kat thought out loud. "Yeah, that's a good idea—sort of a Mister Friskies II. Cats are great listeners. Much better than kids, anyway, and cheaper than a therapist, but isn't Ruth allergic to animal fur or something?"

Kat tripped over an arpeggio.

"Oh, I forgot. Poor, poor Pastor Jon. To lose someone as special as Ruth. The whole horrible thing just doesn't seem possible."

Kat bowed her head in silent prayer, then took up where she'd left off, allowing her memories to drift along with the flow of the music. It hadn't been all that hard for her to lose Dirk. Dirk had pretty much lost himself years before he'd gotten himself incarcerated. Losing Dirk could never be compared with losing Ruth.

Kat sighed. It was the embarrassment of knowing what other folks were saying about her marriage to Dirk which had kept her from attending St. Luke's for years. Although she'd dutifully sent the twins to Sunday school and catechism classes, she'd somehow kept herself off the church *radar* for many years. She realized now she would have remained a lost soul in plain sight forever if Pastor Gebhardt hadn't retired and Ruth Rawlins hadn't come along.

Ruth had made it her personal mission to bring wayward Kat back into the worshiping community. It was the sort of thing both Ruth and Pastor Jon were best at—rescuing lost souls. What else could you expect from such kind-hearted spirits who possessed such firm convictions?

"Ruth was a very special lady," Kat said, and she meant it. There had been both tears and smiles at Ruth's funeral—sadness, because she was gone, but also joy because she was no longer in such pain. Everyone in Germantown knew the heavenly ranks could do no better than recruit Ruth Rawlins as one of their own.

"You know, I was awfully hard on Pastor Jon today," Kat admitted to herself, her hands flowing across the keys. "Those *holey* sweaters make him look homey, accessible, and his tortoiseshell glasses perched on the end of his nose give him a reassuring appearance, and his dated brown loafers are a harmless eccentricity, and the way he sometimes forgets to comb his hair . . . well, we can't all primp like movie stars."

Kat picked up the tempo. "Jonathan Rawlins isn't an altogether bad-looking sort, I guess, but he definitely isn't going to grace the cover of *GQ* anytime soon. On the plus side, folks are never put off by his humble demeanor."

A calming peace wrapped itself around Kat like a sun-warmed quilt. She brought the composition to a close and made a mental note to bring up the cat idea to Darla at choir practice. Darla would know if anyone in the congregation had some kittens to give away to good homes. One for her, one for Pastor.

"Mister Friskies II wouldn't mind a sibling living in the parsonage," Kat reasoned. "After all, it never hurts to have connections in high places."

Four months later

"I've got a secret. I've got a secret," Darla Dierdorf chanted upon entering the choir room.

"That's nice," Kat replied, going about her business. The contents of the music folders were a complete and utter mess. She couldn't fathom why grown adults of average intelligence couldn't put their copies away in some semblance of order. Her eighth-graders at the middle school kept their folders organized better.

Darla grinned and waggled a fleshy finger in front of Kat's nose. "You'll never guess who it's about."

"Who's what about?"

"My secret, of course."

Darla carefully situated her one-hundred-ninety-pound, five-foot-two frame into her seat and made a big production of tossing her lengthy, thick, russet-brown locks over her shoulders. Darla was proud of how she hadn't cut her hair since her high school graduation fifteen years ago, but somehow the Barbie doll hairdo seemed a bit dated.

"You've got really bad hearin' for a choir director, y'know that?" Darla teased.

Smiling, Kat looked up from her sheet music straightening. "It helps sometimes."

Refocusing her attention on her task, Kat wondered what on earth had possessed her to take over as director of St. Luke's choir of the terminally tone deaf. Oh, yes, it was

Ruth. She had done it for Ruth. The cancer treatments had really drained her of her energy, Ruth had said. She'd then expressed such confidence in Kat's abilities that the act of passing the choir director's reins to Kat was *a fait accompli* before anyone knew it. How could Kat refuse?

Some days choir directing was an exercise in patience. Teaching children was one thing—Kat expected kids to stumble and have trouble keeping up—but grown-ups? She'd realized too late that she was too much of a perfectionist to be leading adult amateurs.

"So, do ya wanna hear about the latest news or don't ya?" Darla asked, intruding on Kat's thoughts. "I didn't come fifteen minutes early for choir practice just to warm up."

Kat shook her head. "It'd be nice if you did. You'd be able to hit those high notes with more authority if you did warm up your upper range a little before rehearsals."

"Don't worry none. I'll be able to," Darla assured her with a wave. "Matthias just has to step on my toes and then I can squeak it on up there with the best of them. Now, about my secret, it's—"

The door swung open at that precise moment, and in walked tall, dark, and terminally timid Brenna Bangle. At once, the chatty church secretary stilled her tongue.

"Hello, Brenna." Kat handed a folder to the newcomer and winked at Darla. "You aren't fixin' to tell me your secret with an audience, huh?"

Darla mouthed to Kat, "I'll tell ya later," then swiveled in her seat and diverted all her attention to her fellow choir member. "Why, hello there, Bren. I hear congratulations are in order."

"They are?" Brenna replied softly.

"You've been promoted to line manager at the ice cream factory, or did I get my wires crossed?" Darla queried. "It wasn't someone else, was it?"

"No, it was me," Brenna acknowledged with a shy smile. "But how did you know? I just found out myself yesterday."

"I have my sources, namely my hubby, Dillon. Dilly always lets me in on the good news when it comes to church members at the dairy. Keep up the good work, and you may be kicked upstairs with the paper-pushers before long."

Brenna blushed. "You really think so?"

"I know so, honey. Ain't that the gospel truth, Sally?"

"Probably," Sally Dobbins mumbled. The petite, blue-rinsed matron had slipped into the room unnoticed and taken a seat in the back as usual.

"What day is it?" she asked Kat, glancing nervously back and forth.

"It's Wednesday. It's choir practice, remember?" Kat grinned at the nervous-looking woman, then counted out music folders for the rest of the early arrivals. Sally had obviously forgotten to take her medication today.

"I'm singing in the choir, right?"

"Right beside me." Darla patted the empty chair next to her. "Come sit up here, Sally, so you can help the soprano section."

Sally's doe-like eyes widened. "Can't I just sit in the back?"

"Sure." Kat handed her a folder. "Just don't throw the bass section off when you're singing the descant and not the melody."

"Bass section?" Darla quirked an eyebrow. "Have we captured another male besides Matthias who can belt it out that low?"

Kat shrugged. "No, Neal is going to give singing bass a try. The tenor part is too high for him."

"Everything is too high for him," Darla grumbled under her breath. "Anything with more than one note is too much for him."

"Who will sing the tenor part now?" Brenna wondered.

"I might," Kat said. "Unless you want to give it a try."

Brenna nodded enthusiastically. "I could do that. Most of the time it's well within my range."

"Just don't out-sing the other female parts," Darla interjected. "Our balance has been really off lately."

Kat frowned. She knew Darla relished her role as unheralded assistant choir director too much at times, but they'd received decent comments on their performances.

"Who said our balance was off?" Kat asked.

"I'll tell ya later," Darla whispered, pointing at the arrival of their accompanist and her husband.

"Are we late?" Neal Wallace took a chair behind the sopranos. Thin, graying hair sat atop Neal's thin and graying frame in perfect contrast to his wife Gayle's form. She sported a roundish figure and a bottled golden beehive and green cat-eye glasses.

"We can't be late." Gayle glanced at her watch, taking her place at the piano. "I have seven straight up."

"So do I," Sally added. "Is it time to go now?"

"We haven't started yet," Kat informed her.

Gayle scrunched up her nose and grinned, her fleshy face crinkling like crushed velvet. "Thanks for clearing off the mess on top of this thing. I can actually tell it's some sort of keyboard instrument now and not just a sheet music organizer."

Kat returned the smile. "You're very welcome. Which reminds me, everyone please remember to clear out your folders of old copies from time to time. Just place the old music in the metal basket here on the table." She then addressed her troops in much the same manner she lectured her middle school classes.

"Are we all ready now?" She raised an eyebrow in expectation.

Heads nodded, and folders flipped open.

"I've added the next three Sunday's selections to your folder, so let's do our warm up on *Faith of Our Fathers*."

Neal raised a lanky hand. "Where's Matthias? I need him to show me how to sing bass."

Kat clenched her fists at her sides. Tall, with a commanding presence, Matthias Ringleschmidt's slight graying at the temples and powerful, deep voice only added to his air of authority. It was no wonder he had run unopposed as congregation president for two terms, but they could sit here and chat for hours if she let them. She cued Gayle to begin the song's intro. "I believe Matthias said he'd be a bit late tonight, so try your best for now."

"How's Aunt Mabel getting along? Does anyone know?" Brenna asked in a hushed tone.

"She's doing much better," Darla volunteered. "In fact, she told me the physical therapy is going so well she should be able to stand without a walker by next week."

Gayle continued playing softly but added, "Doris told me that a week or so after Kara delivers her baby she'll be back at choir practice, too."

"Doris and her poor, sick daughter, and poor ol' Mabel and her hip," Sally moaned, rocking in her seat, "and Ruth, dear sweet Ruth, no longer with us. I miss her."

Darla sighed. "Don't we all."

A somber cloud descended over the room. Gayle hit a clunker. Kat flinched. Gayle lifted her hands from the keys momentarily, then continued playing.

Neal scratched his chin. "Didn't Jim Bexley say he wanted to join choir?"

Brenna nodded. "Yeah, I think he did say that a while back, but he's been real busy working overtime at the dairy and —"

"That's wonderful news," Kat interrupted her talkative

assembly. She motioned to their accompanist to start the piece over. "Now, let's begin again. We need to focus on our singing, people. Remember, our fellowship hour begins after practice, not during it."

The look of disappointment on their faces rivaled those of her middle school classes. Her chin dropped to her chest in defeat.

"All right. Y'all can have five more minutes of yakking and *then* we sing. Okay?"

The happy hubbub started up again.

Kat sighed.

I'll wager the director of the Houston Opera never has to put up with this sort of behavior.

"What would I do with my evenings if the church didn't have a board meeting each and every weeknight?"

Jonathan turned from his fruitless rummaging through the semi-barren kitchen cabinets of St. Luke's parsonage. All those wonderful frozen casseroles from the funeral had long ago been consumed, and he had never been much of a cook. He sighed. Ruth had always found such pleasure working in her cozy little kitchen with its blue gingham-checked curtains and china duck motif. He didn't wish to change a thing in it. But every time he gazed at one of her cherished collectibles in the china cabinet he practically lost his appetite. Board meetings with their cookies and coffee at least tided him over on these occasions.

Of course, he didn't have to attend every meeting of every board. A good pastor knew it was better to let the flock handle things on their own without his constant input. But it couldn't hurt to show up every now and then to let them know he was there if they needed him and that he was interested in what they were doing, he reasoned with himself. It showed he cared.

But something had been off-kilter in his existence this past month, and Jonathan knew it. Here it was, Wednesday evening at seven twenty-five, and he'd already attended four gatherings this week and wished there was some other group he could drop in on. It was crazy. People might really talk if he crashed the Ladies' Sewing Circle tomorrow morning.

"I could call Elizabeth for the third time this week," he mumbled to himself, tossing a box of instant macaroni and cheese onto the counter. "Nah, she needs to be resting—not catering to her old man's loneliness."

Jonathan's thoughts drifted once again to what was happening next door.

Choir practice.

He reached above the kitchen work aisle to retrieve a pan.

Kat is there. I do need to ask her about the lessons.

No, now wasn't the right time. He couldn't interrupt the choir's rehearsal just to inflict himself on their lovely director.

"She is lovely, isn't she?" Jonathan heaved a long sigh. He'd caught himself sighing a lot lately. Ever since Kat Dubcek had cast her spell on him that magical Sunday three weeks ago, he couldn't get her out of his mind. He actually wanted to get on with living now.

The season to mourn was over. Summer was here. Just the thought of Kat had Jonathan wanting to whistle, to sing—to play the piano during family gatherings like Ruth had. Then one day this past week it had struck him—Kat was a music teacher. Like all underpaid professionals, she taught music lessons on the side. What better way to get to know Kat than to sit close beside her on a piano bench?

Jonathan glanced up at the clock. Choir practice was about over. Maybe he should casually stroll over and talk to Kat about the piano lessons? It was a foolish idea, but he couldn't help himself. He returned the lonely box of mac-cheese to the cupboard and hung up the pan.

"It's decided," he announced to the rows of comical duck figurines waddling along the china cabinet's shelves. "Kat Dubcek is about to acquire a new pupil."

CHAPTER TWO

"Night, y'all."

Before Kat could gather her things together and make good her escape from the choir room, a pudgy finger tapped her on the shoulder

"Now can I tell you my secret?" Darla asked.

Kat sighed and nodded her consent. "Go ahead. I'm listening."

She did her best to tune out most of Darla's chatter and not act too interested. It didn't take much encouragement to get Darla going, and once she did . . . Kat really needed to go home and get her beauty rest before next week. She busied herself rearranging the metal chairs, then opened the filing cabinet to pull a few selections she wanted to try with the children's choir in the fall.

" . . . And what really struck me odd after that was how Pastor Jon said he was so impressed with your solo on Sunday. Then he came on down here and started going through the music files."

Kat's ears perked up. She halted her fingers' crawl through the filing drawer. "My solo?"

"Yes, Pastor said you did a great solo on Sunday, even after I told him you didn't have one—you were just the only one singing alto since Brenna was out of town and Mabel was still in the hospital."

"Wow." Kat closed the file drawer with a swish of her hip and crossed her arms. "We must have sounded mighty off-balanced if he noticed something like that. Thank him for pointing it out to us. I'll have to remember to shut up when I'm standing in front from now on."

Darla threw up her hands. "Sure, do that, but you're not getting the really intriguing part of what I'm saying."

Kat rolled her eyes and laughed. "Isn't all gossip supposed to be intriguing?"

"Of course it is." Darla looked only slightly hurt by Kat's remark. "I meant, what do you think about Pastor Jon rummaging around in the files and pulling sheet music out? Don't you find it a bit strange?"

Kat stared a full second at her glib informant and shrugged. She had to admit she was curious as to why some of the music files she had just perused seemed a bit thinner than others.

"You're telling me that Pastor Jon came down here and started going through the music files?"

"Yes, odd, isn't it? Doesn't he let you and Gayle handle these kinds of things?"

Kat furrowed her brow, thinking. She had a point there. "Usually."

"I thought so, too. Now here's the real icing on the cake." Darla took a deep breath before spilling the beans. "The really big news is he's been whistling to himself for the last two days."

"Pastor Jon whistling?" Kat couldn't conceive of such an outrageous notion. The idea was simply absurd, ludicrous, insane. She giggled. "You've got to be kidding. Pastor Jon is not the whistling type. He's an okay singer, but he doesn't possess a lot of musical confidence. You must have mistaken someone whistling on the office radio for Pastor."

"He didn't have a radio on, and it was only him and me here in the building at the time, unless . . ." Darla looked furtively around and lowered her voice to a whisper. "Unless we've got ourselves a ghost. You don't think it's the spirit of

25

Ruth Rawlins, do you?"

Ruth?

Kat felt like she had been hit in the stomach. Everyone at St. Luke's seemed to be nursing a terminal case of missing Ruth Rawlins.

Kat did her best to hide the rising irritation in her voice. "Oh, for Pete's sake! What a thing to say. Ruth is *not* haunting our church. She is singing with the choir celestial at this very moment. It's too bad, too, since we definitely could use her strong soprano down here."

Kat snatched up her purse and papers and sprinted up the back stairs toward the choir loft to leave her director's copy on the music stand. Darla followed close on her heels.

"Then there's only one other explanation for his whistling," Darla said, panting, breathless from the short climb.

Kat switched on the lights along the side wall of the chancel area. "What explanation is that?"

"Pastor's got himself a sweetheart."

"A *what*?" Kat took a step backward, tripped over a fallen hymnal, and landed hard on her tailbone.

Darla raced over to Kat's side. "You okay? Shocking idea, isn't it?"

Speechless by her sudden fall, Kat took a deep breath and accepted Darla's helping hand. It was a blessing she was wearing slacks or else she could have received a nasty rug burn on her backside.

"It's not shocking, just surprising," Kat managed at last. She bent to retrieve the spilled contents of her purse and the scattered pages of music. "I just didn't think it would happen so soon after . . ." She swallowed hard. "I mean, he isn't the type who gets out much."

Darla nodded her agreement, then gathered Kat's dropped items. "I know. I know exactly how much he gets out of the office Tuesday through Friday while I'm here. Nada. He even eats his lunch at his desk."

Kat accepted her lipstick, mirror, and address book from Darla, depositing them in her purse before dusting off her derrière with her hands. "True enough. Most folks know when and where to reach him on any given weekday."

"Pastor and Ruth were such a . . . such a team." Darla's pained expression said it all. "It's just such an unsettling thought. I'm flabbergasted he'd even look at another woman, let alone whistle over one."

"Let's not jump to conclusions." Kat sat on the organist's bench and rearranged the scattered pages of her director's copy across the organ's broad music stand. "You know, he may just be feeling better about life in general. The mental fog of losing Ruth is lifting. Maybe he's taking a mood elevator?"

"He's not taking any drugs that I know of," Darla said, biting her lip. She sat beside Kat on the bench and placed the sheets she had retrieved there as well. "I don't think he's hitting the bottle."

"That's a relief," Kat muttered.

Darla raised an eyebrow. "What did you say?"

Kat blushed. "Uh, nothing." Totally discombobulated now, Kat babbled on to hide her fluster. "Maybe he's just happy about his soon-to-be grandbaby. Elizabeth is doing okay, isn't she?"

"Right on track, according to all reports."

"That explains it then. Having a first grandchild can be a very exciting time."

"Oh, I agree."

Kat's smile almost slipped. The memory of her own parents' reaction when she'd told them she was expecting Dirk's child sprang to mind. They hadn't exactly acted excited. Ready to disembowel her, yes, but excited, no. Darla's whoop of laughter pulled Kat back into reality from her painful side trip down memory lane.

"I see it all now." Darla slapped her ample thigh, cackling like an old hen. "Pastor Jon is practicing his whistling so he can entertain his new grandchild."

Kat shrugged. "Explains it."

"Next thing you know, he'll be humming *Rock-a-bye Baby* when some district big-wig like Doctor Keller drops on by." Darla hooted with laughter.

The laughter was contagious. Kat joined in with a chuckle of her own. "Now, that *is* a pretty picture. We'd better pray Doctor Keller doesn't think Pastor Jon's fixin' to go completely around the bend."

"What's this about me fixin' to go around the bend?"

Kat's heart stopped momentarily at the sound of Jonathan's voice behind her. She spun her legs around the edge of the polished organ bench, slid off, and landed square on her derrière in a flutter of sheet music for the second time in less than five minutes.

"Hi, Pastor." Darla hopped down from her perch. "Kat is rather klutzy today."

"Is she now?" Jonathan rushed to Kat's side and retrieved several pages of music. He offered his arm to her to lean on as she stood. "You looked like you'd just seen a ghost or something."

"I-I almost thought I had," Kat stammered, regaining her feet. She accepted the music sheets he'd gathered. "Thanks. I'm a little tired, that's all. Time for me to go home and have some supper and hit the sack."

Jonathan raised an eyebrow. "You haven't eaten yet? We can't let our choir director go on much longer without sustenance, can we?"

Darla grinned, sauntering toward the exit. "Of course not. I'm fixin' to go home and grab some dessert myself and then rustle my rowdy toddlers into bed. 'Night, y'all."

"'Night, Darla." Kat squared her shuffled papers on the

edge of the choir loft and placed the sheet music on her music stand, promising herself she'd double-check the page order before Sunday's service. Gathering the rest of her personal effects, she headed to the door.

"'Night, Pastor."

"Just a second." Jonathan touched Kat on the forearm. "Can you stay a moment and talk?"

Kat froze. An odd yet familiar tingle fizzled at the spot where he touched her, traveling down the length of her arm and throughout her frame. She couldn't quite place where and when she'd experienced the pleasant sensation last, but somehow she sensed it was imperative for her to pull away from him — and fast.

"I . . . I've really gotta get home and feed Mister Friskies," she pleaded.

Darla's laugh echoed from the exit at the back of the sanctuary. "Good one, Kat. I'm still working on getting you a Mister Friskies II, remember? Bye, y'all."

Jonathan observed her through narrowed eyes. Kat gave a feeble chuckle.

"I guess I loved the little fella so much I forget he's not with me anymore."

He dropped his hand. "I understand."

Kat took a deep breath and relaxed. "I'll be seeing you then—"

"So, why don't we go out and eat and chat at the same time?" Jonathan suggested. "My treat."

"You're inviting me out to eat?"

Warmth invaded her cheeks. Kat couldn't believe she'd blurted out what sounded more like an accusation than a question. Now it was Jonathan who appeared as if he'd seen a ghost. He recovered momentarily.

"Yes. Yes, I am. Will you join me for dinner?"

Kat swallowed hard. She had no real reason to turn down

his gracious offer. It was just so . . . so . . . *unexpected*. What would folks say if they saw the two of them together? Probably nothing. After all, preachers often dined with their congregation members. Didn't Ruth invite her and the twins over to dinner once or twice? Here poor Pastor Jon had no one at home to dine with.

Kat plastered a smile across her face and summoned up her courage. "Of course I'll join you for dinner."

"Good." He nodded toward the door. "Let's go."

The best thing about life in Germantown, Jonathan decided, was that there was a variety of eating establishments within easy walking distance of St. Luke's. It hadn't always been the case, but the recent attempts to steal business away from other sight-seeing spots in the Hill Country area had seen a marked increase in restaurants of various kinds. Every old storefront downtown now sported either a café or an antique mall or a gift shop specializing in German-style arts and crafts.

It was all becoming a bit too touristy, though. The town's quiet charm and uniqueness were being drowned out by the blare of neon signs screaming, *Micro-Brewed Beer Using Our Ancestor's Recipe.* Jonathan wondered if they were alive today, would the humble peasant farmers from the Old Country who had settled this town claim it as their own. Probably not.

"Where do you want to eat?" he asked as they exited the church.

They could have gone next door to eat at the parsonage, but somehow it didn't feel quite right to invite Kat into Ruth's kitchen. Instead, he nodded to the west, and they walked toward the downtown area.

"I'm not too sure there's a whole lot of places open at seven-forty-five on a Wednesday evening," Kat said slowly. "It's bingo night over at St. Justin's."

Jonathan cleared his throat. "Ah, yes. We're in the middle of the tourist season, so our chances may be better than average."

He glanced at Kat from the corner of his eye. How long had it been since he had small-talked with a beautiful woman? He and Ruth had only to smile at each other across the table to get their meaning across. His heart beat faster as he realized he'd actually have to converse with Kat on a meaningful, adult level. Was he up to the challenge?

He stopped in front of the first café they happened upon with a brightly flashing *We're Open* sign in the window. "Schroeder's is a really good place, don't you think?"

Kat stared up at the sign. Jonathan flinched. Her face read more along the lines of *Root Canals Performed Without Anesthesia* than *The Best Burgers in Town*.

"Yeah, they're pretty good," she said at last.

"They're open until nine, it says." Jonathan held the door open for his guest to enter first. He wondered if his gallant gesture didn't make him seem hopelessly dated.

"Thank you." Kat skirted inside, allowing a microsecond of hot summer air to wash into the super-cooled eating establishment.

Inhaling a lungful of the frigid air, Jonathan could swear an icicle was forming on the end of his nose.

"A booth for two?" the young waitress asked, one eyebrow cocked in a knowing manner. She was rail thin with a bleached blonde crew cut, several piercings in one ear, and a small green jewel placed on one side of her nose.

The wondrous diversity of God's creation. How does she blow her nose with all the metal?

Jonathan smiled and nodded. "A booth will be fine."

Once they were seated toward the rear of the establishment in a high-backed booth with a minimum of distrac-

31

tions, Jonathan relaxed. He was growing more optimistic by the second. He might be able to pull off a decent conversation and ask Kat about the piano lessons. At least he felt that way until the waitress returned.

"You want the usual?" She glared at Kat.

If looks could kill, Jonathan would have called 911 that very moment.

Kat returned the icy stare with one of her own. "No, thank you. I'll have the chef salad and a diet Coke."

The girl's tone lightened as she turned to face him. "For you, sir?"

"I'll have the Hill Top Burger minus the onions and sauerkraut and sweet tea."

"Our burger special today is the Ostrich Burger. Lower in fat and calories and higher in protein."

"No, I like my burgers to moo rather than hiss at me."

The young woman laughed at his witty remark, then took his menu. She glowered and collected Kat's. Something wasn't quite right here. Jonathan felt uneasy. He had to find out what was going on.

"Do you want to go somewhere else?" he asked.

"No." Kat shook her head emphatically. "Schroeder's has great food. Really, they do."

"It just seems like . . . like you aren't welcomed here. I don't want you to feel uncomfortable."

She flashed a weak smile. "It's all right. I realize that small-town folks can carry grudges a long time. I didn't think a year would be enough time for them to forget about me, but you never know."

Jonathan's stomach flip-flopped—and it wasn't from hunger. "Forget about you?"

Kat politely ignored the waitress returning with their drink order and waited until the girl was out of sight. "I've been here before if you haven't guessed already."

"I sort of figured that to be the case." He licked his lips and ventured forth. "What happened?"

Kat averted her eyes, twirling the paper at the end of her straw for several long moments, then put it on the table to stare at the ice melting in her drink. "You might say I was involved in what loosely could be termed a lover's tiff."

A lover's tiff? Jonathan swallowed hard. He really hadn't been aware that Kat had dated much. He supposed Darla had mentioned Kat's boyfriend to him from time to time, but he had learned long ago to tune out Darla's voice once she hopped on the gossip wagon. Her words were far from kind at times.

"It got a little noisy in here that night," Kat continued. "I got upset with some obnoxious thing my date said about me. When he raised his voice, I picked up my drink and I—"

Jonathan cringed. "You threw it at him?"

"Sort of." Her eyes met his, and she flashed a knowing grin. "It was rather crowded that evening. We were sitting at one of those tables in the middle of the restaurant, and I sort of miscalculated my aim. I hit someone else square in the face with my foot-tall glass of iced tea."

The light dawned in Jonathan's mind. "You don't mean our—"

"Yes, one and the same." Kat rolled her eyes toward the cash register where their waitress now stood. "Sheila's a cousin of the owners, too. They aren't very happy with me as a customer as you can tell, but I think they're over it now and figured it was all an accident. You can't afford to run off business nowadays."

"We can leave if you'd like," he suggested, feeling horrible he'd chosen the restaurant now and not a quiet meal in his own home.

"No, that would only aggravate them more. It's better I go on as if nothing happened and live down my past mistakes.

They only come back to haunt you if you don't."

"It's a very wise philosophy."

"Thank you."

When Kat grins, her whole face lights up.

Jonathan enjoyed conversing with her. Her smile was a lighthouse blazing through the darkness of his life, illuminating the way home.

"Experience makes the best teacher, I always tell my students," she continued. "Besides, I know what the Schroeders are thinking at this very moment. *How much trouble can that woman cause sitting with that nice, calm, polite pastor from the church down the block?*"

Nice. Calm. Polite. It all meant one thing—he was deadly boring. Jonathan tried hard not to frown.

Their waitress returned with their order, perfunctorily asked if she could get them anything else, then left them alone. Jonathan found himself concentrating on his burger to keep himself from staring too much at his appealing companion. Who would have believed mild-mannered Kat Dubcek acted like a spitfire when her ire was up? It occurred to him there was a lot about Kat he didn't know.

Correction, he didn't really know more about her than she knew about him, which was only the side of themselves they presented to the public. A shadowy chill enveloped him. Could some of his assumptions about Kat be off the mark? Could she still be dating the Neanderthal who had upset her in this very restaurant?

Jonathan's appetite slipped away. He continued chewing his food, however, to not arouse suspicion.

"Don't look so scared," Kat teased. "I'm not fixin' to baptize you in soft drinks anytime soon."

Startled, Jonathan returned to reality. "I didn't think you would," he said, purposefully deepening his voice. "By any chance are you still . . . seeing this person who insulted you?"

Kat sighed as she forked a big wad of lettuce from her plate. "Fortunately, no."

"Are you seeing anyone else?" He did his best to pretend it didn't matter to him. "You don't have to tell me if you feel I'm prying too far into your personal life."

"No, I don't mind telling you. I'm not seeing anyone currently. You could say I've hung up my spurs when it comes to the opposite sex."

He tilted his head and stared at her, perplexed. "Your spurs?"

She nodded. "Yep. There'll be no more riding the range for this here cowgirl. No more rolling in the hay with the cowpokes for me. No siree, Bob."

Jonathan almost choked on his burger at such a frank disclosure. Kat reached over the booth table and patted him hard on the back.

"They didn't slip you some of that ostrich burger by mistake, did they?" She flashed him a concerned look.

"No, it just went down the wrong way," he covered, dabbing his damp forehead with his napkin. He took a couple of sips of his drink, then cleared his throat. "Do you really mean it when you say you're not interested in dating anymore?"

Kat bit the edge of her lip in a thoughtful gesture. "I don't know. I occasionally might need an escort to attend some fancy to-do, but it'll be nothing serious. I'm kicking the *going steady* habit for good."

"You shouldn't make a sweeping statement about such an important aspect of life," Jonathan protested. He felt his chances to impress Kat plummeting by the second. "I mean, you're still young. Someday you may find someone . . . someone who won't insult you in public places."

She shrugged. "Possibly. I don't know."

He reached across the table and gently touched her hand.

"You have faith that God works for the good in all things for those who love him, don't you?"

Kat sucked in a sharp intake of breath and withdrew her hand from his grasp. "I suppose I do, but I just don't have faith it'll ever happen to me. I mean, I don't seem to attract the right sort of men. I think God is telling me I need to shy away from the whole lot of them."

A cold sweat broke out across Jonathan's brow. His burger did a back-double somersault in his stomach. He bravely carried on. "What makes you say a thing like that? You're a wonderful, caring person, Kat. You can't let one bad relationship ruin your—"

"It's not just one," she cut in. "All my adult life I've hooked myself up with some real first-class duds." She held up her fingers and sighed. "First, there was my husband . . ."

What was Kat's ex-husband's name? Dick or Jock or something like that?

Someone had mentioned it to him long ago when he'd first come to St. Luke's along with the fact that the man had been killed under peculiar circumstances. But her ex was long out of the picture. Surely she wasn't raking herself over the coals about that experience?

"Then there was my boss at the middle school." Kat shook her head with regret. "How did I not know sleeping with the principal would cause me such grief with the other faculty members? It certainly didn't translate into reaching a higher step on the career ladder."

Jonathan shuddered. His table companion was near tears, but she stoically continued.

"After a long string of easy-to-forget, brief liaisons, there came my last steady, the most arrogant, self-absorbed male to ever walk the face of the earth."

He opened his mouth to cut in, but no words came forth.

"So, don't say I know how to pick them, Pastor," Kat drawled, emphasizing her point with her fork. "'Cause I do.

Unfortunately, all the ones I pick are either users or losers. Losers and users. It's the sordid story of my life."

At Kat's honest admission, Jonathan's heart went *splat* like a burger sizzling on the grill.

CHAPTER THREE

Which one am I? A loser or a user?

Uncomfortable to be forced to choose between two such disagreeable alternatives, Jonathan felt that the walls of the diner were coming in on him. If Kat believed she only attracted cads, what would she make of him? He prayed she wasn't thinking he would ever use her in any way, but a loser? It wasn't a moniker he wanted attached to his name, either.

"I hope I didn't ruin your appetite," Kat said, interrupting his troubling thoughts.

"Oh, no, I'm fine," he answered. He knew his far-off gaze wasn't convincing.

She crinkled her nose at him. "Uh-huh. Don't look so sad. I don't think it's awful going through the rest of my life as a single. Think about the apostle Paul. Didn't he say something like *it is good to remain unmarried and serve the Lord?*"

"Yes, he did," Jonathan admitted. "He also said *it's better to marry than to burn with passion . . .*"

As the last word slipped out, Jonathan bit his tongue hard, mentally kicking himself for blurting out his feelings. The expression on Kat's face which greeted him was one of complete bewilderment. His verbal gaffe put a damper on the rest of their dinner conversation.

They ate the remainder of their meal in relative silence. An occasional glance at the other or a brief mention of the weather, next Sunday's hymns, or how dismal the Cowboy's chances were for reaching the Super Bowl this coming season were their only interruptions. Jonathan forgot all about asking Kat about the piano lessons. It was as if the easy way they had related to each other previously had never existed. He wished now he had never opened his mouth.

"This was really good," Kat said at last, putting her fork down. She stood and retrieved her wallet from her purse. "I better be on my way in case one of the twins is trying to reach me from school on my home phone. They do love making midweek crisis calls."

He tried not to sound disappointed. "Please, put your money away. My treat."

She furrowed her brow. "Oh, no. I can't let you do that. It wouldn't be . . . it wouldn't be right."

"Yes, it would."

He stood, picked up the tab, and pulled out a bill from his wallet to cover both their food and the tip. They both headed toward the exit.

"This was the best meal I've had in a long time. Thank you for sharing it with me, Kat."

She nodded. "You're welcome. See you Sunday."

With her last remarks echoing in his ears, Kat flew out the door like a tumbleweed in the wind. Sighing, Jonathan handed the cashier his money, then slowly made his way home.

"Why did I ever let those two chatterboxes have cell phones at school?" Kat muttered, hanging up from the weekly ranting and ravings of her son and daughter. She looked up at the kitchen clock and yawned, realizing it was almost the witching hour, and if she didn't get some sleep soon she'd turn into a pumpkin.

Plodding through her bedtime routine, Kat caught a quick glimpse of herself in her dresser mirror. She paused. What the heck had been going on between her and Pastor Jon to-night? Why had she allowed her shiny façade to drop? Why had she let him catch a glimpse of her sullied core within? Why had she spilled her guts? Occasionally she had cried on Ruth's arm whenever Kevin had done something idiotic at school, but what she had told Pastor at dinner about her de-funct love life had been so . . . so personal. What on earth had gotten into her?

She stared at the wrinkles forming around the corners of her mouth and eyes. She knew she wasn't as haggard as she felt some days, but it was close.

Still, her form gave some men pause. Didn't BB always tell her that she had a *nice rack with just enough room to rest your deer rifle on*? And her legs? At five-foot-eight, she had always received great comments about how shapely her long legs were, although lately she'd been stuffing them into casual slacks to hide her ever-spreading hips. So what if her lips were a little too fat and pouty and her eyes were fading so quickly into gray they about matched the platinum high-lights in her ash-blonde hair? It wasn't an altogether bad package she was selling here.

"For Pete's sake." Kat threw down her hair brush and padded to the shower. "I sound like I'm peddling myself on a street corner. I'm a schoolteacher and a choir director, not some third-rate hooker. I've hung out for too long with low-lifes like Bradley T. Bradley."

As she turned on the taps, it struck her.

What must Jonathan think of me?

"Jonathan? Not Pastor Jon or the Reverend Rawlins? Oh, crud, I've forgotten the man's title."

Sighing, she plunged her head under the lukewarm shower spray. "What's wrong with me?" she muttered. "I'm thinking of him as just a plain ol' average, red-blooded American male instead of a man of the cloth."

He's still a man under the dog collar.

Hmm, she had a point there. After all, Jonathan Rawlins didn't walk on water. He never claimed to have fed the five thousand with a few barley loaves and fishes. He never admitted to raising anyone from the dead. Whether she cared to acknowledge it or not, he was only a flesh-and-blood man, not a poster child for sainthood.

So why did that fact bother her so much?

Kat turned the faucet to extra tepid and did her best to scrub away all notions of Jonathan being a male along with her top layer of skin.

"The man is still grieving, you idiot," she berated herself, lathering her hair with the over-priced shampoo her hairdresser had said was specially formulated for highlighted hair. "He's lonely, and he's got no one to eat with at home. He misses all those great, home-cooked meals, and Ruth's divine angel food cake with the pecans and chocolate glazing."

Kat sighed. Just the mere mention of Ruth's signature homemade dessert had her mouth watering. She missed Ruth's company, too.

Kat finished bathing and toweled herself off before slipping into her favorite fuchsia and black, rose-patterned silk pajamas. She blow-dried her hair, brushed her teeth, hit the lights, and crawled into her very wide, very empty king-sized bed.

She smoothed the comforter over the mattress, her hand lingering in the dent where BB's ample frame had once been a regular visitor. Poor Pastor Jon. He and Ruth had had to squish themselves into that teeny-tiny, little queen-sized bed in that teeny-tiny, little parsonage bedroom. He was a tall man, too—about six-foot-one or two at least. His big feet must have hung off the end. What size did he actually take in those old-fashioned shoes of his? About a thirteen? Kat fantasized what it would be like to share a small bed with such a tall man . . .

"All right. Stop that train of thought right now." Kat gritted her teeth. "You are not—I repeat not—going to start imagining how great your spiritual adviser is in the sack. Get that through your thick skull once and for all. Goodnight."

She turned to her side and allowed a tired sigh to escape her lips. She had to fight this odd attraction she'd felt tonight as she'd sat across from Pastor Jon in the back booth at Schroeder's. It was ludicrous. Even crazier, she had to fight off the feeling that somehow the attraction was mutual.

Faced with the cold, hard facts, Kat couldn't deny reality. What two types of men had she always attracted? Answer— Users and Losers. While she never once harbored a fleeting thought that somehow Jonathan Rawlins would want to use her in any way, it didn't keep him from being a loser, did it?

"Loser? Pastor Jon? No way." She sat up and grabbed the neighboring pillow to hug close to her chest. "Yeah, so what if his entire closet is filled with ratty old cardigans and rows of brown shoes? Lots of collegiate types dress simply. He's intelligent and kind and a genuine servant of the Lord. You don't label a person a loser because he doesn't look like a movie star or have a billionaire's bank account. You're a loser for even thinking that way, Dubcek."

She slugged her pillow. "You're fixin' to prove to yourself that you're nuttier than a Hill Country fruitcake if you continue talking to yourself. Now, goodnight."

Kat flopped backward and forced her eyes shut. All right, if Jonathan Rawlins wasn't a loser, then did he qualify as a user? What possible use could he have for her?

Okay, sure, but for other things besides that . . .

What Jonathan needed was a companion to stand by his side and help him deal with his congregation. He needed someone who could make all kinds of scrumptious goodies to fill the bellies of church council members, so stressful meetings proceeded smoothly. He needed a woman beyond reproach, well-respected and well-loved by everyone in the community.

In other words, he needed another Ruth Rawlins.

There was no danger, then, that even if there had been an inkling of attraction between them—an attraction on some primitive, chemical level—that a man with the obvious intelligence of Jonathan Rawlins would ever allow himself to act upon it. He had his position to think of. He had his good name, his reputation to protect. Katrina Dubcek was definitely no Ruth Rawlins.

Thing was, was any woman?

"Poor Ruth. Being perfect must have been a real drag," Kat mumbled. Yawning, she curled up in a ball and fell asleep, dreaming of row after row of brown shoes, size thirteen, and mile-high mountains of chocolate-pecan-glazed angel cakes, glistening in the sun.

"Okay, Adam, let's do it again. This time put your fingers on the keys exactly how I showed you." Kat stood and reached for the metronome situated on the spinet's top. "Ready? One, two, three, play."

Kat bit the inside of her cheek in dismay. It was simply amazing. What were the odds that a person could hit every single note wrong in the opening measures of *Mary Had a Little Lamb*? Her pupil, freckled-faced, ten-year-old Adam MacDonald, should be listed in a world record book somewhere.

But a student was a student. Kat couldn't afford to turn anyone away—particularly if their parents had paid a full month in advance. Keeping her two in college was all the motivation she needed to listen to the repeated, tortured tinkling of the ivories. On second thought, wearing a pair of earplugs couldn't hurt.

Adam finished the piece and flashed Kat a troubled smile.

"It's getting there," she said kindly. Her face was going to crack if she had to hold this frozen grin for much longer. Thank heaven the half hour was almost over.

"I ain't very good, am I?"

Kat felt like a villain at his downcast expression. The kid was trying, she could tell, but he just didn't seem to have it in him. She gently patted him on the shoulder.

"I think you meant *I'm not playing well today.* I think you're selling yourself short there. How long have you been taking lessons?"

He slumped over the keyboard. "Since April. It seems longer, don't it?"

"*Doesn't it.*" Kat found it difficult to turn off her school-teacher mind when it came to correcting grammar, even in the summer months. It did feel like she'd been instructing Adam a whole lot longer than three months, but she just couldn't come out and say so.

"It doesn't seem that long to me," she continued. "You have been practicing the assignment I give you after every lesson for twenty minutes or more a day, haven't you?"

He shrugged. "Sometimes."

"Ah, well, that's it. I promise you, Adam, if you practice every day for twenty to thirty minutes, you will play better. You just have to put your mind to it. Promise me this next week you'll try your best to practice every day?"

"I'll try, Ms. Dubcek. I promise."

Kat winked. "Good. Let's try the piece one more time and see how it goes."

After a few false starts, the boy regained confidence in his abilities and hit more right notes than wrong. A soft tap on the front door briefly interrupted his concentration.

"I know I'm a little early," came the voice of Hannah

MacDonald from the hallway, "but Adam's got a softball game tonight, and we're fixin' to have company over for dinner later. You know how it goes."

"Come on in," Kat called. "Adam's about ready to call it a day."

"How's my little Mozart doing?" Hannah's dark eyes sparkled as she tousled her son's rusty patch of hair.

Adam paused momentarily to grin at his mother and then proceeded with the next page of music. It was obvious to even the blindest of people that Hannah's children were the light of her life.

"He's giving it a good run for the money," Kat admitted.

"Do you think he takes after his Great-Uncle Neal in his musical abilities?"

"Hmmm . . ." Kat had forgotten all about the family connection. Poor kid. She held out some hope, as the boy's Great-Aunt Gayle could definitely play the organ. Too bad she was only a relation by marriage.

Kat shrugged. "I guess so."

"Great." Hannah's brilliant smile spoke volumes. "The new suit I bought today for Adam for the end of the summer piano recital will get some good use then."

"Aw, Mom, not a suit." Adam groaned.

"Yes, you're wearing a suit," his mother said through gritted teeth.

"Keep playing," Kat instructed her pupil. She nodded Hannah toward the sofa. Something was bothering the usually bubbly woman with soft, raven-colored curls and the most captivating dimples in all of Hill Country.

"The recital's a formal event, isn't it?" Hannah asked as they sat.

There was no mistaking the anxiousness on Hannah's pretty features. Kat sympathized with the young mother since she, too, had always longed to make the right impression on the natives of Germantown. It was a tough sell. Ten years after the fact, folks could be overheard making the occasional quip about how Hannah and Aaron's anniversary date and Adam's birthday weren't quite nine months apart. Kat had the guts to laugh her own sordid past off when it came presented to her on a silver platter, but that wasn't the case for dear, sweet Hannah MacDonald who took the small-town barbs seriously.

Kat patted her friend's hand. "A recital is indeed a formal event. I wore a ball gown to play at a recital once in college."

"Just like a prom queen, huh?" Hannah teased. She leaned toward Kat and spoke in a loud whisper, "Speaking of formal wear, you'll never guess in a million years who I saw trying on some very stylish clothes in Bronner's Men Store while I was looking for a tie to go with Adam's new suit."

"I give up. Willie Nelson?"

"No, silly." Hannah giggled before lowering her voice again. "It was Pastor Jon."

Kat chuckled. "You're such a joker."

"I'm not joking. I was so surprised to see him there myself that I couldn't believe my eyes at first, but it definitely was Pastor Jon."

A sudden, uneasy feeling came over Kat. First Jonathan had asked her to dinner, and now he was shopping for clothes. No, there could be no connections between the two activities. Absolutely none. She had to get the notion out of her head before it took root and grew into who knew what.

Kat eased back on the sofa and casually crossed her legs. "I didn't think Bronner's stocked cardigan sweaters with elbow patches in the winter months let alone the summer ones."

"They don't," Hannah assured her. "I saw him modeling some very nice sports shirts and some rather flattering casual slacks and some gorgeous cotton sweaters. You know the kind—sort of what yachters wear."

Kat forced another chuckle, then rose to her feet. "Yeah, and what would we know about what yachters wear here in the middle of Texas? You're such a card, Hannah MacDonald."

"You know, Pastor looks like a whole new man when he's wearing stylish clothes." The dark-haired beauty tilted her head and regarded Kat curiously for a moment. "Maybe there's a special lady in his life?"

Kat had reached the side of the piano when the full intent of Hannah's words struck. She grabbed the musical instrument for support before her knees buckled. How many people from church knew she and Pastor Jon had gone out to eat together last night? Only Darla knew—and she had a very big mouth. Kat felt an urge to strangle the meddling church secretary.

"Ta-da!" Adam cried, pounding out the last chord. "How was that, Ms. Dubcek?"

"Very good." Kat helped her protégé gather up his lesson books. "Now don't forget what I told you. Practice every day for twenty minutes or more. Understand?"

"Yes'm. Every day from now on. I won't forget."

Hannah rose, took her boy by the hand, and scooted him toward the front door. "Thanks, Kat. We'll see you next week. Bye."

"Bye, y'all. Now, remember what I told you—practice."

Sighing, Kat leaned against the door as it closed behind them, her fluster over what Hannah had told her about Jonathan Rawlins momentarily forgotten as she eavesdropped on the heated, mother-son conversation happening on her front stoop.

"Adam, what on earth have you been up to for those twenty minutes every night after dinner when your father and I take your little sister out back to play catch? Heaven help you if you've been playing video games."

"Is that a new haircut, Pastor?"

"Wow! Those colors are definitely you!"

"I see you've finally discovered *business casual.* Congratulations."

Jonathan was overwhelmed by the community's response to his attempt to dress more fashionably. One would think he was strolling along Main Street sans clothing from the leers women were flashing his way. When some of the kids from the church youth group honked at him as he'd crossed the parking lot, he'd almost dropped his many bags and bundles. No doubt about it — his new look was causing a minor stir in sleepy ol' Germantown to say the least.

Would it stir Kat Dubcek any?

At last Jonathan reached his car and deposited his spoils of shopping into the back seat. He pulled out onto the main drag and tried his best not to worry about the answer to that particular question. He knew he wasn't doing all of this just to impress people. His change in style was because he had finally taken to heart Kat's comments of several weeks ago when she'd pointed out the *ratty sweaters* hanging in the closet.

The sweaters really needed to go, she'd said, and Jonathan had at last reached the same conclusion. It was time for them to go. And today he felt strong enough to see them go. After all, he couldn't play the *nutty professor* in cardigans and slip-on oxford shoes all his life. It was time he stopped acting twice his age and started acting like how he felt inside. To do anything less would be hypocritical.

Kat was far from being a hypocrite — hadn't she confessed to him the extent of her romantic past over their dinner at

Schroeder's? He could tell she thought she was shocking him as she'd rattled off her long list of love affairs gone sour. Instead, her painful honesty only endeared her more to him and hinted she longed to form a lasting relationship with a man who didn't promise a tabloid type of experience.

Besides, how could anyone be labeled a *nice, calm, polite, boring* man while wearing a jaunty red-white-and-blue-striped knit sports shirt, intensely white cotton slacks, and a sporty pair of navy leather loafers? The only reservations Jonathan had about his new taste in clothing was how in the world he was going to wash the fabrics without fading their vivid colors.

"Oh, well," he contemplated, pulling his car into the driveway, "I can only handle one challenge in life at a time."

Jonathan carefully laid his new duds in his dresser and removed the old. Ten minutes later, he had another three packing boxes filled to the brim with clothing to give away. He prayed the Salvation Army wouldn't pass on them when they glimpsed the drab and dreary contents inside. As he looked into his closet now, it was as if the cold, grayness of winter had at last been driven away to be replaced with the cheery rainbow hues of summer.

He sighed.

Would Ruth be proud of me?

CHAPTER FOUR

Jonathan swallowed a lump in his throat. Ruth would have been proud of him no matter what, he reminded himself, whether he was attired in ratty sweaters or colorful Henley shirts or mud-and-grass skirts. She had loved him for who he was inside.

Thing was, Jonathan had relied too much on people who knew him in the past. It hadn't occurred to him until recently how hard it might be for a person of today to get to know someone who dressed like he'd been born in the nineteenth century. From now on, he'd act like a more modern, more approachable person. Surely his new appearance would attract an equally modern, approachable person like Kat Dubcek. Wouldn't it?

Shaking his head, Jonathan stared hard at the dapper man staring back at him from his mirror. The haircut had helped. Slightly graying at the temples with only a handful of wrinkles, he had a remarkably rugged look about him. Not quite a rodeo star, but maybe if he wore his cowboy boots and jeans more often?

"The glasses have got to go," he muttered, removing the heavy frames from the permanent dent in the bridge of his nose. "They have *loser* written all over them."

He squinted at his image in the mirror. Did they prescribe contacts for men his age? The very least he could do was purchase some new frames. Those lighter weight wire frames would subtract years from his face. He'd call and make an optometrist's appointment today.

"It's back to the grind now, Mr. Fabulous," he joked, pointing to himself. He slipped his spectacles back on and winked at his reflection before heading out the door.

"Whoa! Pastor Jon, is it really you?"

Darla jumped up from her desk chair, cat-calling and clapping when Jonathan entered the church office. "So this is what your *personal errand* was all about?" Her sharp gaze raked over his form as he revolved to show off his new outfit. "I like, I like."

"Thank you. I wasn't quite sure if I should go all out and replace my entire wardrobe, but then I thought, why not?"

She smiled. "Sure, why not? You deserve it."

He laughed. "I thought so, too."

Darla sat and returned to her typing. Jonathan picked up his mail from the corner of the desk only to pause at his office door. He turned around and crossed his arms, a nervous tic growing at the edge of his grin.

"Pastor?" his secretary asked a moment later.

"Darla, how do you think folks will react when they see the new me?"

She tilted her head and shrugged. "I don't know. Does it matter? The thing is, you obviously enjoy your new threads. I think everyone will be happy for you. You seem to be acting more like your old self this week."

My old *self?*

Jonathan cringed.

Here I am trying so hard to get away from that old *business.*

He sighed. Hopefully others, such as Kat, would come to an understanding that *old* was not a permanent part of his personality.

"I am feeling a lot more like myself these days," he said proudly.

"And it shows." Darla winked, then returned her attention to Sunday's bulletin layout.

"Good." Upon entering his *sanctum sanctorum,* Jonathan settled himself into his comfortable desk chair.

"There's only one thing that has me wondering, though," Darla called out from the front office a minute later.

"What's that?" Jonathan replied.

Her circular face peeked around the door. "Why all the whistling lately?"

"Whistling?" Jonathan's brow furrowed in concentration. Had he been whistling out loud?

"You know what I mean," Darla insisted. "You've been whistling to yourself at your desk all this past week. And then you went downstairs and started going through the music files the other day. Is there some kind of connection?"

Jonathan's cheeks heated slightly. "Between my whistling and looking at the music files?"

"Yes."

"There is."

"And?"

How could he explain his actions without making himself look like a total idiot or embarrassing Kat? "I . . . I was thinking of some familiar hymns Ruth used to play on our piano at home when the kids were visiting. I decided I wanted to study the music."

"Oh." Darla tapped her fingers along the edge of the door. She didn't act too convinced. "Pastor, you don't even read music."

"It's true," Jonathan acknowledged. A bead of cold sweat trickled down his back. "That's why I was whistling. I was trying to figure out how the tunes went in relation to the words."

She nodded. "I see. You're going to sing them a cappella?"

"Maybe. I was thinking of learning to play the piano, too."

"Really?" She quirked an eyebrow. "You'll have to take lessons, lots of them, and that's not easy. I should know — my mom made me take piano lessons for years, and it never took. At least I can read music, and it helps with singing in the choir."

Jonathan relaxed. Darla had bought into his cover explanation. If Darla bought it, Kat would, too, with any luck.

"I figured a few piano lessons would help my singing," he agreed.

"That's great. Do you need to know the names of some piano teachers in town?"

"No, I have a lesson lined up already."

Darla's eyes narrowed. "You do? With whom, pray tell?"

"Kat Dubcek," Jonathan replied, calmly scribbling a note to himself on his desk calendar. "My first lesson is tonight."

Kat stood motionless, gazing out of her kitchen sink window as ruby-throated hummingbirds buzzed about the morning glory blossoms climbing the trellis beside the back deck. To be so colorful, so carefree . . . and here she was trapped inside with the A/C, doing her dinner dishes because it was just too hot outside to do anything else.

She glimpsed outside again at the birds. They were gone now. A sudden stab of pain sliced her forehead. It didn't look like rain on the horizon — and the end of the world wasn't predicted for this evening — so why did she feel a massive tension headache coming on?

As soon as the phone rang, she knew why.

"Hey, Mom," Kevin grunted. "How's it going?"

Kat switched the phone to speaker and lowered herself into a chair at the table, rubbing her throbbing temples in preparation for the worst.

"It's going fine, dear. I heard from your sister last night. I figured y'all had decided it was her turn to give me the low-down about things this week. What's up?"

"Can't a fella call his mom every now and then just to hear her voice and not get the third degree?"

"Sure he can, but you usually don't."

A pregnant pause, then, "Man, you're good. How did you know? Did Keely tell you?"

Kat felt her blood pressure rising. "Did Keely tell me what?"

"About my flunking English again this term."

Kat grimaced. "No, she didn't prepare me for that one. She was too busy yakking about her own troubles in advanced music theory."

"Oh. Well, I'm glad you're not angry then."

"I never said I wasn't angry." Kat forced the words out through gritted teeth. "I'm very angry, Kevin. You know you can't get a degree in secondary education without passing the basic English requirements—even if you're only going to be a PE teacher."

"You make it sound like becoming a high school football coach means I'm a total idiot." Kevin sounded like a whiny little boy instead of the strapping, six-foot-four, two-fifty solid wall of muscle that he was. "I'll have you know I've attended every tutorial session and even asked for extra credit to get a passing grade, but the prof says this isn't high school."

"It isn't."

Kat clenched her fists. Kevin was so like his father—better with numbers than words, but even better with a football in his hands. She shouldn't have let the Longhorns take him on when he would have been better off attending junior college at home for the first two years to get his basics done under her care and supervision. She had to admit what he had been given at UT was a once in a lifetime opportunity. How many average high school students were offered free college tuition just because they could sack a quarterback in seconds flat?

Kevin's deep mumble brought her back to reality. "Don't worry, Mom. I can retake English again in the fall. Third time's the charm, they say."

Kat shook her head, her son's cockeyed optimism eliciting an exhausted sigh from her lips. "Yes, they say that, but I don't think they had an athletic scholarship hanging in the balance."

"What?"

"Listen, honey. I just want you to graduate this coming spring with your sister. I can't afford to pay for your living expenses much longer than that. You think you can swing it?"

"I'll try, Mom. Honest, I will. I think I could have passed if Keely would have helped me out with my term paper."

Kat straightened in her chair and crossed her arms. It was so unlike her daughter not to help her brother. "You're telling me your sister refused to help you out?"

"Well . . ."

Kat's head spun. Keely had practically walked Kevin through the basic secondary education classes they'd both needed. Keely had received all A's, of course, while Kevin maintained a passing B- average. Without Keely's help, Kevin would have needed to retake at least a few of those classes. Now that Keely was concentrating on her music classes and Kevin on his physical education requirements, she wasn't always able to tutor him. But English? She had helped him before. It seemed unthinkable she wouldn't help him now.

Kevin lowered his voice. "It's not so much Keely refused

to help me as it is she's been way too busy to help me this term. Way, way too busy with late-night extracurricular activities, if you get my drift."

"Keely?" Kat frowned. "She's never let her activities get in the way of schoolwork before. She join another string ensemble?"

"No, not really. She joined up with a field goal kicker with one hell of a foot named Nigel."

"Nigel? Who or what is Nigel?"

"He's a Jamaican exchange student," Kevin said with unabashed enthusiasm. "Nigel came over here to study and play some soccer, but when Coach got a look at how he could kick a ball . . . well, let's just say Coach snatched him from the soccer team before they knew what hit 'em."

"You're telling me your sister—your serious, studious, sedate twin sibling—is dating a Jamaican field goal kicker?"

"Yep. Nigel's a real good sort. He's not jumping her bones for the heck of it. I really think he cares about her and wants to stay in the US and settle down."

Settle down?

Kat felt a tense, dry cough coming on. A feeling of mind-numbing dread reverberated throughout her body. Her heart raced. No, her baby girl wasn't ready to make important life commitments like marriage just yet—especially if they had anything to do with foreign exchange students who wanted to stay longer than their student visas allowed.

Kat had long ago made a vow to herself that she would never stand back and watch her daughter's life be ruined by marrying a no-goodnik like Kat's own parents had permitted her to do.

"I understand now why Keely said she was having trouble concentrating on her studies," Kat said through clenched teeth. "Why didn't she tell me about her boyfriend? Why all the subterfuge?"

Kevin sniffed. "Beats me, Mom. I guess she knew you

wouldn't approve of Nigel. He's a nice guy. You'll like him when you meet him."

Kat bit her lip. What on earth had happened to her daughter's good judgment?

"I believe I will—meet Nigel, that is." Kat cleared her throat. "All right, now hear this—I'm giving you two fair warning. I'm fixin' to come for a little visit this weekend. So you'd better start weeding the books and dirty clothes from the chairs now so I'll have a place to sit when I get there."

An hour after Kevin's call, the extra-strength ibuprofen finally started working its wonders on Kat's headache. She lounged aimlessly in front of the TV, not caring what was on the screen. It had taken a good soak in the bathtub to relax the tight knot in her stomach which had begun at the first mention of Keely's secret boyfriend.

Kat sighed, flipping television channels like a football fanatic between games. Her body was feeling a lot calmer now, but her mind was still spinning in turmoil.

Why had her most trustworthy child deceived her? Kat had expected Kevin to sneak behind her back when it came to his love life, but he had been surprisingly honest with her since he'd left home. He'd told her bluntly he was too busy keeping in peak athletic form to keep his spot on the football team to start any real serious relationships and that their coach had warned them of the dangers of groupies. Kat believed him.

But Keely? From day one she'd announced her studies came above all else. She'd declared she was a *career woman*. No man dare get in her way. Kat had felt so proud. Her daughter would never make the same mistake she had in dropping out of college to get married.

Now a threat clouded her daughter's rosy horizon— Nigel. Keely was putting her studies, her future career plans aside and focusing her energies on a relationship that would only bring her pain in the end.

It hurt Kat to think of how her baby girl would cry when her lover boy headed back home to the sunny Caribbean after his schooling was over, but it hurt Kat more to admit to herself how little she knew about her children at times.

The doorbell added a somber note to Kat's sad musings.

"Perfect." Kat scrambled to her feet after the third ring and shuffled toward the door. "It better not be one of those missionaries with their black ties and white shirts. I'll knock 'em over the head with my church pictorial directory if it is . . ."

"Good evening, Kat."

Kat's eyes bulged in surprise. Her jaw dropped. "G-good evening, Pastor," she stammered at last. "Um, what can I do for you?"

"I have a proposition for you." He opened the storm door an inch. "Mind if I come in?"

"Please do."

Kat did her best to pull her eyes back into her head as she glanced at her unexpected guest's attire. Hannah MacDonald was right. This new and improved version of the Reverend Jonathan Rawlins stood in front of her dressed positively high-fashion. The casual Columbia blue knit shirt and navy chino slacks fit perfectly. She'd never noticed just how svelte his waist and how broad his shoulders were, either. His former garb of ratty sweaters and baggy trousers had successfully camouflaged a very masculine frame—what a shame.

He caught her staring and smiled. Kat blushed.

"You like my new clothes?" he asked.

"Oh, yes, very much so," Kat jabbered, tearing her gaze from the striking male image in front of her. She guided her guest to the sofa and switched off the tube with the remote.

"Who played Henry Higgins to your Eliza Doolittle?"

He raised an eyebrow as he sat. "Henry who?"

"You know, the musical, *My Fair Lady*. Somebody must have helped you make your clothing selections. The colors are very flattering, and the fit is . . ."

Kat sat in the overstuffed chair opposite and rested her teeth on the tip of her tongue to keep it from hanging out.

"The fit is?" he queried.

She swallowed hard. "The fit is excellent, if you ask me."

"Thank you. Those two sharp young guys down at Bronner's—Bill and Ted—are the real geniuses." Jonathan happily smoothed his new slacks across firm, muscular thighs. "I must say I'm very pleased with the way I turned out, and so were they. I practically bought out the store."

Kat chuckled. "You cleaned out all those ratty sweaters in the closet, didn't you?"

His eyes twinkled. "I did. Out with the old, in with the new."

"Good for you."

His voice held a warm, honeyed tone. "It is good for me. Don't you think so?"

"Definitely . . ."

Kat's voice faded away. She stared down at her hands, suddenly uncomfortable with sitting in her own living room. Jonathan Rawlins had, of course, visited her home before on several occasions, but he'd always come with a crowd—like at the Christmas choir party she'd hosted last year. Somehow, his being here alone tonight in her home signaled something was out of the ordinary. Although nothing had really changed since they'd eaten dinner together, Kat couldn't deny that something in the air between them felt different.

"Do you want me to explain my proposition?"

"Of course," she said, grinning like a fool. "Go ahead."

He cleared his throat. "First, though, let me compliment you on the lovely outfit you're wearing. It's really quite flattering."

"My outfit?" Kat blinked in slow motion, then looked down, realizing the awful truth of her situation—

She wasn't wearing any outfit at all. She was wearing her favorite lounging-around-the-house attire, consisting of her royal-blue satin pajamas without the benefit of proper undergarments. The synthetic-silk of the cloth clung like a second skin to her every curve, accentuating every line, bump, and dimple on her body. The plunging neckline revealed the creamy, smooth flesh between her breasts, and it was more than obvious from her nipples poking through the thin material like two pearl buttons the air conditioning was doing its job more than adequately, too.

"Oh dear," she whispered, springing to her feet and racing toward the bedroom.

"Where are you going?"

"I'm sorry," Kat called out, breathless. "I forgot—I'm not dressed to entertain company. I'll be back in just a moment."

The door slammed behind her.

Jonathan grinned and crossed his arms, sinking comfortably into the couch. "Hmm, I don't know about that. I certainly was entertained."

CHAPTER FIVE

What on earth do I wear?

Flustered, Kat's mind twirled around and around, gaining momentum like a cyclone on the plains. After practically flashing her spiritual advisor, should she err on the side of caution and put on a full-length gunny sack and veil, or should she make light of the situation and slide into a black, spandex mini skirt and a sheer, ivory, low-cut blouse?

Kat stifled a scream.

For Pete's sake. What has gotten into me?

She settled on wearing the clothes she'd worn earlier in the day—practical stretch cotton jeans and a floral-printed t-shirt covered with violets. Making sure her bra was on and securely fastened, she finger-combed her hair in the mirror, took a deep breath, and shoved her feet into her canvas flats before calmly reentering the living room.

"Very nice." Jonathan rose, then sat as she reclaimed her seat.

Kat didn't know whether to feel relieved or disappointed he hadn't said he preferred the way she had been dressed—or rather undressed—previously.

"Thanks. Now, about this proposition. It wouldn't have anything to do with the choir singing for both services every week, would it? 'Cause if it does, I can tell you right now they've complained to me enough about singing for both Easter sunrise and—"

"No, it's nothing to do with the choir at all," Jonathan cut in. "It's something I want you to do for me personally."

Personally?

Kat rubbed at the throbbing pulse in her temple. "You want me to do a favor for you, Pastor?"

"Yes, but first you must promise me one thing," he said.

"What's that?"

"Stop calling me Pastor. You can call me Jonathan, Kat. I do have a regular first name like most folks."

Kat bit her lip and screwed up her eyes. "I-I don't think I can do that."

"Why not?"

His hurt expression cut her to the core.

"It's just that I'm not used to calling people I work with by their first names," she explained. "I call our principal Mister Pfeiffer since we teachers are supposed to model how we want the children to address those in authority. Giving someone a title is a sign of respect."

"Yes, but Mister Pfeiffer is quite a few years older than his students, I believe." Jonathan looked as if he was struggling to keep from frowning. "We're actually very similar in age, Kat, and technically, I'm not your boss."

She forced a grin. "True. Matthias signs the checks at church, doesn't he?"

Jonathan's furrowed brow relaxed. "He sure does. You can't miss his signature on the bottom line, either. John Hancock could have taken lessons in calligraphy from Matthias."

Kat couldn't help but laugh at the wisecrack. "Matt probably thinks it makes his name harder to forge, but why bother? His last name is hard enough to spell correctly as it is."

"So, it's Jonathan from now on, all right?" He raised an eyebrow in expectation.

Kat took a deep breath and nodded. "Okay, Jonathan it is. Now, Jonathan, what can I do for you?"

Jonathan turned to a folder of papers lying beside him on the sofa cushions that Kat hadn't noticed earlier. "I want to learn how to play some of these hymns. Do you think you can teach me?"

"You want me to teach you how to play the piano?" Kat widened her eyes. Most of her pupils were high school age or younger. She hadn't taught an adult student in years.

"I'll pay you for your time, of course."

"It goes without saying," Kat mumbled. "I mean, I charge a standard rate for a half hour lesson."

"Can I double up and have hour-long lessons? I want to be able to play something by Christmas."

"I guess I could schedule you for two-lesson blocks, but why the big rush? Why do you want to become a proficient piano player by Christmas?"

Jonathan shuffled through the sheet music and drew out a copy. "It's like this. We have an old family tradition of gathering around the piano on Christmas Eve and singing carols and hymns like this." He showed her a yellowed copy of *O Holy Night*. "This one is Elizabeth's favorite. I've found a few others that I know Eli would like, too."

A tear welled in the corner of Kat's eye. She blinked it away.

"I didn't want the kids to forego a family tradition just because Ruth isn't here to accompany them on the piano, so I thought I'd . . ."

As his voice trailed away, Kat knew in her heart that she had to do this for Jonathan. Jonathan—she could think and say his name now without hesitation. He was a father and soon-to-be grandfather who cared about his family so much he was willing to subject himself to the pain and torture of learning a musical instrument later in life.

Not that much later in life.

She herself had learned how to play the guitar and the recorder when she'd returned to college to finish her degree in music education. It shouldn't be too hard to help Jonathan learn how to pick out some familiar tunes within the next six months or so.

"When do you want to start?" Kat cringed at her impulsiveness. Was her eagerness to earn some extra income so transparent? She paused, regrouped her thoughts, and began again. "I mean, are Tuesday evenings okay with you? I'm free to give longer lessons on that night. We can start this coming Tuesday at seven, if you like."

"Tuesday it is." Smiling, Jonathan gathered his music together and arranged it before closing the folder. "I suppose I should be off now. You have other students to teach tonight?"

"No, my last student on Thursday comes in the late afternoon. It gives my poor ears a chance to recoup before Friday's onslaught." She rolled her eyes for effect. "I do mean onslaught."

He quirked an eyebrow. "You have a full schedule on Fridays?"

"Most of the time."

Now, why did I say that?

Kat had only a couple of little girls taking lessons in the morning tomorrow and nothing scheduled for this coming Monday, but she liked the idea of having her three-day weekends to herself in the summer, especially since this weekend she was making a trip over to Austin to check up on the twins.

Jonathan rose. "I'll let you get back to your recuperating now. Thanks, Kat, for taking me on as your pupil."

Kat stood and opened the door for her guest. "You're most welcome. With such enthusiasm, I'm sure you'll become my best student."

"I plan on it." He gave her a mock salute, then crossed the threshold and headed down the drive toward his serviceable, sedate gray sedan.

At the sound of the engine starting, Kat remembered she needed to tell Jonathan about her trip this weekend.

"I almost forgot to tell you," Kat shouted, stepping onto the front stoop. "I'm fixin' to visit the twins at UT so I won't be at church Sunday. Darla will fill in for me."

The car screeched to an abrupt halt. Jonathan leaned out the window. For a split second, Kat could have sworn the look on his face was sheer devastation.

"Darla didn't tell me you were going out of town."

"No, she doesn't know. It just now came up. I had a phone call earlier this evening. I need to spend some quality time with Keely and Kevin and see what's going on in their lives over at UT."

He nodded. "As a parent, I understand. I'll see you when you return from Austin then."

"Yes. Bye, Pas—"

His frown stopped her mid-word. *Old habits die hard.*

"I mean, goodbye, Jonathan."

He smiled. "That's better. Bye for now, Kat." He waved as he drove off.

"Now, what all should I pack for Austin?" Kat mumbled to herself, heading back into the house. There was something needling her that she needed to write down on her calendar, but whatever it was had slipped her mind.

Preaching a sermon is very much like riding a bicycle.

Jonathan took his place in the pulpit Sunday morning.

If you get right back on after you fall off, it just keeps getting easier.

The cheerful faces of his supportive congregation certainly gave his ego a boost. Jonathan glanced over at the choir loft. His heart fell. The church seemed emptier without Kat directing, but at least the front left pew was occupied this Sunday. A fragile hand waggled a finger at him mid-sermon. Jonathan winked at the elderly occupant.

Bless your heart, dear Aunt Mabel.

After the service and several dozen hearty handshakes, there came a firm tapping on Jonathan's shoulder.

"Pastor, there's something we need to discuss about the roof," Matthias Ringleschmidt announced in his deep, commanding voice.

Jonathan strolled toward his office. "Can't this wait until the next trustees' meeting, Matt?"

"It could, but by then we might be needing a whole new Sunday School building instead of just a new roof."

Jonathan shuddered. He nodded for Matthias to come into the room and shut the door.

"I never realized it was so bad," he said after hearing more about the problem. "Here the trustees have been arguing about the roofing expense for over a year now."

"It wasn't a wasted discussion," Matthias assured him. "We know now exactly what we can and what we can't afford."

"Which is?"

"Precious little without going deep into debt."

Jonathan plopped into his desk chair, motioning Matthias to take the chair opposite. St. Luke's had held a long and proud tradition of never going into debt over major building projects, but times changed — and so did the costs of labor and materials. It was past time for the congregation to be let in on the crisis and learn they needed to be more generous in their giving.

"The church district can always help us with the loan process," Jonathan suggested.

"No, Pastor. We've never done things that way at St. Luke's, and I don't think folks around here want to start now."

"Matt, let's get serious. Wasn't forty thousand the most reasonable estimate we received for redoing the roof? To replace the whole building . . ." Jonathan spread his arms wide in a helpless gesture. "I don't have to tell you how much more it would cost."

"I know, I know, but I was talking with Rocky Rockford, the fire marshal, the other day, and he told me that the way the Sunday School building is wired, it may not be able to pass the new county fire code regulations."

Jonathan sighed. "Isn't there such a thing as a grandfather clause anymore?"

Matthias scratched his head. "In our case, it'll have to be a great-great-grandfather clause. The building is just plain old. Whether we like it or not, it'll have to be replaced eventually. The question is whether it should be replaced now or later."

"What are the advantages to both options?"

"To be blunt, the advantage to a whole new building is we lessen the church's chances of being sued when the roof caves in on the kindergarten class after a heavy rain or we injure a score of children by smoke inhalation if the wiring fails or—"

"Enough already!" Jonathan cried, putting his hands to his aching forehead. "I get the picture. You're saying the building is a death trap. How come we haven't discussed its more dangerous faults before at a trustees' meeting?"

"Well, the trustees are mighty proud at how they've been able to keep the ol' gal together all these years. The building has its share of history—just ask the older folks about all the good classes they attended in that building. It's a monument to all that is good about St. Luke's."

"It's a sad testament to what needs to be updated," Jonathan muttered, shaking his head. Wonderful. Knock over the Sunday School, and half the congregation would withdraw their contributions out of hurt. Leave it standing and run the risk of losing the other half—the younger half—of the congregation from possible disaster. It was a classic no-win situation.

"Don't worry," Matthias said, interrupting Jonathan's troubled thoughts. "I have an idea on how we can raise the funds for a new building."

Jonathan looked up. A small seed of hope blossomed in his heart. "You do?"

Matthias leaned over and rested his big hands on the desktop. "We'll host an Oktoberfest."

"Oktoberfest?" Jonathan scratched his chin. "Don't the volunteer firefighters already hold one on Labor Day?"

"Yes, they do, but we could have ours in July. This town could easily handle two Oktoberfests in one year. Plus, it's the tourist season. Not all the funds will be coming out of our neighbors' pockets."

"True, very true." Jonathan stood and removed the church activity calendar from the side wall. "July's a busy month, but it looks like we could plan something the weekend before Vacation Bible School starts. Then we could hand out flyers advertising VBS as well as use the Oktoberfest as a building fund-raiser."

"I was thinking we could use the back parking lot for the stage area."

"Yeah, Matt, that's a good idea. I believe there are several polka bands in the area who'd probably play for a reduced rate or free just to help us out."

"That's the spirit, Pastor." Matthias stood beside Jonathan and slapped him on the back. "I'll take care of getting the necessary permits and start drafting people for set-up, promotion, and patrolling."

"Patrolling?"

The congregation president dropped his gaze, shuffling his feet as he plunged his hands deep in his coat pockets. "If we serve beer we're going to have to have some policing going on—official and otherwise. We can't let our Oktoberfest get out of hand like the volunteer firefighters' does on occasion."

"Does it get out of hand?" Jonathan really didn't know. It wasn't the sort of function that had attracted either him or Ruth in all the years they'd lived in Germantown.

Matthias shrugged. "Not often. But it can."

"Couldn't we host a *dry* Oktoberfest and avoid the hassle?" Jonathan wondered.

"We could, but we probably wouldn't raise enough money to build an outhouse, let alone a whole educational wing."

Jonathan nodded. "You're right, but I think we should emphasize the fund-raising and cultural aspects over the drinking ones in our advertising campaign. I don't want members of the county council of churches looking down their noses at me at the next meeting. You know how some folks still believe dancing is a mortal sin in these parts."

"You mean it isn't?" Matthias grinned.

Jonathan laughed. "For those of us with big feet and no rhythm, it probably is. All right, Matt, you get to work on getting this thing together to present to the church members next Sunday, and I'll do what I can to smooth the way in the meantime." He stuck out his hand. "Deal?"

"Deal." Matthias firmly shook Jonathan's hand. "One more thing, Pastor."

"What's that?"

"I wanted to compliment on how well you preached today. You seem to be acting your old self lately."

Jonathan flinched. The *old* word again.

"Thank you. I am feeling more myself—my *younger* self, that is." He patted the church president on the back and nodded toward the exit. "Now, you'd better get on home before Denise's Sunday pot roast burns."

Sighing, Matthias trudged toward the door. "Like the old

Sunday School building, burning it could only be an improvement."

Kat schlepped into the house Tuesday noon and plopped her suitcase beside the washing machine. She'd have to hurry if she was going to grab a bite to eat and change clothes before her one o'clock voice lesson arrived.

She dumped the pile of mail and newspapers wedged under her arm onto the kitchen table. How she wished she had the time to take a shower! Even after sandblasting the twins' apartment shower stall with lime-remover to scrub off the water deposits, Kat still didn't feel clean whenever she bathed at their place. How they could stand the mile-high mesa of dirty dishes in their kitchen sink and the reeking Everest of Kevin's workout clothes in his bedroom, she'd never know — nor did she ever want to.

Kat grabbed a banana from the fruit bowl on the table in the kitchen and headed for her bedroom. She must have spent a fortune in quarters at the Laundromat washing their linens and on purchasing plug-in air fresheners. The twins' noses must have ceased functioning properly upon entering college. It explained the moldy pizza box sitting in the back of their practically empty fridge. After a weekend of mucking their place out for them and helping restock their cabinets with canned goods and macaroni dinners, she was more than ready to come home to solitude and fresh air.

Although Kevin had been the more slovenly of the two before, this term it appeared Keely had caught his slob disease in regards to their shared public areas. The only halfway maintained room was Keely's bedroom. Perhaps the real reason why Keely's room looked pristine was she hadn't been sleeping in her bed much lately?

Kat threw her damp, scoop-necked t-shirt and jeans shorts

in the hamper with more *oomph* than necessary, reaching for her deodorant stick. She just couldn't cope with the idea of where—and with whom—her daughter occasionally slept right now. She didn't want to think about it.

Grabbing a fresh, powder-blue checked cotton crepe blouse and matching solid-blue slacks from the closet, she buttoned it as she returned to the kitchen to make herself a low-cal turkey salad and watercress sandwich. Mid-sandwich, the doorbell rang. Just her luck, Kristy had arrived ten minutes early. She gulped down her Diet Coke as she opened the door and escorted her star pupil into the living room before parking her hips on the piano bench.

Kat couldn't stay irritated for long. Kristy Kershaw's enthusiasm was the highlight of her week of otherwise mind-numbing private music lessons. The towering teen with the gorgeous flowing, curly auburn hair and captivating green eyes had a lovely soprano voice—crisp, clear, and true to pitch if not a bit thin in her top range. After an hour of demonstrating to Kristy how to breathe from the diaphragm and telling her to use her whole body to support her sound rather than forcing it, Kat felt a bit light-headed.

"Remember what I told you, Kristy," Kat said, guiding her protégé to the front door. "Relax your vocal cords and your abdominal muscles when you do your exercises. Don't tense up."

"I'll try," Kristy promised. "It's so hard to relax sometimes when my mother watches me all the time and keeps making comments about trying out for the Houston Opera."

Kat sighed. She'd always wanted to try out for the opera herself. "I know, dear, but isn't it nice to know your mother realizes what a sunny future you have? You are truly blessed. Goodbye now."

Kat stifled a yawn and returned to the kitchen to finish her lunch and continue sorting through Saturday's and

Monday's pile of mail. No time for a quick nap, she had a trio of piano lessons that kicked off in another fifteen minutes.

Kick off.

The image of Nigel Morgan, field goal kicker extraordinaire, immediately sprang into Kat's mind. Nigel Morgan, her daughter's so-called one true love. Nigel Morgan, the boy who could ruin her daughter's sunny future.

Kat had tried to act nice toward the boy all weekend long, but it had been difficult. Flashing his pearly teeth in a perpetual smile, Nigel had been open and honest enough about how he wasn't even planning to graduate until the year after next.

The acid in her stomach churned. Didn't he have any ambitions other than playing professional sports? Keely's student teaching period was next spring, and her advisor had said she was practically assured a spot in the graduate program the following term. Getting her master's in music education and starting her own academy for strings was all Keely had talked about since high school. There wasn't any need for her to complicate her life with a boyfriend at this point in the game.

An ad flyer under a stack of bills on the table caught Kat's eyes. The photo of a tall, dark, and handsomely smiling male model promised, *We'll make your teeth their most dazzling white in one session or your money back.* Frowning, she crumpled the junk mailing into a tight ball and pitched it straight into the trash—two points.

Kat had decided Keely didn't need a freeloading boyfriend keeping her away from her dreams no matter how charming and polite he acted. Besides, they were complete opposites. Keely was serious and studious and driven. Nigel acted altogether too laid-back and jovial, seeped in a live-and-let-live atmosphere since birth. It would never work.

At the knock at the door, Kat stilled her troubling

thoughts and slipped back into her piano teacher persona.

"Come in, come in, come in." Forcing a grin, Kat flung open the door for the Marquez sisters' weekly invasion of her quiet abode. "Who's up first today?"

A small hand attached to a slightly cross-eyed, six-year-old girl wearing light pink frames zoomed into the air.

"Okay, Wendy? You take the bench, dear. Mindy and Lindy? You two sit quietly on the couch and get out your paper keyboards and try to play along with your sister best you can. Ready?"

Why Kat had ever agreed to host the energetic threesome in back-to-back sessions she'd never know. Well, it wasn't quite true. She'd done it for the money, of course.

At the end of the ninety-minute marathon music session, Kat felt exhausted. She was long overdue for her nap. Straightening the piano's music rack and bench, she then turned out the lamp above the keyboard and headed for her bed.

Kat fluffed up her pillow and, with her other hand, rubbed the back of her neck. Sleeping on the twins' lumpy futon sofa cushion against the living room wall they shared with their late-night, stereo-blasting neighbors had been a genuine horror. The only other time in her life she'd ever suffered from such exhaustion and pain was when she'd been married to Dirk, the pain-in-the-neck master himself.

Dirk. Hadn't her parents warned her they were complete opposites? Had she listened to their dire predictions? No, of course not.

Kat kicked off her canvas flats and crawled under the top sheet and closed her eyes. Night and day, north and south . . . Keely's and Nigel's mutual attraction wasn't really all that different from hers and Dirk's. There was something mysterious, something dangerous, something attractive about a man who acted entirely contrary to everything you'd ever been brought up to find desirable in a mate. The magnetism of a ne'er-do-well's personality sucked you into his brawny arms and straight into his bed . . .

Oh, Lord. They'd better not be doing everything I did.

Luckily for her, Dirk hadn't been averse to getting married when she'd told him about the baby. He hadn't even blinked when she'd informed him a month later the ultrasound had identified that she was, in fact, carrying two babies. Both she and Dirk had been in their wild-eyed romantic phase then. Giving up her chance to ever make it in the world of professional music to carry her and Dirk's children to term didn't seem too big a sacrifice to make at the time. After all, they'd been in love.

Dirk's gambling and drinking were only minor pastimes at that point. His family—poor Hill Country ranch workers—had been happy to call her their daughter, welcoming the newlyweds into their humble home. How useless Dirk had ever sprung from such gracious seed, Kat was never certain, but she'd loved her in-laws dearly. When both passed away within several years of Dirk's death, she'd grieved as if it were her own mother and father whom she'd lost.

Kat drifted off to sleep in the softness of the mattress and the solace of silence, only to be awakened by the incessant ringing of the doorbell at six-forty-five.

"Huh?" She rubbed her bleary eyes and stared at her alarm clock. Who the hell could it be at this hour? She pulled herself groggily from her comfortable bed and shuffled to the front door.

"I'm ready for my lesson," Jonathan Rawlins announced.

Still laboring under the heavy influence of sleep, all Kat could do was stare back.

Jonathan quirked an eyebrow. "My piano lesson?"

Kat mouthed his words. She had another lesson today? Then it came flooding back to her. She blushed and startled fully awake.

"Oh, yes. It was tonight, wasn't it?" She stumbled back-ward and motioned for him to enter. "Come on in and sit yourself down at the piano. I'll be right with you."

Kat rushed to her bathroom, splashed her face with cold water, and grabbed her hairbrush.

"For Pete's sake. Every time the man comes over, I'm ei-ther half-undressed or half-asleep . . . a regular schlep, noth-ing like I usually am in public. Whatever must he think of me?"

Jonathan seated himself at the low piano bench and rammed his knees against the underside of the keyboard.

"Ow!" He shifted his long legs outward, toward the sides. They fit — barely. Placing his sheet music on the rack, he at-tempted to rest his gangly fingers on the keys. They didn't seem to fit, either.

"This is never going to work." He sighed. If he couldn't sit on the piano bench properly or move his fingers on the keys correctly, how in the world would he ever learn to play? How could he ever hope to make a good impression on Kat if he was such a hopeless case?

"What's not going to work?" Kat briskly reentered the liv-ing room. "You having trouble with your knees hitting the underside of the keyboard?"

Jonathan nodded, trying his best not to frown. "Yes, I am."

"No problem. I have an adjustable stool that's suitable for taller folk. I apologize for forgetting to remove the bench af-ter my last pupil. The stool's in the storage shed out back. I'll go fetch it."

She darted from the room before Jonathan could protest. He noticed Kat had brushed her hair and reapplied her makeup. She'd made an attempt to look nice for him. It was a good sign, wasn't it?

He stood and carefully moved the now wobbly piano bench over to the side against the wall. Oh, no . . . his weight must have loosened one of the legs—correction, all four legs. Jonathan smacked his forehead in disgust. Here it was less than five minutes into his first lesson, and he'd already broken Kat's furniture. What kind of evening did that threaten?

Straightening himself, he caught a glimpse of a small framed photograph hanging at eye level among a montage of family portraits. It must have been taken several years ago as both Kevin and Keely looked to be about age five . . . and Kat? Kat simply looked, more or less, her same beautiful self with the possible exception of her hair color, which was a bit more ash than silvery-blonde at this point. The background appeared to be a park shelter. They were dressed in t-shirts and shorts, apparently attending a picnic.

On Kat's right stood a brooding older gentleman, and beside him a scowling woman of approximately the same age. They must be Kat's parents, Jonathan decided. The frowning couple shared many of the same facial characteristics as both Kat and the children save one—they didn't seem to possess an inkling of a smile between them.

Jonathan cocked his head to the side, taking in the strapping man wearing a muscle shirt standing on Kat's left. No way on earth this blond Adonis could be her brother. Jonathan had never seen a photo of Kat's husband or even heard a physical description of the man before, but judging by the way Mister Muscles in the picture possessively draped his bare, brawny arm across Kat's shoulders there could be no mistaking their relationship. Now he knew exactly where Kevin got his athletic prowess—from this strong, intimidating-looking man with flashing hazel-green eyes and an almost devilish grin.

Jonathan's broad shoulders slumped as he stepped away from the photograph. There was no comparison. He may have an inch or two over Kat's late husband in height, but Mister Muscles appeared to have worked out in a gym regularly or possibly he worked on a ranch. No clunky spectacles hid his handsome face, and with his rugged physique there was no need for him to wear designer clothes to get the ladies to notice him. Mister Muscles oozed movie star charisma and probably had attracted women to him like flies to honey.

Jonathan shook his head. No wonder Kat had never remarried. How could any man hope to compete against such a memory? Unless . . . unless he bit the bullet and got himself *buffed up* as well?

"Sorry for the delay." Kat deposited the stool in front of the piano and twirled the seat around and around to lower it. "This old thing was hiding in the back under some of Kevin's free weights. I wish he would have taken them to college with him. They'd make excellent paperweights."

"Can I help?" Jonathan bent to assist her, a flood of guilt washing over him as he realized how difficult removing the weights to get at the stool must have been.

"No, I'm fine. It's a one-woman operation." Kat stood and dusted her hands together. "All you need to do now is sit and see if it's at the right height for you. You need to feel comfortable while sitting at the piano. No knee cracking, no straining to keep your hands on the keys. Keep your elbows at a ninety-degree angle as much as possible."

Jonathan gingerly sat and stretched his hands across the keyboard. He smiled. "It's the perfect height. How did you know?"

"A lucky guess." Kat stood perpendicular to the piano at Jonathan's right. "You're about six-foot-one, six-foot-two?"

"Try six-three. You'd never know by the way I stand

sometimes, would you?"

Her eyes widened. "Really? I bet they had you playing center in high school or college."

"No, whenever a basketball coach saw how thick my glasses were he immediately put that notion out of his head." Jonathan shrugged. "Long hands and fingers aren't detrimental to playing the piano, are they?"

"Goodness gracious no." She grinned her encouragement. "In fact, you'll be able to easily reach every note in a chord which is something most of my pupils can't do very well. I'll show you."

Kat placed her right hand in the middle of the keyboard, resting her thumb on the key clearly marked *middle C* with a small piece of masking tape. She stretched out her hand until her pinky barely hit a key about two to the right of a key marked with tape *high C*.

"See? I have to try really hard to make it across ten keys, and that's not too shabby. You'll be able to reach farther."

"Like this?" Jonathan overlapped his right hand over Kat's, stretching until his pinky hit two keys above hers. He felt sorely tempted to take her delicate hand in his, to hold on to it and caress its softness and warmth, but he thought the better of it. Instead, he tilted his chin upwards and gazed deeply into her eyes. "How's that?"

Frozen in place, Kat returned Jonathan's gently probing look with one of her own. "How's what?"

"Is that a good stretch?"

Kat shook her head, slipping her hand out from under his. "Yes, it's great. Now, I want you to relax your hand a bit, but keep your thumb on the key marked middle C. One finger on each key. Try to keep your hands cupped, lifted off the keyboard, sort of like you were holding a rubber ball in your palm. Press down firmly on the keys like this, one at a time."

She demonstrated the technique on the octave above and motioned him to do the same. After two false starts, Jonathan played each of the corresponding keys along with Kat several times.

"Bravo!" She clapped. "You're a natural."

He quirked an eyebrow. "Natural? Me? At piano playing? You've got to be kidding."

"No, it sometimes takes a whole lesson to get some of my students to do what you just did. The quicker you catch on, the better your aptitude."

"Well, I'll be." Jonathan chuckled. "So, how come my parents never signed me up for lessons?"

"Did your family own a piano?"

He stroked his chin. "No, they didn't. Probably the closest one was located some ten miles from our farm at the church. My dad always had more than enough chores for me to do after school. I guess it explains why I haven't gotten around to playing piano until later in life."

Kat rifled through some papers stacked on top of the piano and pulled several free. "Just remember, it's never too late to learn. I taught myself guitar and a few other instruments when I went back to school to finish my music education degree."

It's never too late to learn.

Jonathan gazed at Kat in admiration. Was it too late for her to learn to see him in a different way? Too late for her to consider him anything but a doddering old fool?

"Here it is." She placed a sheet of music on the stand in front of him. "This is a beginner's exercise page for the right hand. I'm sorry I didn't go out and get you a lesson book, but this is probably a better route to take, being that you are so much, uh, so much . . ."

Jonathan cringed.

Say it. I'm old. It's what you think of me — old, boring, half-dead Jonathan Rawlins.

"So much more mature than my other pupils," Kat finished diplomatically. "You can read a little bit of music, right? You follow along on hymns quite well, I've noticed."

Jonathan took a deep breath and dismissed his self-deprecating thoughts. "All I know is that the white notes are held longer than the black ones, and when they climb the fence, the pitch goes higher."

"The fence?" A light dawned across her face. "You mean the notes on the staff. Very clever analogy. I'll have to use it with the kids sometimes."

He smiled. "Be my guest. It's not copyrighted as far as I know."

"That's good. I'd hate to be sued for infringement," she teased, rolling her eyes. Leaning over Jonathan's shoulder, Kat pointed to the top line of music on the page with a pencil. "Now, looking at this measure, place your right hand on the keys and play exactly as you did before."

Jonathan did as he was instructed. Was that all there was to it?

"Ta-da. You're reading and playing music, and it hasn't even been the full hour yet. My best pupil yet."

Jonathan's cheeks warmed. "Aw shucks, ma'am. I just happen to have the world's best teacher, that's all."

She laughed. "Flattery will get you everywhere, mister."

He raised an eyebrow. "Will it now?"

Kat caught herself the second before she practically threw herself into Jonathan's lap. What the heck was getting into her? Was she openly flirting with her student? And for some unknown reason, the room had become stifling hot. She reached to open the top button of her blouse, then thought the better of it.

"Excuse me a second. I need to go check the A/C. Why

don't you go over the same measure again and try to make the notes sound more even, more connected this time."

Kat dashed straight to the kitchen whereupon she gulped down a large glass of water. Had it been the touch of Jonathan's hands as they'd met hers or the way he had looked deep into her eyes like he could read her mind which had affected her so?

Maybe this was all something hormonal? Her doctor did tell her the last time she went in to be on the lookout for hot flashes. More than likely the heat she felt pulsing through her frame, lingering a little longer than necessary in her belly, was simply caused by a power surge blanking her programmed thermostat and shutting down the air conditioning. She went into the hall, hit a few buttons, and checked the readout on the climate control panel. Funny, it seemed to be doing its job.

Rubbing the cold glass against her warm forehead, Kat listened to Jonathan's playing in the next room. It sounded like he was trying to pick out the melody of *Amazing Grace*.

"You didn't tell me that you could play by ear," she said, a this-is-a-pleasant-surprise smile splayed across her face.

Jonathan started at her entrance but continued with his hunting and pecking. "No, I'm just using my fingers like I do on a keyboard. It's not the most efficient way to play a piano, I've discovered."

"You got that right. It does help, though, if you have some notion as to how the song you want to play goes already." She crossed to stand beside the piano once more and waited as he finished his impromptu concert. "There's a beginner's book of favorite hymns I think you'll want to get. After a few pointers on how to read the music, you'll be able to play a more recognizable version of *Amazing Grace* before you know it."

His eyes mushroomed in amazement. "You actually could

tell what I was trying to plunk out?"

"If I can tell someone's playing *Mary Had a Little Lamb* while missing practically every note, then I can make out what you were attempting to play."

"I'm that good, huh?"

Kat felt drawn to him like a magnet to steel. Her gaze settled on Jonathan's full lips as he spoke. Would their touch be as electrifying as the feel of his fingers sliding over hers across the keyboard?

"Good?" She blinked twice to break the warm, damp fog settling in her brain. She really needed to finish her nap. That explained it. She was sleep-deprived. "Yes, you play quite well."

Kat's gaze drifted toward Jonathan's lips again, then lower. Six-foot-three with hands that could easily reach twelve keys and possessed an almost magnetic touch—what kinds of things could he do with those hands?

Kat pounced on the stack of sheet music he'd brought to the lesson. "Um, would you like me to play the version you brought?"

"Please do."

She sorted out the copy from the others and opened it across the music stand. "Sorry, but we need to switch places. I need to sit where you're sitting to play properly."

Jonathan stood and side-stepped over to the left to give her access to his stool.

Kat flashed him a grin in gratitude and sat without looking. Immediately she found herself deposited on her rear end on the floor.

"Ouch!" she cried, rubbing her bruised tailbone. "I missed."

"You seem to be doing quite a bit of falling on your backside lately." Jonathan chuckled. Placing his large hands under her arms, he lifted her to her feet in one easy motion.

"There you go. You all right?"

"I . . . I'm fine," she managed, taking a step back. The warmth of where his palms contacted with her bare flesh lingered, sending tingles of awareness down her arms. "I just need to adjust the height a little."

Kat bent to twirl the stool to raise the seat. To her horror, it stuck.

Jonathan grimaced. "Did I break it? I apologize if I did."

She straightened slowly and shook her head. "Don't worry. It isn't broken. It probably needs to be greased a bit. Why don't we try relocating the bench?"

Jonathan removed the stool. Kat grabbed the bench and dragged it into position. Without a word, both seated themselves side by side, thighs touching.

Kat shuddered at the delicious sensation of Jonathan's near presence.

This isn't the appropriate time or place for playing footsies, but wouldn't it be nice?

Swallowing hard, Kat focused her attention on the music. Just as she was about to turn to the first page over there came a small moan of wood, then *snap!* The wounded bench decided it couldn't handle their combined weight any longer. The back leg collapsed. The seat tilted left, throwing her against Jonathan's hard body as they tumbled to the floor.

CHAPTER SIX

"Oh!" Kat cried, landing in a heap on top of her student.

"You hurt?" Jonathan asked.

"N-no . . ."

She raised her spinning head and gazed into his big brown eyes mere inches from her own. Kat's breath caught. An amused expression danced in their depths rather than a mortally injured one. There was something else, too, a glimmer of some kind, a glimmer of *desire*? Could *she* be the cause of that glimmer? An eternity passed until either spoke or moved.

"I'm so sorry." Kat scrambled to her feet and brushed herself off.

"No harm done." Jonathan smiled at her, then stood. He picked up the bench and turned it over to examine the damage. "I'll have this thing fixed for you. It's the least I can do."

She placed a hand to her heart and willed it to stop beating in cut-time. "Why thank you, but please, don't blame yourself for the bench's demise. It was long overdue for service. I know a place in town where I can get it fixed. I should since I've had it done often enough."

He wriggled an eyebrow at her, then placed the seat to the side. "I guess you'll have to try the stool again."

"Yes, it does look that way. I'll have to sit on a book or a cushion, though."

Jonathan cleared his throat. "You could just sit on my lap," he suggested.

"What?" Kat blushed. "Uh, yeah, it's adjusted for your

height, isn't it?"

He scooted the stool over to the keyboard, seated himself, and swung his legs toward the piano. "If you don't mind, I certainly don't."

Kat took a steadying breath and nodded. There were no bones about it—this had to be the most awkward situation of her entire teaching career.

"Very well," she said at last. "If you're sure you don't mind. It *is* a rather short hymn."

The lights in his eyes mesmerized her.

"I don't mind at all. In fact, I insist."

Kat bit her lip, summoning her resolve. She gingerly seated herself atop Jonathan's long thighs. The heat of his breath tickling the back of her neck almost drove her mad before she could play a note—the fascinating bulge poking close to her posterior excited her. It was almost more than she could bear.

"You comfortable?" His voice sounded deep, husky.

Kat cleared her throat and stretched out her arms. "Quite," she lied.

Steeling her nerves, she began playing *Amazing Grace* in a slightly faster than normal tempo. As she came to the repeat sign, somehow she found herself playing all the verses, her hands lingering forever on the last chord.

"Beautiful. So very beautiful . . ." Jonathan sighed as she finished. "It certainly beats my picking out a song one note at a time."

He reached out both hands and placed them on either side of Kat's on the keyboard, essentially trapping her between himself and the instrument. "How long until I'll be able to play with both hands like you do?"

Kat gasped. Her mouth formed a small O of its own volition. His closeness, his heat, his arms encircling her, enveloping her . . . she knew she should pull away, run away, but she liked it. She really, really liked it.

"You'll be able to play with two hands eventually," Kat replied, melting farther into the warm comfort of him. "We start out with the right hand so you can learn the melody before we progress to playing the harmony."

"How do you know how to make your hands move up from middle C to hit those high notes?" Jonathan demonstrated by gliding his silky, long fingers over hers.

Kat shivered, her head tilting ever-so-slowly toward his face, her lips subtly parting, dying to meet their counterparts.

"You make it look so easy," he said softly.

Easy? He thinks I'm easy?

Kat froze. Somewhere in the rational part of her brain she realized she was acting like it didn't take much to get her motor running and on the road to the boudoir. If Jonathan didn't hold a jaundiced view of her before when she'd answered the door half-asleep, or how she'd practically flashed him in her silk pajamas the week before, then he most certainly would now if she did as her body told her to.

She withdrew her hands from the keys and made an effort to stand. Jonathan dropped his arms, allowing her to make good her escape.

"It takes practice," Kat said, regaining her composure. She scooted over to the side and gathered a few information sheets from the piano top. "Practice and time. Anyone can learn to play the piano if he's willing to take the time to practice."

She handed Jonathan the papers and averted her eyes. "Here you go. This tells you what books you need to purchase by your next lesson and where you can buy them. There's also a little exercise you should try practicing for about ten minutes every day until your next lesson. I'll let you go now so you can go look for your materials."

Jonathan nodded. "Thanks again—for showing me the basics of piano playing, that is."

A rising warmth flooded her cheeks. "You're welcome."

"I promise I'll practice every day," he pledged, raising a long-fingered hand. "I want to be your best pupil—your best pupil ever."

He sauntered to the door, then exited.

"No problem," Kat said breathlessly, staring at the closed door and hugging herself tight. "There's really no competition. No competition at all."

Jonathan carefully lifted the bow-like exercise contraption from the trunk of his car and deposited it next to the back wall. The garage seemed as good a place as any to store the thing, although after summer really got going he might change his mind and drag it indoors to the air-conditioned comfort of the family room. He slammed the trunk closed and stepped into the house so he could sit and digest the plentiful, full-color illustrated information on how he, too, could have rippling biceps and firm abs in six weeks or less as advertised on TV.

What would Ruth think if she could see me now?

He poured himself a tall iced tea, minus the sugar, before spreading out on the couch. Here he had spent half the day in Austin and half a fortune on exercise equipment and music books. Ruth wouldn't have found fault in him for improving both his body and his mind, would she? Between body-building and piano playing, Jonathan was determined to make a new—and much more exciting—man out of himself in six weeks or less or at least die trying.

Jonathan downed his drink and sank deeper into the comfortable overstuffed sofa, desperately trying to decipher the whys and wherefores of the fancy exercise equipment he'd just purchased. After perusing the literature for fifteen minutes, he concluded the basic idea of the contraption was to force his muscles to bend steel rods, thereby bulking him up into a Charles Atlas lookalike as he progressed from the lightest rods to the heaviest. It seemed a straightforward enough course of action. Reading a little further, he was chagrined to discover that weight training alone would not burn off his middle-age spare tire.

"Rigorous, aerobic activity, such as jogging, biking, inline skating or mountain climbing is necessary to increase metabolism and accelerate weight loss," he read, stroking his chin thoughtfully. "Mountain climbing is definitely out of the picture, and I don't own inline skates or a bike that isn't in a thousand pieces and rusting. Jogging doesn't sound too awful, and I already own some good sports shoes, so jogging it is."

With that matter settled, Jonathan rose to make himself a late dinner, promising himself it would be more nutritious than the meal he'd consumed last night after his piano lesson. For some reason, he'd been ravenous after he'd left Kat's home, hankering after something sweet and feeling like an extra-large ice cream sundae with plenty of nuts and gallons of chocolate syrup from the local ice-cream stand. While it had been more than filling, he'd found himself on a sugar and caffeine high until the wee hours of the morning. Ice cream for dinner was no way for a man his age and condition to get into shape.

Retrieving the free sample of *muscle-building powder supplement* from the sporting goods store bag, Jonathan read the label contents. *Ugh.* He definitely could wait to sprinkle the odd concoction on his bran flakes tomorrow morning. Tonight, he felt like a steak and promptly went to digging through the freezer to see if anything fit the bill.

"This thing is long overdue to be defrosted," he mumbled, flipping over package after package of frozen hamburger in search of sirloin. "Bingo." A few minutes in the microwave to thaw the hard lump of meat and he'd be all set to barbecue.

There was still a bit of propane left in the tank Jonathan happily discovered. He removed the cover and slapped his steak onto the grill's surface. With some fresh corn on the cob, a recent gift from of one of his flock, and some grilled Texas toast, he actually had something resembling a decent meal.

Jonathan stood entranced as the flames licked at the sizzling steak. Images of last night—hot and steamy memories of Kat falling on top of him and then agreeing to sit on his lap—sprang vividly to life. He'd been joking when he'd suggested she sit on his lap. All right, half-joking. He truly had been concerned for her safety when he'd stretched out his arms on either side of her. He hadn't wanted her to fall on that gorgeous rear end of hers again, her very nice, curvy rear end . . .

Jonathan gulped. He flipped his sirloin over to cook on the other side, dabbing it with barbecue sauce. He needed to get in control of himself. He didn't want to frighten Kat away after only one piano lesson and one dinner date of sorts. It was difficult for him to stop thinking of Kat in that way, that same way he'd thought of Ruth earlier on in their marriage.

There was no use denying it anymore. Ruth's plaid flannel nightgowns and woolen socks to bed in the winter were never much of a turn-on for him, but she had suffered from poor circulation, so they had become a necessity in recent years. He wondered, what did Kat wear to bed on a chilly winter's eve? Possibly the same body-hugging satin pajamas she'd had on the other night? In the summer? What must it be like to lie next to her soft, voluptuous body on a hot summer's night, comfortably attired in nothing God didn't grace her with upon her birth?

Jonathan found himself drooling. It had to be the smell of his well-done steak, he decided. He forked it and a corn cob onto a plate and grabbed his bread and went indoors to eat at the dining room table away from the flies and skeeters. He missed not having anyone to talk to during mealtimes, but mostly he missed having Ruth there to wait on him hand and foot and offer him seconds before she'd even finished her firsts.

He cut into the sirloin and tried not to think of his waistline. No wonder he'd put on so much weight over the years. If Mother Ruth and her selfless indulgence of his appetite were still around, his plan for shedding a few extra pounds and getting in shape would be lost. Ruth had forever told him he didn't have a weight problem and she liked him just the way he was, but in recent years, whenever Jonathan looked in the mirror, he hadn't been happy with what he saw, and it had been difficult for him to express that thought out loud to Ruth or to anyone. Perhaps the reason God had called Ruth home early was to rouse him from his lethargic lifestyle, to light a fire under his lazy backside?

Dismissing his troubling thoughts, Jonathan cleaned his plate, then rinsed it off and placed it in the dishwasher. At the rate he filled the machine up, it would be another two weeks before he ran the thing, so he decided to be extravagant and go ahead and start it. Yes, it was a waste of precious resources like water and electricity, but Ruth wasn't here to remind him of that fact.

Jonathan's shock at his own disloyalty lasted a whole ten seconds before the phone rang.

"Pastor, the evangelism committee is having a little problem," Darla informed him. "Can you come on over to the church and see if you can't help straighten things out?"

He bit back a sigh. "What's the trouble, Darla? Surely you

all can work things out among yourselves. You're all adults."

"We know, but still, we could use your input. Without Ruth as our chairperson, things sort of get out of hand at times, and I don't know what to do to get them back on track."

"All right. Give me a few moments, and I'll be over."

Jonathan put the phone down and shook his head. If Ruth had always been Mother Ruth, then there could be no doubt his congregants wanted him to continue playing Father Jon.

Kat clenched the receiver in frustration and swallowed a scream.

"For the millionth time, BB," she repeated, "I don't want to go to the party with you. Can't you get that through your thick skull?"

"*No lo comprendo, bebe,*" Bradley T. Bradley drawled.

Even over the telephone, Kat could tell he was smiling like an imp, thinking he'd cornered her good and she couldn't say no.

"It's only the hottest ticket of the year for the County Democratic Fund-raising Committee. You do want me to win a third term in office, don't you, sweetheart?"

Kat gritted her teeth and rolled her eyes in disgust. "Enough with the terms of endearment, or else I'll be tempted to use my own special nickname for you in public sometime."

A pause. "You wouldn't."

"I most certainly would. Don't try me, Mister Floppy."

This time, it was Kat who grinned at the sound of BB gritting his teeth.

"Look, Alley Kat—er Baby Doll, um, darlin', I didn't mean to go off with that bimbo in Austin. I got carried away when the governor shook my hand and said I was the best darn county DA in the whole state. You know how things like that go to my head and all."

To other parts of your anatomy as well?

Kat remembered. Even after all this time, his betrayal still stung worse than a scorpion bite.

"Yes, I'm sure. And who could ever imagine the governor was that ill-informed about a member of his own party?"

"Hey, Angel Cakes, there's no need to get nasty with me—"

"Then stop calling me Angel Cakes, Puddin' Head!" Kat shouted. She dropped the receiver to her side and drew in a steadying breath before continuing. "Look, BB, it's over between us. O-v-e-r, over. I don't want to date you anymore. I have better things to do with my time. So, please, take my number off your speed dial and get yourself a new girlfriend. *Comprende?*"

"Oh, all right, Kat. Whatever you say, but if you ain't interested in escorting me to the dinner-dance tomorrow night, then how about a couple of drinks at my place on Saturday?"

His audacity stunned her. "You-you w-want me to come over for drinks at your place? Are you insane? What did I just now tell you?"

"I'm lonely," he whimpered. "Look, honey pie, I promise I'll make it worth your while."

Kat rubbed her temples. "BB, if I came over to your place and warmed your water bed one more time, I'd charge you exactly what that hooker in Austin charged you that night."

A pause, then, "You would?"

"Yes, I would."

"Well, dang it, sweet cheeks. I knew you still liked me some." BB sniggered with glee. "Hot dawg! I'll go change the sheets right now. I'll put on the purple ones you like so much."

"Aaaaargh!"

Kat slammed the phone down and kicked the side of the garbage can for good measure. Almost at once she paced the kitchen floor to burn off her frustration.

"What is wrong with that man?" she muttered. "He's intelligent enough to graduate law school, get himself elected to office, but he can't understand the simple word *no* for the life of him."

Kat paced back and forth, but it was no use. Five minutes after holding a conversation with Bradley T. Bradley, and she still felt like kicking everything in sight, and her tile floor couldn't take much more wear and tear. A breath of fresh air would clear her head. Picking up her cross-trainers from the back doormat, Kat headed to her car.

It had been too long since she'd jogged the trail at Germantown City Park. She pulled her car into a parking space not far from the trail's entrance and switched off the engine. Opening her driver's side door wide, she swung her legs around to slide on her walking shoes. At the sight of the pale-gray sedan parked next to hers, she did a double-take.

"Could it be? No, it couldn't be, could it?"

Kat finished tying her laces, stuffed her purse under the front seat, and locked the doors. Casually strolling around the back of the pale-gray car, she spied a Clergy Parking bumper sticker courtesy of one of the local hospitals. What was Jonathan Rawlins doing in the park on a Thursday night at seven-thirty?

Kat scanned the picnic table area. Wherever Jonathan was, he wasn't nearby. Possibly he was beyond the small woods over at the softball diamonds watching one of the little league teams play. Yes, it was probably the meaning behind his visit to the park. He wasn't following her around.

She sighed. For some reason the notion that Jonathan wasn't pursuing her disappointed her. She'd half expected to see him again after choir practice last night to invite her out for dinner and was half relieved when he hadn't showed. She didn't like to admit it, but the other half of her had wanted to see him.

"Get over it," Kat muttered as she jogged across the field toward the entrance of the walking trail. Nestled in a small valley along scenic limestone ledges in a grove of live oak and ash juniper, the track had quickly become the favorite pathway for pedestrians. She fell into an easy loping stride and allowed her mind to wander.

Tuesday's piano lesson had had a mesmerizing effect on Kat. The feel of Jonathan's arms around her waist, his hands touching hers, his breath warm and sensuous against her neck—she shuddered. Here it was, ninety-plus degrees, and she was actually shivering, shivering with desire at the recollection of how Jonathan had made her feel Tuesday evening.

No man had ever made her feel so aware of her body's responses—not Dirk, not BB, not anyone. What was it about Jonathan that made her feel so alive? She'd never seen Jonathan Rawlins in such a light before while Ruth had been alive. But now? Now he was practically all she could think of.

Kat halted and grabbed her knees, gasping for breath, at the first park bench located a dozen yards along the trail.

God should strike me dead for such wicked thoughts.

Here she was, lusting after a man who was still mourning his late wife—his late wife who was a saint by anyone's standards and was still sorely missed by one and all. She should feel ashamed of herself. Really, she should.

But somehow, she didn't.

Kat started jogging again. The exercise would purge her of these impure thoughts or at least make her too tired to act on them.

"You know, it wouldn't be too forward of me to ask him over for dinner some night," she reasoned. "I could just tell him I wanted to make sure he was eating right."

You could tell him that he'd never have to eat another meal alone. Ever.

Kat gulped and blinked hard, hastening her pace. Good Lord, her estrogen levels must be completely whacked. She was acting like a silly teenager who harbored a secret crush on her teacher. She was fantasizing about becoming Jonathan Rawlins's main squeeze.

"I've *got* to get over this."

Kat tilted her head back and let the rays of dying sunlight streaming through the trees bathe her face with their warmth. She focused her concentration back into the tempo of her footsteps falling on the path. Right, left, right, left, right, left. Up, down, up, down over the rolling hillsides . . .

Her breathing slowed. A calming blanket of sanity wrapped itself around her raging hormones. Her mind solved her present dilemma. It was simple. She was an adult—he was an adult. Two adults having the occasional dinner together was a perfectly natural, wholesome activity. Hadn't he invited her out to eat once before? She could say she was returning the favor. It wasn't anything to be ashamed of—

"Look out!" a familiar male voice shouted, rousing her from her daydreaming. Too late.

Kat tumbled over the large, man-shaped obstruction in her path, sliding and tumbling in an unladylike jumble of limbs and legs among the carpet of wood chips only to land spread-eagled on her well-bruised backside.

"Kat? Are you all right?"

Jonathan's voice sounded like it was coming from somewhere near her right temple, but Kat couldn't be too sure. Was she hallucinating? After all, hadn't she been thinking about Jonathan a moment before she'd fallen?

A large hand caressed her cheek. "Kat? Speak to me, please."

Kat slowly opened her eyes and looked to her right. Jonathan Rawlins's face hovered mere inches from her own.

"Thank Heavens you're still with us." He sighed. "For a moment there, I thought you might have been knocked unconscious."

"I'm conscious?" Kat managed after a moment. Somehow, it didn't seem real, lying on her back on the ground, peering up and seeing the tops of trees and Jonathan's concerned face so near hers.

"Yes, you're conscious, and we're a bit tangled up. Here, allow me first."

Jonathan slid his shorts-clad legs from beneath Kat's, sending a ripple of delicious sensation sizzling throughout her body as flesh rubbed against flesh. He carefully removed one arm from beneath her back and slid the other across her breasts and stomach. Kat's breath caught. His fingers had the same effect on her whether they were playing the piano or playing her.

He rolled to his knees, then stood. "There. We're untangled now."

Kat pulled herself up to her elbows and shook her head to clear the cobwebs. She had landed practically on top of him like the other day. She must be dreaming.

"I do believe I'm a jinx." Jonathan offered Kat his hand and pulled her to her feet. "Every time I've seen you this past week, you've landed in a heap on your backside. I hate causing you to injure yourself so."

She raised her hand. "Oh, no, please don't blame yourself. It was my fault. I wasn't watching where I was going. Not many folks use this path on a weeknight, so I didn't think I'd run into any . . . any obstacles."

He grimaced. "My shoelace came untied, and I bent down

to take care of it. I'm sorry."

"No apology necessary." Kat glanced down. He was wearing cross-trainers the same as she. "I didn't know you were a jogger."

"I didn't know you were one, either." Grinning, he motioned with his eyes down the path. "Shall we continue our exercise together?"

Kat inhaled deeply and nodded. "All right."

A few yards later, she was forced to call it quits. They hobbled over to a nearby park bench and sat.

"I think I may have twisted something," Kat groaned, rubbing her right shin. "You'll have to go on without me."

"Nonsense. We can wait here until you feel like you can walk again."

"It might be a while. I think it's more of a muscle pull than a sprain. All I can do is wait for the spasm to pass."

"Would a drink help?" He handed her his half-empty water bottle.

She accepted it with a smile. "Yes, it most certainly would. Thanks."

Jonathan was never more glad to have brought his sports container than he was today as Kat flicked open the snap top with a long mauve nail and lifted the bottle as if in slow motion to her full, mauve-tinted lips. He was fascinated watching her gulp the icy liquid. Drops sensuously slid from the corners of her mouth, around her chin, and down her lovely, long neck to collect in the V of her cotton tank top. He sighed. What he wouldn't give to be one of those water drops trickling into Kat's cleavage just about now.

"You're a lifesaver," she gasped at long last, handing the container back to him while licking her lips. "I hope you don't mind my slobber all over your bottle."

"Not at all. I'm glad I had it with me."

Jonathan swallowed hard. He was grateful for his new baggy shorts tonight and not his old skin-tight ones. The bagginess of the cut allowed him to cross his legs.

"How often do you go jogging?" Kat asked.

Shifting his weight to one side, Jonathan barely managed to bring his right leg over his left without tapping his seatmate with his number thirteens. "I jog only occasionally. I'm hoping to do more exercise this summer."

"Me, too."

He arched an eyebrow. "Jogging?"

"Or walking."

Kat placed her foot up on the bench, stroking her calf muscles in a slow, deliberate motion. Jonathan felt powerless to tear his gaze away from Kat's luscious lower limbs.

"Walking is easier on your joints," she commented without looking up while she continued her self-massage.

"I've heard that, too," he agreed, his eyes practically on stalks.

"There." Kat straightened her legs and stood, flexing her ankles one way and then the other. "I think my charley horse has passed."

"Can you make it?" A heroic image of sweeping Kat up into his arms and carrying her for the remainder of the trail sprang into Jonathan's mind, but he quickly dismissed it.

Kat grimaced as she put her weight on her injured side. "I should be able to. I may limp a bit."

Jonathan gallantly offered his arm. "Here, lean on me. I make a good crutch."

"Do you?" Kat clasped Jonathan's elbow and took a tentative step forward. "You're tall and thin like a walking stick."

She thinks I'm thin.

Jonathan reveled in the sentiment. God had performed at least two miracles today. First, the Lord had dropped Kat straight out of the heavens to tumble over him without being seriously injured. Secondly, the Almighty had changed her heart so Kat didn't think of him as the out-of-shape, washed-up, middle-aged has-been Jonathan thought he was. What could be more miraculous than that?

They continued down the trail at a leisurely pace. "I can't think of a better person to fall on top of me than you," he said, smiling.

Kat colored and flashed him an odd look. "Uh, thanks."

A bead of sweat crossed his brow. That hadn't come out the way he'd meant it. He sounded like a first-class lecher, not a preacher. How could he convince her otherwise?

"I meant if you're going to trip, you might as well trip over me." She was still giving him that odd look. Jonathan sighed. "I didn't mean to imply you're a klutz in any way," he tried explaining again.

"It's all right." Kat grinned. "I didn't take your comment the wrong way."

"Good, since you're not a klutz at all. In fact, you're quite . . . quite . . ."

"Coordinated?" Kat volunteered.

"Exactly."

"You mean the way I can play piano with both hands at once?"

"Yes, that, too."

Her eyes narrowed. "That, too?"

Dumbfounded, Jonathan bit the inside of his cheek. What he had been thinking was how Kat could play the piano while simultaneously giving him the biggest thrill of his life by sitting in his lap but he couldn't come out and say such a thing out loud at this point in their relationship. It might scare her off.

"You coordinate your time well in serving both the choir and the social concerns committee," he babbled on for lack of a better thing to say. "The congregation sincerely appreciates it."

Her grin wavered ever so slightly. A distant look clouded her once-shining eyes. "Thank you. I try my best for the congregation."

An uneasy silence descended over them as they limped along the remainder of the path. Other than a few brief comments about church committees and upcoming choir anthems, they didn't seem to have much to say to each other.

Jonathan was grateful when he spied the open field at last. He helped Kat to her car, made sure her leg didn't need medical attention and she was able to drive home, then quickly said his goodbye and climbed into his own vehicle.

"Why is it that whenever she's beside me I say the most stupid, inane things?" He ground the engine to life. "I should shut my mouth before I stick my big foot into it again."

His heart sank lower. He pulled out of the park and headed homeward.

"Dear Lord, why is it that I can't just come out and tell Kat I'm attracted to her and want to get to know her better? I'm used to speaking on my feet. Why do my mental faculties seize up whenever she's near?"

Because it isn't your mind that's involved, it's your heart. Try again. Pray for courage.

At once, Jonathan's jangling nerves ceased their clamoring. A sense of inner peace overcame him. He smiled.

"Yes, that's it. I'll pray for courage — and for discernment. I'll definitely need discernment to recognize if and when the right opportunity to declare my intentions comes along."

"Why is it that whenever he's near me I act like the most brain-dead person to ever walk the face of the earth?" Kat wondered as she drove out of the park. "Why can't I just tell Jonathan what's really on my mind and get it out in the open? Why am I suddenly playing little Miss Hard-to-Get?"

Because you *know you're not hard-to-get — but* he *doesn't.*

Yes, that was it in a nutshell. Jonathan respected her as a colleague. A principled, honorable man like Jonathan Rawlins could never in a thousand years possibly fathom how depraved her soul actually was. He thought only good things about others. He'd never accept a dinner invitation from a woman like her if he knew what she was really like.

Who needs to deal with a man with such a condescending attitude? Remember, BB's putting purple sheets on his bed.

Stopped by a red light, Kat slapped her steering wheel in disgust. Blasted Bradley T. Bradley! He was wearing her down with his nagging about going to just one more political function with him.

The light changed. Kat slowly accelerated the car, keeping her frustration in check so she wouldn't cause an accident.

"All right, it's time to come clean," she said, sighing, trying hard to be completely honest with herself. "BB's offer of a night of no-strings-attached whoopee is tempting. It's been so long, but I can't do it."

Kat bit a lip as she thought back to her tumble in the woods today. Once the stars had stopped twirling about her head, she'd been sorely tempted to switch places and jump on top of Jonathan and beg him to make love to her right then and there.

What had gotten into her? She knew it wasn't right to practically rape a man just because she hadn't experienced any physical intimacy recently. It simply wasn't done.

"All this time I've known Jonathan I've only desired his respect," she reasoned with herself. "I've only wanted what's best for him. So I can't jeopardize his reputation by pursuing a fruitless affair. I must let go of these *feelings* I have for him. I have to forgive myself for being weak and forget the whole darn thing."

Kat whipped into her driveway, cut the engine, then

marched into the house. A beep from her answering machine greeted her upon entering the kitchen. She knew who it would be before she even pressed the play back button.

"Kat, it's BB. Listen, I want to apologize for ragging on you earlier this evening. Can we still be friends? I promise, if you accompany me to this party tomorrow night, I will not make any moves on you that you don't want made. Okay? Give me a call back if you're agreeable. I swear on a stack of Bibles that I won't bother you again after this. Promise. Bye now."

Kat slumped against the wall and rubbed her aching temples. It figured BB would get all apologetic on her and act like a decent human being now, wouldn't it? How could she say no?

She reached for the receiver, then hesitated. What about Jonathan? Hadn't she just told herself she wanted his respect above all else? Would he respect her if he knew she was going out with a man like BB?

Remember, BB's putting purple sheets on his bed.

"What's wrong with attending one little dinner-dance to do an old friend a favor?" Kat quickly punched in BB's number before she could change her mind.

He picked up on the third ring. "Huh-loo."

"BB? This is Kat. I've had a moment to calm down and to think about your invitation. I'd love to accompany you tomorrow night. What time will you be picking me up?"

"How about six-thirty? The cocktail hour goes until seven-thirty with the dinner around eightish and dancin' and schmoozin' afterward. We don't need to stay too, too late if you get to feeling a bit put out by the whole affair."

Affair?

Kat gulped. Heat crept across her cheeks as a once familiar warmth grew in her belly. Perhaps going out with BB again was the only way to get this crazy notion of jumping Jonathan's bones out of her mind once and for all.

"Sounds great," Kat said. "I'll be ready."

CHAPTER SEVEN

"Why did I let that salesman talk me into a dish antenna?" Jonathan grumbled, tossing the TV remote aside on the couch. "A million channels, and there's still nothing worth watching on a Friday night."

The collie pup lounging at his feet barked his agreement.

"You think so, too, don't ya, Rolf?" Jonathan laughed and petted his new companion. Purchasing Rolf from Old Man Ringleschmidt was probably the best thing he had ever done. Now Jonathan had someone to talk to even if the frisky canine didn't know what in the world he was saying.

Curled up at the foot of the bed, the pup would keep his toes warm at night. It wasn't quite the same as having a real, live, flesh-and-blood woman lying beside him, but it would have to do for now.

Jonathan shook his head and sighed. He couldn't deny it any longer—he wasn't getting anywhere fast with Kat Dubcek. He wasn't making any good impressions on her. In fact, his spate of recent debacles had probably *un*impressed her.

Maybe it wasn't possible for a man and a woman to take what had always been a professional relationship and change it into something friendly. Maybe this was God's gentle way of telling him to give that part of life up. If religious aesthetics could live their entire adult lives without a spouse, then he supposed he could, too.

The memory of Kat slowly sipping from his water bottle sprang to mind. A crystal-clear image of cool, sparkling droplets of moisture trailing down her long neck, trickling across the top of her full, round—

"Okay, that's enough daydreaming," Jonathan command-ed himself. "I don't want to give her up. Not yet anyway. But perhaps this is a case of *once friends, always friends* and I'd better get used to it."

Rolf looked up at his new master oddly, cocking an ear as if to question the validity of his master's insights.

"You don't believe me, do you, boy?"

The collie barked again and jumped up on the sofa. Jona-than petted the pup briskly between the ears and grinned at him.

"You want to go for another walk already? We just came back."

Rolf yipped the affirmative, his whole body wriggling its pleasure.

"Okay, sit for a spell and give the old man a few more moments' rest. Then we'll go out."

At least he wouldn't have to worry about running into Kat again on the trail in City Park, as there were no pets al-lowed there by order of the town council. After all, who wanted to side-step through doggie messes on a jogging path? It looked like he and Rolf would have to stick to the sidewalks for their strolls.

Jonathan glanced sideways at the instructions for his new exercise equipment on the coffee table. Already he had re-neged on his plans to bulk up. He'd discovered that a hot, stuffy garage wasn't a particularly good place to work out, but it hadn't been his main excuse. In reality, he just couldn't quite bring himself to rearrange Eli's room in order to trans-form it into a home gym.

Ruth's good taste was evident in the room, from the navy plaid drapes, matching bedspread, and oak furniture, right down to the coordinated navy throw rug beside Eli's bed. It wasn't as if Eli would be using his room anytime soon. His son was twenty-one years old and stationed at Camp LeJeune. Eli probably couldn't care less if his childhood bedroom hadn't changed a bit since he graduated high school. Jonathan knew his son would love the chance to work out on the bench during his leave, too.

"About the only person who suffers guilt at not wanting to change things around the house is me," Jonathan said. It had been difficult to give away his old, ratty sweaters, but he'd done it and had felt better after he had. He needed to do this, too.

"A new dog, a new wardrobe, and a new gym. It's not every day a man practically reinvents himself." He smiled at Rolf, scratching him behind the ears once again. "Time to burn a few more calories, eh, fella?"

Rolf barked his reply. Jonathan rose to retrieve the leash from the key rack by the back door as the phone rang. He picked it up in the kitchen and held it out a foot from his ear to prevent further hearing loss.

"Dad? Where on earth have you been?" Elizabeth Rawlins-Rice nagged. "I tried you earlier tonight, and the answering machine picked up."

"I love you, too, precious," Jonathan replied gently. "So, you're the rude person who didn't leave a message. I must have been out walking Rolf."

A pause, then, "Who is this Ralph, and why are you walking with him?"

Jonathan knelt and slipped the leash on his canine companion. "Rolf is my new playmate. He enjoys catching a thrown stick and digging up things in the backyard as well as having his ears scratched."

"A dog? You got a dog?" Elizabeth's tone ratcheted up a notch. "You know how much trouble pets are—the fur, the dander, the stains on the carpet, the chewing on things—"

Jonathan gave Rolf another good scratch between the

ears. "You know, Elizabeth, you sounded just like your mother there for a moment."

"Thanks for the compliment," she muttered, "but you know I'm giving you wise advice. You don't need to encumber yourself with a creature who only makes messes and doesn't contribute to the general welfare of the family at this time in your life."

At this time in your life?

Jonathan almost bit his tongue in half at the backhanded comment. He couldn't let the gentle dig at his feebleness go unanswered.

"I suppose that's why we finally kicked you and your brother out of the house, huh?"

"Ha-ha, very funny, Dad."

Jonathan stood and leaned an elbow against the wall, sighing his frustration. Elizabeth really had taken after Ruth in many ways—in her good looks, in her intelligence and organizational abilities, but particularly in her occasional total lack of humor.

"Don't forget it's my home and not yours anymore," he reminded her, "and I could use the company. I promise Rolf will stay in the yard when my grandson comes to visit."

"That's good, but don't get your hopes up too high. We don't know for certain it's a boy yet. We've got a girl's name picked out just in case."

"Really? Tell me."

"Bailey."

"Bailey?" He furrowed his brow in dismay. "It sounds like the name of a liquor. Why not name her Ruth after your mother? After all, you said it was Joshua Jonathan if it was a boy."

"I don't think I could name my child after Mom. It's still hard for me to think about her being gone."

Jonathan's heart ached at hearing the pain in his daughter's voice. "You'll heal soon, sweetheart."

"I know I will. Besides, Ruth is a rather old-fashioned name. Using last names for girls' first names is all the rage these days. I don't want my daughter's name to be out of style."

"How about Ruth as a middle name then?"

"Possibly, but it's a moot point at the present. I've got a couple of months to go yet, remember?"

He smiled. "I'm counting the days—as I'm sure you are, too."

"Yes, I am. They go so slow when you're forced to lie in bed a good portion of the day," Elizabeth moaned. "I wish the doctor would take me off this forced bed rest. I want to help Josh finish decorating the nursery."

"The baby couldn't care less if his or her room doesn't look like the one in the magazine. Take it easy like the doctor says. I want you both to be healthy and happy."

"I know you do, Dad. I want the same for you, too. The dog's helping you get in shape, huh?"

Jonathan reached over to the counter and pitched a squeaky chew toy to occupy his overactive puppy. "Yes, Rolf's excellent at getting me off my duff. I got myself one of those home gym benches, too. I plan to be a big beefy hunk before the end of the summer."

"Yeah, sure."

Elizabeth's snort of laughter pierced his fragile male ego. Why did those nearest and dearest to him find it so hard to believe he was actually quite the athlete beneath his academic façade?

"You don't think I can do it, do you?" he challenged her.

"Oh, it's not that. It's just tickled me to think of you walking around with massive pecs and biceps straining the seams of your robe." She broke into another uncontrollable fit of giggles. "Can you imagine the looks on all the little old ladies' faces in the congregation? You'll have them swooning in the aisles."

There's only one woman I want swooning over me.

Jonathan tuned out Elizabeth's voice. His mind's eye wandered back to Kat lying beneath him on the woodchip-covered trail, her long legs entwined with his as he'd removed his arms from across her body. Where was Kat tonight? Maybe a little jog over to her home to introduce Rolf was in order?

Elizabeth's chuckling turned into hiccups. "At least once you've become a muscle man or something, Josh and I won't have to worry so much about you not being able to take care of yourself."

This was the final insult. Jonathan could take the ribbing no more.

"You two don't think I can take care of myself? What am I? A hundred and seventy-five-pound weakling or something?"

"I didn't mean it that way, Dad," Elizabeth said, calming down. "I know you can take care of yourself, but it's like Eli said to me in an e-mail the other day. *We need to keep in touch with the Old Man to make sure he's looking after himself properly between visits.* So, I'm doing my best to check-up on you."

He frowned.

Old Man, huh? You'd be surprised to know your old man could run circles around you two still.

"Thank you, honey," Jonathan acknowledged, wisely keeping his angry words to himself. "I appreciate it. Now, if you don't mind, I need to be going. Rolf looks like he's about to stain the carpet."

"By all means go," she commanded him. "I'll call you in a few days. Hopefully we'll see you in a couple of weeks if the doctor says it's okay for me to travel. I love you. Bye."

"I love you, too. Take care of yourself. Bye."

Jonathan replaced the phone receiver, then tossed a bacon-flavored doggie treat to his patiently waiting pet.

"Thanks for giving me an excuse to hang up, Rolfie. Old Man, my foot. Where do they come off saying a thing like that about me? They're not going to get away with it for much longer."

Leading the pup out the door, Jonathan found himself walking toward Kat's house. "We'll show 'em all, won't we, boy?"

Rolf happily howled his reply.

The incessant car honking outside her front door woke Kat from her daydreaming. BB's classic obnoxiousness didn't surprise her one bit. A quick peep out the window confirmed that at least he was trying to be on his best behavior tonight by picking her up in his jet-black foreign sports car and not his perpetually mud-splattered SUV. Cinderella that she was, though, Kat thought how nice it would be someday to be escorted to a ball by a handsome, well-mannered prince in a golden carriage instead of an impatiently honking, loud-mouthed lawyer driving a blatant status symbol.

"About time, sweet cheeks," he greeted her as she opened the passenger door. "Judge Holbreicht is hostin' this shindig, and I wanna impress him with my promptness."

He lifted his white felt Stetson and ran a beefy hand through his slicked-back, thinning blondish hair, simultaneously raking his hungry gaze up and down her frame. "Nice. Very nice. I always said you had a great set of legs."

"Thanks."

Kat crawled inside the luxury sports car and pulled the hem of her cocktail dress lower. It was a bit warm to be wearing pantyhose, but there was no way she was going bare-legged in her sapphire-blue, spaghetti-strapped outfit.

BB hit the gas pedal and raced out of town, easily going twenty miles over the speed limit. A moment later, Kat remembered the other reason she'd decided to wear stockings.

"You look very nice, too," she mumbled, removing his hand which he'd attempted to rest on her thigh. "Is that a new tux jacket?"

"Yeah, it is. Old one got wine stains on it at the last dress-up function I attended down in Austin. Mel over at the cleaners couldn't get it out."

I bet it was more like lipstick stains, and they were probably all over your lapels, too.

Kat rolled her eyes as she turned toward the side window.

"Luckily, this party is Texas Tuxedo, and I can wear my jeans and boots."

BB attacked the next bend in the road like a professional race car driver. For a second, Kat could have sworn they'd taken the turn on only two wheels.

"I know I always feel more comfortable in my boots," BB continued. "I don't know how you're fixin' to dance in those high heels."

She nudged another one of his pudgy fingers off her knee. "I don't. I plan to find me a nice table in the corner and hole up there. I can kick my shoes off, and no one will be any the wiser."

"I'll be." BB licked his lips. "Is that an invite for me to do likewise?"

Kat cringed. "Goodness gracious, no. You pull your boots off, and Judge Holbreicht and the rest of the party faithful will pass out from the fumes. Think with your head for once, and not the lower half of your anatomy. I thought you were trying to impress the man."

"I am, I am," he protested, casting an unabashed leer of longing toward her silhouette. "It's just seeing you again brings back so many wonderful memories."

Sighing, BB stretched out an arm across the back of the seat, lightly tiptoeing his fingers across her bare shoulders.

"We were always good together, Kat. Whatever happened to us?"

Kat edged away from his caress. "Simple—I had enough of your pawing and treating me like I was about as bright as that perpetually burned-out street lamp in front of the courthouse. So, I said *Adios* and vamoosed. Remember?"

He frowned. "Oh yeah. You didn't say it in those nice words either as I recall."

"No, I didn't," she admitted with a tinge of guilt. "Sorry about that."

BB roared the sports car's engine like a child's plaything and passed a slowly moving vehicle ahead of them, blindly careening over a steep hill without a thought to oncoming traffic. White-knuckled, Kat gripped the edge of her leather seat and hung on for dear life.

"Well, that's all water under the bridge now, isn't it? To-night proves it." He removed a hand from the wheel and squeezed her shoulder once more, flashing her a suggestive grin. "Can't we start up where we left off?"

Kat suppressed a groan and batted away his hand. The man was practically drooling. Why on earth had she decided to take BB up on his invitation?

Oh, yes, the possibility of experiencing some casual sex to forget my growing attraction to Jonathan Rawlins. A really smart plan.

Ten minutes into their date, and already Kat was reconsidering the wisdom of her actions.

"Tonight proves nothing, BB," she emphasized, "except that I want to hear a good band play, eat some food I didn't prepare myself, and I care enough about the party to see that you don't make a total ass out of yourself before you run for reelection."

BB abruptly whipped the car around the last curve of the winding ranch road and crossed under the wrought-iron gate which proudly declared they had at long last reached the Holbreicht Ranch. Kat gazed in awe at the impressive homestead. The renowned two-story house rose as serene and commanding as its owner, District Judge Harold Holbreicht, as they crested a small hill.

Dating a man in power did have its advantages, Kat had to admit. She would have never experienced more than the outside of the Holbreicht's gorgeous Victorian-era edifice if she hadn't known BB and hadn't been asked to attend exclusive functions like this one.

BB parked by another equally upscale vehicle in the long drive and switched off the engine. He turned to her, and Kat witnessed something that possibly could have passed for hurt glimmering in his dark, beady eyes.

"You don't mean you don't want to ever see me again after tonight, do ya, sugar?"

Kat sighed. For a user, sometimes BB seemed to possess half a heart. She hated being cruel to anyone, but this was Bradley T. Bradley, legal eagle, and not to put too blunt a point on it, noted liar.

"Don't tempt me," she said firmly.

They exited the car and strolled toward the house.

BB placed his hand at the small of Kat's back and whispered in her ear, "Why not? You sure the heck tempt me, darlin'."

Her back muscles tightened, but she plastered a how-do-you-do smile across her face and allowed herself to be escorted up the magnificent red sandstone steps and onto to the long, covered verandah.

A waiter appeared from nowhere and immediately placed a tall glass of Llano Estacado wine in Kat's hand and pointed out the brimming appetizer buffet to them. She left BB's side and meandered toward the food, chatting briefly with some members of the school board before filling her plate and grabbing another glass. She excused herself from the porch and sat at a lawn table near the pool. There she could sip her drink and enjoy her stuffed jalapeño and mushroom *hors d'oeuvres* with a minimum of interruptions.

The breeze shifted momentarily, allowing a whiff of the barbecuing brisket from the pit out back to assail her nostrils. Kat drooled at the delicious aroma of roasting brisket but continued to eat her appetizers slowly, all the while observing her date's lively behavior.

BB was in rare form tonight, flattering judges' wives, slapping colleagues on the back, and joking loudly again and again with the political movers and shakers of the county without breaking a sweat. Truly, he was a sight to behold. There was something to be said for having a boyfriend with money and power. Kat sighed.

"Another glass?" a roving waiter suggested.

"Yes, please." A warm, relaxed feeling spread throughout her body, numbing her nose and fingers. She dismissed it as she sipped the liquid refreshment. Texas wine was good. It would be a shame not to support a growing state industry.

A few minutes later and Kat had polished off her stuffed jalapeños and wanted more. She shakily rose to her feet and headed toward the buffet. It was a great party. She glanced around the patio area and waved to a friendly face in the crowd as she refilled her plate with spicy chicken wings and taquitos. Sitting back down, she declined another glass of wine from a passing waiter and kicked her heels off.

The warm, relaxed feeling had spread from the tip of her nose to her toes now. The intoxication was taking control of her judgment centers. Kat placed her half-empty goblet on a table. If she wasn't careful, she'd be as drunk as a skunk and as flat as a Texas speed bump—otherwise known as the armadillo—before she knew it.

If only I wasn't so weak . . . such a sinner.

If only she had a good friend like Ruth with her tonight to help her resist temptation.

Kat slowly sipped the remainder of her wine. BB wasn't all that bad, she had to admit. When BB was in a really good mood—which was usually the first fifteen minutes after they'd made love—he was open to granting her about any wish her heart desired so long as it didn't totally break his bank account. A man of Jonathan's humble means certainly couldn't keep her in the manner she longed to become accustomed to.

The numb feeling in her nose had spread to the top of her head now. She shook her head. Nope, no matter how else decent, civil, and downright handsome Jonathan appeared compared to rude-talking, big-mouthed, nimble-fingered Bradley T. Bradley, he just didn't possess the same bank account and earning capabilities of a lawyer. His humble lifestyle was clear in the small gray sedan he drove, a far cry from BB's big black foreign sports car.

Although a well-respected member of the community, Jonathan didn't hang out in quite the same social echelon as BB. He didn't regularly hobnob with people who owned cars that cost about as much as her house. He'd probably cringe if he saw her dressed the way she was at this moment. Her cocktail attire was a far cry from the girlish, high-necked, lace-collared, floral-printed dresses Ruth always chose. Would Jonathan find her morally bankrupt if he ever discovered she didn't own a single flannel nightgown or a plain white pair of panties? She giggled at the scandalous thought.

"Wine?" a server asked, clearing off Kat's now-empty glass.

"Yes, it's great," Kat agreed but declined another libation.

As she watched the crowd of local movers and shakers, she contemplated how different BB was compared to Jonathan. Lawyers met all kinds of interesting people—criminals and otherwise. Pastors led lives far from one of glamour and excitement—most of the time, unless she counted the time the ceiling fan blade had rattled its way out of its base and came crashing on top of the lectern just moments after Jonathan had finished his sermon. Now that was exciting, but it wasn't something anyone could depend on happening on a regular basis.

BB—excitement. Jonathan—dullsville.

Kat shakily ambled toward the barbecue pit. Yes, she could do this. She could get back into BB's good graces and forget all about Jonathan Rawlins in every other way except as her spiritual advisor. Yes, she could do it. She would do it. Tonight.

"Here you go, little lady," Judge Holbreicht drawled, handing Kat a plate full of brisket and beans. Silver-haired and silver-tongued, the judge enjoyed playing the humble servant, particularly if a possible photo opportunity was involved. "Haven't seen you at one of these to-dos in quite some time. That shyster BB treating you kindly?"

"He treats me just fine when I let him," Kat acknowledged with a shrug.

The judge laughed heartily and handed her a wedge of cornbread. "I see. Well, you'd better eat up now, so you got the strength to handle him later. Speak of the devil, here's the big-mouth ambulance-chaser now."

"My ears are burning." BB grinned like a fool as he approached the pit. "I hope it's only good things being said about me behind my back."

Kat stumbled slightly in her heels and righted herself against the condiments table. "You know I would never say anything bad about you in public, BB."

His grin dropped for a moment, but he rebounded, smoothly turning to accept a plate of barbecue brisket and focusing all his schmoozing capabilities on their host.

"Thank you, Judge. It smells simply delicious. You know, I forgot to tell you the other day how much I admired your ruling on the Simpson case. It was an inspired judicial appraisement. Let me tell you why . . ."

Kat wandered back to her seat, carefully planting her foot each and every step so as not to drop her plate. Despite a slight headache coming on, her stomach growled. She sat, kicked off her heels once more, and wolfed down her dinner. A few minutes later, BB joined her at the table.

"You having a good time?"

She speared a big forkful of pinto beans and shrugged.

"You wanna dance?" he asked.

"Probably not." The world in front of Kat's eyes was doing quite a good a disco number of its own. "Unless you're volunteering to carry me."

His breathing caught. "Sure thang, sweet cheeks. I'm glad you're feeling more *friendly* now. I can't wait until this meet-and-greet is over with."

Pounding her chest with a fist, she let out a burp. "That's better." Narrowing her eyes, she leaned over her empty plate to take a closer look at BB. Yes, alcohol definitely improved his appearance. "What are we waiting for then?"

"You mean, you want to go now?" BB cried, his brows knitting. "While I'm sorely tempted to leave with you this very second, I've got to think of my career. I've got a few more hands to shake and a few more backs to scratch. Can you hold out a tad longer?"

Funny, when had Judge Holbreicht's pool patio become a spinning, twirling, giant carousel? Kat grabbed the table's edge. If she could keep herself from dropping her face into her plate, she guessed she could wait for BB to finish his politicking.

"Sure. Go ahead and yackety-yak some more with folks. I ain't fixin' to budge from this spot. No, siree."

BB put down his fork and stood. "All right now. I'll be back in a few. Don't leave without me, y'hear?"

117

Kat saluted him goodbye and slumped in her seat. Memories of the good old days came flooding back — the dinner-dances, the political fund-raisers, the late-night drive back to her place, the predictable sex, BB's quick getaway the next morning. Of course, it worked the other way around at times — her quick getaway the next morning if she spent the night at his place. Neither wanted to give the neighbors any reason to talk.

Maybe they both had grown up a little since then?

She swiveled in her seat to view the verandah action and caught sight of BB in a deep conversation with a buxom brunette. Could she be a colleague of his from court? If so, then she had a lot to learn about how to dress to impress men with her intelligence. The piece of cloth she called a cocktail dress barely covered more than a swimsuit and possessed an indecently low neckline.

BB's eyes were on stalks now, practically falling out of his head and into the brunette's ample cleavage. Kat gritted her teeth, angry steam rising from her ears. Campaign fund-raising was the last topic on earth they were conversing about. More than likely some other kind of activity was being discussed, as BB leaned forward and whispered some witty remark into the giggling vixen's ear. Kat rested her head in her hands.

"When will I ever learn — the more things change, the more they remain the same."

"Would you like another glass?" another passing waitress enquired a moment later.

"No, I've had more than my fair share," Kat said wistfully, growing more sober and sorrier by the moment. "What I'd really like is a ride home."

"No problem. The judge hired several of us to act as designated drivers for just such an occasion," the friendly server informed her. "You know, Judge Holbreicht got into office due in large part to his tough stance on drunk-driving laws."

"True enough." Kat slipped her feet back into her shoes and slowly stood. "Do you think you can give me a ride home now? I think I've experienced enough politics for one night."

"Slow down, boy. You're pulling my arm out of the socket."

Jonathan jogged to keep up with Rolf. It was crazy, but the lively pup seemed to gain more energy as the sun set and the cooler night air was stirring. Dog-walking was an aerobic activity.

"Whoa, fella," he said softly as they approached Kat's house. It hadn't been a conscious thought, but something had drawn him toward her home. Nine o'clock at night wasn't exactly a proper time to show up at a person's door, but Jonathan had made up an excuse on the walk over. He'd knock politely and show her Rolf and say how much he wanted to introduce her to his new dog.

They wouldn't even have to go inside. After all, what woman would want an unknown dog traipsing about in her house? At least he'd get a chance to see Kat, talk to her unlike he could talk to her at church on Sunday. About the only thing they had time to grunt to each other there was, "Skip the last verse on the offertory anthem," or "Tell Gayle to turn down the volume on the pedals." Not exactly great pick-up lines.

Jonathan reined in Rolf until the canine was strolling sedately at his ankles as they crested the knoll. They came down the back side of the hill, and he spotted a large, unfamiliar car parked in Kat's driveway. A sudden pain of anguish stabbed his heart. Who on earth could be the owner of the gold-accented, chrome, crimson-colored Caddy?

Slowing to a crawl, Jonathan fought with Rolf's pulling

harder on his lead.

"Easy boy," he soothed, bringing them both to a halt. "It looks like Kat has company tonight. We'll have to come back another time."

Rolf whimpered his disappointment. Jonathan's gaze glued itself to the back window of the Caddy and the two occupants chatting inside.

"Thanks so much for the ride, Bobbi," Kat said, clambering out of the borrowed car. "I'll be sure to let you know if I hear of a good used piano coming on the market. Your little girl sounds like a natural. 'Night."

She slammed the door shut and waved the friendly catering assistant goodnight before heading to the front door.

"Man, are my feet ever killing me . . ."

The unexpected sound of a dog barking close by startled Kat. Her reflexes dulled by too much drink, her house keys jumped out of her hands and catapulted themselves into the bushes.

"Great day in the morning! I've lost my only door key."

Kat kicked off her heels and set them on the stoop, then slowly knelt to get a better look into the bushes. Lucky for her, she had turned her porch light on before she'd left home, but its small bulb couldn't chase away all the shadows.

"Here goes nuthin'." She plunged a hand into the dark shrubbery and patted around the roots area and the soil underneath. "If I get bit by a rattler or spider, I'm fixin' to be mighty ticked off at one Bradley T. Bradley."

After groping blindly for what seemed like several minutes, Kat decided to crawl halfway into the shrubbery to further her search.

"Can we help?" The familiar, deep, rich tones of Jonathan

Rawlins sprang out of nowhere.

Kat instantly backed out of the bushes and jumped to her feet as if she'd been goosed by a cattle prod. A sudden coolness on her right shoulder betrayed the fact that the strap of her dress had been caught on a branch of the holly and torn it in half. She grabbed at the remnant of her straps, doing her best to keep her bosom from escaping in its entirety.

"Oh, hello," she mumbled, trying hard to act natural. How in the world she could look natural shoeless, with dirt on her knees, and holding up one side of an already revealing dress she didn't know, but she was determined to make a good impression. "I had a little accident. You think you could help me find my keys?"

Jonathan smiled. "Of course. Maybe Rolf here can help." He let the lead go slack, giving the pup momentary freedom. "Check the bushes, Rolf. There you go. No, stop!"

"Down boy!" Kat cried.

Rolf's cold nose jutting up her skirt gave Kat an instant case of the giggles. Jonathan pulled the dog away and pointed his muzzle toward the bushes.

"I don't know what it is about dogs," Kat drawled, "but they always seem to poke their hooters right in your—uh, you know what I mean." She tied the loose ends of her dress straps together and smoothed her short skirt over her thighs, praying the darkness hid the blush creeping across her cheeks.

Jonathan cleared his throat. "I apologize for my dog's rude behavior. I guess it's a case of pups will be pups."

Kat quirked an eyebrow. "Eh? This huge beast is only a puppy? I forgive him then—especially if he finds my keys. Can you do that, boy?"

Rolf answered her with a happy yap and a howl.

"I think he has them." Jonathan bent to retrieve the shiny object from his pet's mouth and dangled them by the fob. "A little slobbered on, but here are your house keys."

Kat accepted them cautiously. "Ooo, thanks. Ralph, is it? You're a real lifesaver."

"He is, isn't he?" Jonathan laughed. "It's Rolf, like the puppet dog on TV. You remember *The Muppet Show*, don't you?"

"Oh yeah. The big floppy-eared dog on the piano. How could I forget? I really loved that show."

Kat slipped the damp key into the lock and pushed open the door. "Y'all want to come in for a cold drink? I don't mind animals in the house, provided they stay on the tiled areas."

"I'd love a drink of water, but I can't vouch for Rolf's ability to stay on the tile. He's still learning."

"Aren't we all? Rolf's my hero tonight, so I'm willing to take a chance. Just follow me to the kitchen."

Jonathan pulled Rolf tightly to his side and followed Kat across the front hallway on through to the kitchen area. Once there, she dropped her high heels alongside her garden clogs and opened the sliding door to the screened-in porch. The pup immediately raced over to the window to gain a better view of the backyard.

"You sure you want him on your porch?" Jonathan asked.

"He's fine. My cat always liked sitting on the old wicker sofa on the screen porch at night. It and the old gas grill are beyond repair, so don't worry about him hurting anything."

"All right, if you don't mind."

Kat crossed to the refrigerator. "Want some pink lemonade?"

"Yes, please."

Jonathan sat at the table and watched with interest as she poured them both a glass. In flattering, body-hugging sapphire blue, Kat was a long drink of cool water on a scorching summer's day. He took a sip of the liquid, and his lips immediately puckered.

"I apologize if it's rather tart." She took a seat beside him and passed him the ice container. "Add a little ice to water it down. I tend to like my lemonade rather strong as you can tell."

"Strong isn't quite the word for it," Jonathan managed after forcibly unfolding his screwed-up face. "Industrial strength might be better. How come it doesn't seem to affect you any?"

Kat sighed. Her wine-induced glow was rapidly fading. "It takes more than lemonade to make my lips pucker these days," she admitted.

Jonathan dropped several ice cubes into his glass, twirling them around with a finger to dissolve them. "Maybe you should try making it with a different kind of lemon?"

"Is there such a thing?"

Jonathan took a quick swig of lemonade to bolster his confidence. Watered down, it was still tart but a bit more palatable.

"Lemons aren't all the same," he began. "Some kinds have a bit more meat to them, some a bit more juice. Some are sweet, and some are sour. You've just got to be willing to taste a new variety."

Kat narrowed her eyes. "Are we talking about actual lemons here?"

Warmth flooded Jonathan's cheeks. "Of course."

"Good. For a moment there, I thought you were speaking metaphorically." Yawning, Kat put down her glass and languidly stretched her arms over her head. "I'm afraid my mind's still a little bit fuzzy from sampling the judge's wine cellar earlier this evening."

"The judge's wine cellar?"

"Yes. I was at a political fund-raiser at Judge Holbreicht's spread. He has such a beautiful ranch and simply gorgeous home. You ever see it?"

"No, not up close, but I've heard Darla mention it a few hundred times over the years."

Jonathan took a long drink of his lemonade, observing Kat closely from the corner of his eye. She was utterly breathtaking in blue. Had she worn that flattering outfit for the sole benefit of the host?

"Is the judge a good friend of yours?" he asked.

"Judge Holbreicht? No, he's the party big-wig in the county. I'm only a little cog in the machinery. Since I doubt I'll be invited to any more shindigs in the future, I decided that I might as well enjoy myself."

Kat closed her eyes and rubbed her temples in slow, circular motions. "I think I enjoyed myself a little too much and now I'm reaping the rewards."

Jonathan rose and came around the back of her chair. "Here. Let me help you get through the worst of it."

Kat started at Jonathan's touch on her neck and the sides of her face, gradually relaxing as he gently kneaded the knots from her shoulders and smoothed away the ache at the top of her spine.

Jonathan possessed healing powers in his hands. Kat sank farther into her chair, allowing her head to loll to one side. His fingers feathered out with light spiraling motions to the sides of her face. She could sit here all night, gladly soaking in the delicious sensations his caress engendered within her. Her disappointment at leaving the party early without her date vanished in a sigh of deep contentment.

"Feeling better?" he whispered.

"Hmmm, much, much better . . . Jonathan?"

"Yes?"

"I could stay like this forever, but we've got to think about Ralph."

"Ralph?"

"Yes, your dog. I think he's whimpering to go home."

Jonathan paused, then continued with his massage. "Nonsense. He's fast asleep on your old wicker sofa."

"Really? That's good. I wonder what that sound I heard was then."

"I think it was you. You seem very comfortable in my arms."

"I am, I am. I just wish . . ."

"Wish?"

Could she just blurt out that she wished Jonathan would stay and massage her shoulders forever? No, that was out of the question.

"I wish I hadn't left before I got to hear the band," she covered. "I hear tell they're quite good."

"You enjoy dancing?"

"Occasionally. With the right partner."

Now it was Jonathan's turn to sigh. "I wish I could oblige, but I am terminally afflicted with two left feet."

Kat peeked out of the corner of her eye. "Nonsense. It doesn't look that way to me. Anyone who's coordinated enough to massage my hangover away like you just did is coordinated enough to dance. Let me show you."

Kat gently removed Jonathan's hands and rose from the table. "Follow me."

Leading him into the living room, Kat crossed to the stereo and slipped an instrumental recording into the CD player. To the strains of *Strangers in the Night,* she placed Jonathan's hands in the correct positions on her shoulder and the small of her back and began with a simple box step.

"There. That's not too hard, is it?"

125

"No, it isn't." He raised his focus from his feet and gazed into her eyes. "You make dancing feel as natural as breathing."

Suddenly shy, Kat lowered her eyes. "It is in a way. All you have to do is let your feet follow the beat of your heart— er, the music. Yes, the music, I mean. Everything else will follow."

"Will it?" Jonathan stopped, tilting her chin up to explore her expression. He gathered her closer to him and lowered his head toward hers.

"Jonathan, I . . ."

His lips tenderly grazed across hers, sending a tremor of delight coursing through her veins. For a moment, Kat clung fast to his form, fearing she'd fall into a bottomless pit of nothingness if she pulled away. As his mouth settled deeper, her cares evaporated. Her soul ached with a burning need to reciprocate his kisses.

Rolf's howling from the back porch shattered the delicate intimacy of the moment.

"Rolf, be a good dog," Jonathan commanded. "There's nothing to be scared of here."

A rush of hot air from the front door pushed the dancers farther apart.

"Mom? Pastor Jon?" Kevin Dubcek cried. "What are you two doing in the dark?"

CHAPTER EIGHT

"Kevin! What a surprise."

Kat bolted from Jonathan's embrace, racing toward her son at close to the speed of light, turning on a lamp and switching off the music along the way. "Anything wrong, dear? I wasn't expecting you home this weekend."

"I know, but I couldn't stand the thought of messing up our apartment after all the work you did to clean it up last weekend." He dropped his laundry bag at his mother's feet and nodded at Jonathan. "Howdy, Pastor Jon. How's it hangin' these days?"

"It's hangin' fine, Kev."

"You look like you're doing some weight lifting. Am I right?"

"It shows already?" Jonathan flexed a bicep and smiled. "I've taken up jogging and got me a dog to walk now."

"Wow. So that's the wolf I heard howlin' out back. You fixin' to go hog-wild on working out, aren't ya?" Kevin shook his head and laughed. "I never pegged you as a fitness geek before. Something about wearing that dress in your line of work."

"It's not a dress. It's a robe," Kat reminded him. "You wore one when you were an acolyte, remember?"

While she was always glad to see her children, Kevin's appearance knocked Kat for a loop. She and Jonathan had crossed a threshold of sorts—a tantalizing beginning to a new kind of relationship. She could have stayed in his arms and kissed him for an eternity if first Rolf and then Kevin hadn't destroyed the moment.

On second thought, however, who knew what would have happened between her and her newest piano student if her son hadn't interrupted them? What with her raging hormones, she might have jumped Jonathan's bones and not let him up for air until she'd her fill of him. Kat shuddered at the thought. Kevin's untimely arrival was for the best after all.

"I know it's not a dress, Mom," Kevin was saying as Kat returned to reality. "I was just kidding. Pastor Jon has a great sense of humor. He had to have one to get me through confirmation classes. Isn't that right?"

Jonathan winked. "Right you are, Kev."

Kat stood tall and placed her hands on her hips. "Well, go on and lug your dirty duds into the laundry room. I'm not going to pull my back out carrying your stinky gym clothes through the house."

"All right, all right," Kevin groaned, slinging the bag to his shoulder. "Looks like your outfit could use some washing, too. Is that dirt on your knees? What happened to your dress strap?" He took a step forward, narrowing his eyes. A worried expression flashed across his face followed by a suspicious glare at their guest. "Mom, you sure you're okay?"

Kat sighed. "I'm fine, Kevin. I dropped my keys in the bushes and had to go crawling about for them. That's why I appear the way I do. Pastor Jon's dog helped me find them."

He glanced at his mother's smudged lipstick, then at Jonathan's slightly colored mouth, then back again at his mother.

"So, you two were celebrating when I arrived, huh?"

"Something like that." She grabbed Kevin by the elbow and steered him toward the kitchen. "You hungry, baby? Let me make you something to eat."

Kevin's stomach always overcame his curiosity. "How

did you know?"

Following close behind, Jonathan grinned at the parent-child interaction. It was good to see Kevin again. He'd always enjoyed the boy's company. Kevin may not be the brightest light bulb in the box, but he certainly possessed a loving heart. Jonathan could tell Kat relied on her son's stalwart strength and support more than she admitted.

The evening wasn't a complete loss. He'd held Kat in his arms, and he'd kissed her—and she'd kissed him back, but why did she act so formal, so cool toward him now? She talked to him like he was a child when she told him to sit beside Kevin. Jonathan sensed something wasn't quite right, but he couldn't place a finger on it, and just when it seemed he was on the right track when it came to romancing Kat Dubcek.

"Mom, I'm fixin' to drop out of school and join the Peace Corps or something."

Kat calmly took another long sip of her morning coffee. She'd had a bad feeling last night when Kevin had arrived on the doorstep that some cockamamie plan was brewing in his brain.

"Don't they want you to have a college degree to serve in the Peace Corps?"

Kevin shoveled another forkful of scrambled eggs and sausage into his mouth and frowned. "Uh, maybe," he mumbled. "I'm not exactly sure. I just know I'm not going to be able to pass this English class without Keely's help."

"Whether or not Keely can help you, you can still give it your best shot. Did you bring home your text and syllabus? Perhaps I can help you—or maybe Mr. Jones over at the high school could help? He got you through senior composition class in one piece, remember?"

Kevin's face lit up. "You think he makes house calls in the summer?"

"I don't know, baby. I guess you can give him a call and see if he's willing."

"All right. I'll do it. Right after I finish this last bite."

Kat stood and headed toward the mountain of dirty dishes piled in the sink. "Good for you."

After she had prepared a three-course meal for both Kevin and Jonathan last night, the used pots and pans were practically stacked a mile high. Kat was always astonished by how much food her son could put away, but Jonathan had held his own fairly well, eating like a man who was starving for more than just food.

She opened the dishwasher and stacked plates and cups. Normally, she would have felt resentment for having to clean up after her son's late-night snacking, but somehow today she didn't. It was odd, but the sight of the two men chatting amiably at her kitchen table, polishing off several plates of spaghetti and meatballs apiece, had seemed so natural. Her house had seemed an actual home for the first time since she could remember. Maybe the first time ever?

"Thanks, Mr. Jones. I'll be there in five minutes," Kevin said, hanging up the phone.

Kat started from her daydreaming. "Mr. Jones agreed to help you with your coursework?"

"Yes, he did. I told him I'd meet him at the county library with my stuff."

Kevin dutifully gave Kat a peck on the cheek and collected his papers and books together. "This may take a while, so don't wait around for me, Mom. You go ahead and do what you normally do on a Saturday."

Kat flashed him a wry smile. "I will. I usually do laundry

on Saturday."

"Good, then I didn't get you out of your rut any. See ya later."

The sound of the back door slamming signaled to Kat that she had the rest of the day to herself. A day to stay in her rut as Kevin had put it so eloquently. She headed to the washing machine and started in on Kevin's dirty duds.

My rut.

It irked her to think her own child thought she was hopelessly stuck in a cycle. Was she so predictable? So boring? Didn't she possess at least an ounce of excitement, a spark of creativity? If she didn't, then what had Jonathan seen in her last night when he'd had held her in his arms and kissed her?

Kat switched on the washer and one by one pitched filthy gym socks into the tub, mentally making a checklist of what had happened last night that led up to—and explained—their kiss. Maybe Jonathan had simply been caught up in the thrall of the music, the moment. Possibly she'd reminded him of someone else he'd held in his arms long ago. Ruth?

No. It couldn't be. There was no way on earth Jonathan could ever confuse her with Ruth. Other than a shared love of music, they were polar opposites in looks, temperament, and personality. Ruth was good and sweet and polished, and Kat was . . . she was a bit rough around the edges. Sure, she put forth a more *together* front in public when she was acting like a schoolteacher, but it was painfully obvious from her actions last night that she didn't have it together at all. To clinch it, there had been no goodnight peck on the cheek, no phone call this morning saying he'd meet her later to continue what they'd started.

Kat sighed as she measured out the laundry detergent and poured it into the water. Jonathan probably blamed his madness last night on the moonlight. The kiss had meant nothing to him, and so he assumed it didn't mean a thing to her, either. It was better left unspoken, forgotten.

But it had meant something—at least to Kat it had. With Kevin underfoot, she couldn't very well come out with it last night. She couldn't have said it out loud to Jonathan that she'd been thinking about him in a more-than-friendly way for some time. So, the moment was lost, never to be seen again.

It's for the best.

Starting an affair with your minister wasn't a good thing—anyone would tell you that much. She should feel relieved that Kevin's interruption had halted an improper thing dead in its tracks. Instead, all she felt inside was empty.

Rubbing his eyes, Jonathan leaned back in his desk chair and sighed. Here it was, going on ten o'clock at night, and he hadn't finished his sermon yet. Most Saturdays he'd be done by now, and after a long walk down Memory Lane, he'd crawl into bed, read a little, and go to sleep, prepared to face his congregation bright and early tomorrow morning, but yesterday had changed him somehow.

It was all he could do not to call Kat and invite her out on some kind of date today. Not that there was any place or anything particular he wanted to do. It was just that he wanted to be near her as much as possible, to do any activity that afforded him the chance of her falling into his arms like she had last night when they'd danced.

Something akin to a brick wall prevented him from picking up the phone. Kat had looked so shocked, so chagrined when Kevin interrupted them. Jonathan was certain she'd been embarrassed. Yes, embarrassment explained it. She'd been embarrassed to be seen with him in a romantic situation. Hadn't she acted somewhat uneasy with him when he'd first asked her out to dinner? Hadn't she completely clammed up on him after he'd gotten so talkative on the jogging trail in the park? Kat could tolerate him only so much until her embarrassment factor worked its way to the surface, effectively killing the magic of the moment.

"What can I do to get her so interested in me she doesn't care what others think?"

He reached down and scratched Rolf between the ears. The puppy peered up at him with a look that seemed to be a cross between the canine expressions of gratitude and hunger. Jonathan switched off his desk lamp and headed toward the kitchen.

"Come on, boy. I'll get you something to eat, and then I'm going to call it a night. I'll have to wing parts of my sermon tomorrow. That should make it interesting."

Rolf scampered happily to his food bowl and after a good chow down padded over to his sleeping blanket in the corner of the family room. For some reason, he didn't seem to care for sleeping at the foot of Jonathan's bed.

Jonathan sighed. "It sure is fixin' to be a long, cold winter."

He turned out the front light, then headed down Memory Lane in the dark, not bothering to pause at Ruth's portrait tonight. He knew she was there, watching him, waiting on him to get his life back in full swing. There was no need for him to continue to beat himself up about it.

He got undressed, switched off the bedside lamp, crawled under the covers, and turned to set the alarm clock. He didn't usually need it on Sunday mornings, but lately he'd found himself waking up in the middle of a dream, feeling groggy and confused. Too bad he didn't feel comfortable asking anyone how he could help Kat get over her uneasiness when it came to others seeing them together.

Why would you think I'd ever be remotely interested in the likes of you?

Jonathan's dreams weren't usually so vivid, but tonight Kat's dusty mauve lipstick positively glowed with color — as did her electric blue dress. She slowly twirled around a shiny black grand piano alone in a spotlight on a darkened stage, huge diamonds adorning her ears and her throat, pulsating like airplane beacon lights. The rock on her slender, graceful hand could hardly be missed, either, as she waved it slowly in front of his eyes, hypnotizing him into a paralyzed trance.

I'm used to the best. I can take care of myself. Why would I choose some sweater-wearing, Bible-toting preacher man as my date when I can have the cream of the crop?

Kat continued to move to the tribal beat of drums, drums that tattooed a haunting cadence as she pulled out a neon-pink feather boa from inside the musical instrument and wrapped it around her neck.

What an odd place to store accessories.

Oh yeah, this was a dream. He'd just sit back and watch some more and see what useful ideas he could get out of it.

Kat twirled the ends of the boa as she strutted around the piano. She hiked up a leg and placed a stiletto-heeled shoe onto the bench, suggestively leaning into the pose. *I certainly don't want to be tied down . . . unless I'm in the mood for it.*

Kat grabbed an up-until-now invisible black silk cord and pulled. A line of Hollywood hunks marched out, bound hand and foot, prisoners to her whims. Each stopped in front of her, flexed his bulging muscles, and handed her a sheet of music. She glanced up and down their physiques, tore the paper out of their hands, and threw it way, then pushed them aside one by one with a shake of her head. Jonathan gulped. If she didn't care for the looks of these muscle-bound types there was no way he'd ever stand up to such scrutiny.

All meat, no substance. Why can't a man offer anything else?

Then Jonathan did a double-take, for there at the end of the line stood a scrawny, sweater-wearing buffoon in oxford shoes carrying a large, gold-foil-covered, heart-shaped box of chocolates and a dozen glowing red, long-stemmed roses. His doppelganger bowed low, offering tribute to his queen.

For me? Why thank you. Here, you can sit beside me on my pi-ano bench.

No! Wait! Don't! he screamed at his identical twin, but it was too late.

The bench shattered into a thousand pieces beneath their combined weights. This time, however, Kat didn't land squarely on top of him. In fact, she didn't land at all. She simply disappeared in a puff of smoke, leaving Jonathan ly-ing all alone in a smothering pile of splintered wood, scat-tered flowers, and squished chocolates. He fought his way to the top of the rubble and sighed. Then he spied the silken cord within reach. Something inside told him Kat must be at the other end. He pounced on the slippery rope and pulled and pulled and —

The sound of the alarm clock rudely dragged him back in-to reality. He jolted awake and stumbled toward the shower.

"If ever I felt at the end of my rope, it's today."

At the church office, Jonathan gathered the rest of his thoughts together and finished his sermon notes. A knock at his door brought a smile to his face.

"Can you make this little announcement for me?" Aunt Mabel asked, handing Jonathan a small slip of paper. "I've been trying to catch up with my Ladies Guild duties that I missed while I was in the hospital and I'm afraid this one is a bit late."

"Nonsense. I'm sure whatever it is it's just in time."

He put an arm around the old woman, guiding her to her

seat in the sanctuary before going to the vestry to don his robe and collect his papers.

The golden halo of light poured through the stained glass once more and rested on Kat as she stood to direct the choir in the offertory selection. A lump formed in Jonathan's throat. Did she realize that she was simply breathtaking? No, of course she didn't. How could he go about telling her that without causing her to back away like the other night?

As the last haunting notes of the closing hymn died, Jonathan rose to give the benediction and to read the announcements.

"For all those who are teaching, don't forget the Vacation Bible School planning meeting tomorrow night at seven, and now here's something for the Ladies Guild members — don't forget to give your *secret sister* a little gift or a card over the summer. We'll reveal ourselves at the Christmas banquet in December, but your sister will appreciate knowing she's being thought of in the meantime.'"

Jonathan glanced over at the front pew, left side, and winked. "Thank you, Aunt Mabel, for reminding us that everyone likes to be appreciated. Go in peace."

Jonathan's gaze roved toward the choir loft, and he caught sight of Kat's back. She followed the members down the side steps to the music room below the sanctuary to remove their choir robes and cool down.

Did Kat have a secret sister, he wondered, heading back to his office after shaking hands. Deep down, did Kat really feel loved for being herself and not for what she could do for others?

"That's what the dream means," he whispered. "She's tired of people demanding something of her all the time in return for their affection—she simply wants someone to appreciate her as she is. Why didn't I think of this before?"

"Who are you talking to, Pastor?" Matthias Ringleschmidt stood in the doorway and raised an eyebrow.

"Um, no one in particular," Jonathan covered. "What can I do you for, Matt?"

"I wanted to tell you that I'm on top of organizing the Oktoberfest Festival. I've already got our permits lined up, and the funeral home said we could borrow their tents for our dance floor and eating areas."

"You're certainly jumping the gun—we haven't even announced it to the congregation officially yet, let alone to the community."

"We've got to act fast if we're going to do this in less than a month's time. I think it would be better to have the money in hand, too, when we start planning the new Sunday School building. Randy says we can make a better deal on it if we pay material costs up front."

Jonathan nodded. "Randy, your cousin in the construction business, right?"

Matthias shifted his weight back and forth on his heels. "Yeah, that's him. He's willing to act as our general contractor for next to nothing if we let him advertise on our flyers for the festival, too."

"I see. Well, then, how can we refuse such a generous offer? We'd better announce this to the congregation at large soon so we can start signing up volunteers."

"I knew you'd see it my way, Pastor." Matthias smiled. "I already have one volunteer for the entertainment."

"I thought we were hiring a real polka band."

"We are, but in between sets Kat Dubcek said she'd dust off her accordion and play a little."

"I didn't know Kat owned an accordion." Jonathan scratched his head at the thought.

"She says she doesn't get around to playing it much anymore." Matthias chuckled. "She's actually a closet polka fanatic, or so she tells me. Can you imagine that? Hear she once tried out to be in an opera."

"She did?" Jonathan was learning something new about Kat every day.

"Yeah, it's why Kat's such a great choir director. My daughter in the middle school choir adores her. She's very talented, you know."

"Yes, I know." Jonathan absentmindedly headed for the exit. "Polka fanatic, imagine that."

"It takes all kinds," Matthias agreed, following him outside. "See you at church council, Pastor?"

"See you then, and thanks for all your hard work. The new building is going to be worth it. I just pray we can convince all our members of that fact."

Jonathan waved his faithful church president goodbye, then quickly jogged home to let Rolf out for some fresh air and exercise.

"There you go." He held the back door wide open for the playful pup to scamper outside. "I'll be with you after I change my clothes and check something out online. You know, there's got to be a website on all things polka that might be of interest to a diehard fan. There's just got to be."

"Are we singing the song next week?"

Kat longed to turn her back on Darla's prying. What she wouldn't give for no interruptions while using the church's copy machine for making duplicates of song sheets, but the copier was in a walk-in closet next to the office. The busybody secretary's constant snooping into other people's business was enough to drive even a saint mad. About the only person she could think of who had never acted visibly perturbed with Darla's antics had been Ruth Rawlins.

"No, this music is for the children to sing at Vacation Bible School. Why aren't you at your desk working on something?"

Darla sniffed and tossed her long tresses over her shoulder. "The bulletin is all done—including the insert on how much better off we'd be constructing a new Sunday School building rather than putting a roof on the old firetrap, but I'm sure the old timers won't think so. I'm just waiting for three o'clock and the postman to arrive and then I'm outta here."

"Must be nice to be caught up." Kat pulled out the stack of printed song sheets, double-checked to see if they were all legible, then handed them to Darla. "Can you staple these pages together and stick them in Denise's basket for me? Thanks."

"Will do, but first," she looked right and left, then lowered her voice. "I gotta tell you something I know you'll find simply fascinating."

Kat gritted her teeth into a smile. If there was anything she'd learned from Ruth about dealing with pesky people, it was that you could always smile and nod politely at them until they ran out of steam or walked away.

"Look, I don't have time right now. Just hold that thought until choir practice, all right?"

"I don't know if I can," the church secretary drawled. "You'll really want to hear this. I promise you that."

Kat sighed. How could she tell the dear woman she didn't feel like listening to gossip today, particularly since she had to rush home and get ready for pupils this afternoon? Especially since she'd picked this particular time to come by the office to borrow the copier since she knew this was the time Jonathan visited sick members in the hospital and wouldn't be in the building?

She glanced at her wristwatch. "Okay, you've got three minutes."

Darla grinned and leaned forward, placing a finger to the side of her nose. "It's got something to do with you and Pastor."

"Really?" Kat tightened her fists at her sides.

"Yep, really. He came up to me first thing this morning and asked what I thought your favorite song was."

A chill of apprehension ran up Kat's spine. "My favorite . . . song?"

"Uh-huh. I said I thought it was something by a current pop star. I figured he meant a pop song, not church music."

"Oh, sure." Kat wasn't particularly fond of anything recently released but knew Darla was fond of pop music.

"Then Pastor sort of mumbled *rats, I don't think they have it* and went back into his office." Darla crossed her arms over her ample chest. "You'll never guess what he did about ten minutes later."

Kat retrieved her sheet music from the copy machine and tried not to stare Darla in the face. "He took a coffee break?"

"No, silly, he already had a cup by then. He popped his head around the corner and wanted to know if I knew what kind of perfume you wore."

"He must be allergic to it," Kat covered. She flipped open her music portfolio and crammed the paper into a folder and started toward the exit. "I've really got to be going now. I have a lesson in less than fifteen minutes and —"

"You're missing the good part again," Darla scolded, waggling a finger. "You don't wear perfume. Remember? You said it causes people's throats to get all clogged up and they can't sing. You tell us all the time that no one sitting in the choir loft should wear anything with a lot of scent."

She was right. It was the standard speech Kat gave at least once a month to her choir members.

"I went ahead and told him you like expensive perfume." Darla winked. "If someone is going to give you an anniversary present, then you might as well go for broke."

All at once, Kat's throat felt drier than a creek draw after a ten-year drought. "Anniversary?" she managed at last. "What anniversary?"

"Why, it's fixin' to be nigh on to a year come this fall when you took over directing the choir from Ruth. You haven't forgotten, have you?"

Kat giggled, biting her lip. "How could I forget? So you think that's why he asked?"

"Of course. What else could it be?" Darla smiled. "Our Pastor Jon is such a nice person. He remembers lots of little things like that. Why, he gave me a chocolate sampler on Secretaries Day last year."

"How nice."

"I just wish it was the large-sized box and not the medium!" Darla howled with laughter, then pointed to the clock on the wall. "You best be getting on now. Your three minutes are up."

Kat slowly backed out the door. "They most certainly are. Bye now."

"I'll see you at practice Wednesday. I'll let you know when you can expect your anniversary present. Remember—act surprised."

"Don't worry. I will."

Flustered, Kat hurried to her car, promptly dropping her portfolio case in the parking lot. "Rats. I have no luck at all today."

She crouched and gathered up the chaos of sheet music before a sudden wind gust could blow everything into the next county.

A moment later, a dark shadow fell across her path. A man's shadow . . . a very tall man's shadow.

Chapter Nine

K at, having read numerous e-mails at work relating horror stories about criminals jumping defenseless females in parking lots, was prepared. Before his hands could wrap themselves about her neck, she twirled around and struck him full-force in the shins with her heavy leather purse, knocking the legs out from under her stalker. The menacing shadow crumpled and flopped flat on his back.

"What hit me?" Jonathan moaned, staring up at the noonday sun.

"Jonathan!" Kat screamed, rushing to his side. The music sheets fluttered in the breeze. "Are you all right?"

"For the most part, yes." He took her hand and sat up, rubbing his tailbone with the other. "Why on earth did you hit me with your purse?"

"I-I thought you might be one of those muggers who prey on defenseless women in parking lots."

Jonathan regarded her with suspicious eyes. "You're not defenseless. Your bag must weigh at least a ton."

"Sorry," she mumbled. "I forget to clean it out occasionally. It contains an electronic pitch pipe, a cell phone, and several dozen ungraded tests from last May."

"Talk about your concealed weapons." He smiled and squeezed her hand. "It's nice to know you can take care of yourself, but remember, it's okay to accept help from a friend every now and then."

Putting a hand under his elbow, Kat helped him to his feet. "You're right. To quote the great and wise Fab Four, *I get by with a little help from my friends."*

Jonathan quirked an eyebrow. "You like the *Beatles*?"

"Of course. They're the best rock band in the history of mankind. Who *doesn't* like them?"

"Who indeed." He chuckled.

Kat bent to retrieve what was left of her music portfolio.

"Here, let me help you, *friend.*"

Jonathan reached for the same paper as Kat. Their fingertips brushed against each other, sending a delicious ripple along the nerve endings of her hands, up her arms, and down her spine. Before she knew what she was doing, Kat yanked the paper away and stood straight.

"Thanks, but I think I can manage. You really ought to go into the church kitchen and get some ice to put on your bruises before they start to ache."

Jonathan rubbed the back of his neck. "Hmm, the whiplash *is* starting to set in. What will Darla think?"

"Darla?" Kat froze.

He grinned. "She's going to think you're beating up on me to get my attention."

A cog clicked in Kat's brain.

I'd never, ever beat up on anyone like my ex, Dirk, did.

"That's Darla for you," Kat muttered, shaking her head and snapping the portfolio closed. "Listen, I've got to run now, Pastor. I've got some—"

"It's Jonathan," he cut in, a sadness clouding his eyes. "You don't have to call me by my title, remember? I thought—"

"Yes, well, um, I've really got to fly."

Kat crossed to her car, glancing over her shoulder as she unlocked the driver's side. Jonathan's shoulders slumped. They seemed lower than they had in months. In fact, she couldn't remember seeing him stand so slumped, not since she'd helped him pack up Ruth's clothing.

Guilt stabbed at her heart. She was acting selfish, trying to avoid him like this because she felt uncomfortable about his kiss last Saturday night. He was still grieving and probably never meant anything by it. She was a big enough person to forgive and forget.

Kat approached him. "You sure I didn't break anything?" She smiled. "I can take you to the emergency room if you like for an X-ray?"

He shook his head. "I don't think anything needs a cast on it."

"Let me make it up to you somehow then." She averted her eyes and cleared her throat. "Since you were so nice to take me to dinner the other day, maybe I can return the favor? Will you have dinner at my house tonight?"

Jonathan's chin rose a notch. "You're inviting me to your home for supper?"

"Yes. Yes, I am."

"How about seventy-thirty? The council meeting should conclude by then."

Kat nodded.

What am I doing?

"Seven-thirty will be fine."

"Good. I'll see you then."

Jonathan had forgotten what falling in love had been like — all the ups and downs and sudden heartaches, only to be healed by the touch of her hand or the lilt of her smile. For a moment this afternoon, he'd really thought Kat was upset with him — that she wanted to avoid him at all costs, but then something happened. She'd turned around and invited him to her home for supper. What better way to check out some more of her favorite things?

Church council went on too long, as usual. Jonathan tapped his foot impatiently under the long table as the discussion dragged on and on. Matthias and several other

council members kept rehashing the arguments for constructing a new Sunday School building instead of simply
patching the roof on the old one for another few years use.
Jonathan's wandering attention focused on Matt's pale-
yellow golf shirt similar to one he'd recently purchased. Yellow would look good with his chestnut-brown slacks and
leather boat shoes tonight, he decided. He wasn't showing
up at Kat's in his collar and suit.

"We're all agreed then, correct?" Matthias' booming voice
broke into Jonathan's reverie. "Pastor?"

"Yes?" He looked one by one into the curious faces of his
parishioners. From the way they were all staring at him, one
would think he'd forgotten to wear clothes to the meeting.
"Oh, yes, we're agreed. We need to construct a new Sunday
School building."

A ripple of chuckles circled the room. "We agreed on that
point over an hour ago," Matthias said, smiling. "I was talking about the Oktoberfest fund-raiser festival. We're all
agreed that we will seek permission from the city to sell beer
at the event."

Jonathan quirked an eyebrow. "We are?"

"I'm not so sure," Charlie Zaye grumbled. Charlie, a mirror image of the Marlboro Man at age seventy and the elder
statesman of St. Luke's, was known for his outspokenness.
"The dry churches in the county are going to chew us up
and spit us out about selling booze for years to come. I say
we stick with soft drinks, sweet tea, and bottled water. I like
my bratwursts and sauerkraut and German potato salad
washed down with a cold coke myself."

"Hear, hear," several other councilmen agreed.

"What is the cost for the permit to sell alcohol?" Jonathan
asked. His eagerness to depart evaporated as the importance
of the discussion sunk in. "What are the liabilities? I mean,
what if someone drinks too much beer at the Oktoberfest

and ends up driving their pickup into a bar ditch on the way home? "

"See?" Charlie rapped the table with the gnarled knuckle of an energetic rancher. "I told y'all we're fixin' to get into a whole heap of legal trouble if we get into the booze-selling business."

"The permit itself isn't expensive, but the costs of patrolling if the police department thinks extra officers are needed aren't included." Matthias looked decidedly uncomfortable. "I take it we're all not agreed on this issue then?"

A general grumbling in the room indicated otherwise.

"We're going to lose the younger set—and potentially all the tourists in the area if we don't allow beer," Matthias warned. "After all, this *is* a fund-raiser. We need to make as much money as possible."

"Then how about a compromise?" Jonathan suggested. "We'll allow people to bring their own beverages—provided they show proof of age. That way, those who like chowin' down on brats with beer are happy, and the youth group said they'd be happy to handle the soft drink sales, and the men's group is handling the barbecue. With the Ladies Guild handling side dishes, we pretty much got everything covered."

"I vote for that," Charlie concurred. "Nobody is going to shame themselves in public by bringing in too much of the Devil's foul brew to a church-sponsored event. It'll help our drinkers moderate their consumption."

Jonathan could see the numbers rolling around in Matthias's businessman's head as he spoke.

"I suppose we could ask Rudy's Convenience Store to put a donation can on his counter for the building fund?"

A consensus nodded their approval, and the matter was soon assigned to the appropriate committees. Jonathan stood and took advantage of this opportunity to call the meeting closed with a short prayer. A quick shake of hands and he was out the door, departing for home for a quick change and an even quicker drive over to Kat's house.

"Seventy-forty-five," Kat said to herself, checking the kitchen wall clock while tossing the salad in slow motion for the tenth time in as many minutes. "He said he'd be here at seventy-thirty. Did he chicken out or did something important suddenly come up?"

For Pete's sake! You're conversing with yourself again. It's past time to replace Mr. Friskies.

No, it isn't. Jonathan owns a dog now, remember? Dogs and cats tend not to get along with each other.

Jonathan doesn't live here. You do. You go ahead and get you a cat now. It's going to be a long, cold winter without a nice, furry, purring fuzzball warming your feet at night.

The doorbell interrupted her self-haranguing.

"Please forgive me for being late," Jonathan said, smiling in a cheery yellow casual shirt. "Church council had a disagreement on the Oktoberfest refreshments. Speaking of which" — he handed her a chilled bottle of red sparkling grape juice — "here's my contribution to the meal."

"Thank you. It's okay you're late. The lasagna had to cool anyway." Kat nodded him inside. "Come on in."

Jonathan followed her into the dining area. Kat could tell he was making a mental note of her good china place settings, white linen tablecloth, and the highly-polished silver candlesticks as she placed the bottle beside them.

"I don't get too many visitors so I sort of thought I could take them out of the cabinet and exercise them a bit," she explained, gesturing at the table. "These things all belonged to my grandmother."

"They're very lovely — like their present owner."

Kat blushed. It was amazing how just like a school girl

she felt whenever Jonathan complimented her. "Thanks. I guess you can sit down. Help yourself to the salad and breadsticks. I'll go get the main course."

"Can I help?"

"No, you stay put and rest your backside. It's probably still sore from our little altercation earlier today."

Funny, but I don't feel a thing.

Jonathan settled himself in the closest chair. He felt free like a hawk drifting with the warm currents above the eternally azure skies of the Texas Hill Country. Nothing could bring him down tonight. Nothing.

Kat reentered the dining area momentarily and placed a good-sized casserole dish on a hot pad in front of him. "I hope you're hungry, 'cause I defrosted a big one." She covered her mouth as she dropped into her chair. "Oops. I shouldn't have let on this wasn't homemade."

"It makes no difference to me. I'm just happy I didn't have to cook. Shall I say grace?"

"Please do."

After a quick blessing, Jonathan poured them both a small amount of grape juice.

"I hope this stuff is good. It was a Christmas present I didn't even think of opening until today."

"They say wine improves with age, so it should be at its best by now, right?" Kat lifted her glass. "*Salud.*"

Jonathan raised his likewise. "*Salud, dinero y amor.*"

He brought his cup closer to hers. "You're supposed to toast to health, wealth, *and —*"

The glass slipped from Kat's fingers as their goblets clinked together.

"Oh, I'm sorry," she cried, jumping up to blot the spill with her napkin. "I'm such a klutz at times." She righted the long-stemmed glass. "Will you look, I splattered the front of your shirt."

"No big deal. I've been baptized with a lot worse before." He smiled, then frowned, his hostess frantically trying to erase the results of her accident.

"It won't ruin your tablecloth, will it?"

"It will if it sets in. Red grape juice is among the worst-staining drinks there is." Kat put down her napkin and placed her hands on her hips. "There. I got most of it blotted up. I need to get this in the washer with some of that expensive stain remover I bought off late-night TV right away. Can you help me take off the plates and candlesticks for a sec so I can slide it out?"

"My pleasure."

Jonathan lifted items off the tablecloth, then put them back down. Kat gathered the once-spotless linen into her arms and hurried into the kitchen. Sighing, he glanced down at the sprinkle of blood-colored spray staining his new shirt.

"Can I use your bathroom to wipe off my shirt?" he called out.

"Go ahead. It's the second door to your left down the hall."

"Thank you."

As Jonathan made his way to the bathroom sink, he was careful to note how different Kat's home décor was from Ruth's. Most of the knick-knacks in her living area had something to do with the twins. There were sports trophies courtesy of Kevin's athleticism and contest ribbons and plaques courtesy of Keely's musical talents. Even the artwork on the side tables looked like it had been crafted in art or shop class at school. Her bedroom hallway wasn't covered floor to ceiling with photographs of various family members like his, either. There were only one or two portraits of each of the kids. It seemed apparent that Kat's whole existence centered on raising her son and daughter.

Where could he fit in?

Jonathan took a wrong turn and ended up in what he assumed was Kat's bedroom, so he headed to the master bath. He picked up a washcloth on the counter and scrubbed at the dribbled red stain on his front to no avail.

"This isn't coming out," he mumbled. He put down the rag and pulled the shirt over his head, taking in the contents of the bathroom as he worked on rubbing out the stains. "Well, there's nothing labeled Channel No.5. around here. I think Darla's dead wrong about Kat's preference in perfumes. It looks like she's more into good old-fashioned cocoa butter lotion and baby powder."

After several minutes of scrubbing under the cold-water tap, Jonathan wrung his shirt and held it out at arm's length. He couldn't very well put it back on in the soggy state it was in. Maybe he could throw it into the washer along with the tablecloth?

He reentered Kat's bedroom and scanned the dresser top. No, no perfume bottles here, either. The antique pinwheel quilt hanging above the bed seemed to be the only non-twin artwork in the entire house. His gaze followed the busy pattern down the wall to the solid dusty-rose-colored comforter stretched across the mattress.

It must be a king-sized bed. Why did Kat need such a big thing to sleep in all alone by herself, unless . . .

"You get lost?" Kat shouted from the dining area.

"Sort of." He hurried back to their dinner. "Can I throw this shirt in with your table linen?"

Kat stood behind her chair, mouth agape, staring at Jonathan's half-clad visage. He held the damp shirt over his hairy chest.

"Sorry about my state of undress. I figured it was the best way to get the stain out."

She blinked in slow motion once, twice. "Sure. Makes

good sense. Give it to me."

Jonathan averted his eyes and handed the shirt to his hostess. Kat spun around and raced into the kitchen, opened the washer, flung in the shirt, then darted out again.

"It'll be ready in a little while. Shall we sit down and eat before you get cold — I mean, before the food gets cold."

His cheeks reddened. "If you have an old shirt of Kevin's around here, I could put that on."

"Oh. Yeah. That's an idea . . . a good idea."

Kat dashed out of the room and down the hallway, returning a minute later with a football jersey.

"The *Cowboys*. I approve." He smiled, quickly donned the shirt, and sat. "They told me before we moved here that if I ever said a bad thing about them, I'd be out of a job and kicked out of Heaven to boot."

"They don't call them God's team for nothing," she agreed, taking her seat. She passed him the casserole server. "Please take as much as you like."

Jonathan dished himself a decent amount of lasagna and salad and reached for the sparkling grape juice bottle. "Don't worry. We don't have to clink glasses again." This time, he poured them both a generous amount.

Kat grinned. "Thanks. It's been a long day."

After a few minutes of eating, Jonathan decided to broach a topic that was of no small interest to him.

"Tell me about the blond gentleman in the family photo on the wall by your piano."

"Blond gentleman?" Kat frowned. "I think you mean my late husband, Dirk." She took a bite of food, then completely changed the subject. "Have you been practicing your piano, by the way?"

"A little. A very little." Jonathan shrugged. "You make it seem so easy. Some things don't come naturally to us nonmusical types, and we get easily frustrated."

"Well, don't be. Everyone starts out slow and works their way up to a decent performance level eventually."

He had to know. "Was Dirk a musician?"

She rolled her eyes. "Good gracious, no." She cleared her throat and put down her fork. "I know you're curious about Dirk and I don't know what all Darla and the rest of Germantown might have told you about him, but rest assured he did possess a few good qualities."

Jonathan swallowed his bite of lettuce hard. The man only had a *few* good qualities? It had never occurred to him that Kat could have been trapped in a horrendous marriage to a selfish lout and the reason she had stayed single all these years wasn't because she'd simply lost her faith in the male gender. Perhaps she'd been so hurt by a man she could never think of truly giving her love to another?

If Jonathan didn't think so before, it was imperative now he do something nice to show Kat how much he appreciated her.

"Kevin takes after Dirk in the athletic arena, doesn't he?"

"Yes, he does." She sighed. "It's amazing how much of that nature versus nurture theory seems spot-on. I put musical instruments in both twins' hands early on, and only Keely seemed to have a feel for it. Kevin picked up a football off the playground in kindergarten and . . ." She shrugged. "Well, the rest, they say, is history. The boy can sure play ball. It about breaks my heart."

"You don't want Kevin to become like his father?"

"No, it's not that exactly." Kat looked off into the distance. "I'm proud he's been gifted in the physical fitness area, but I want him to be a more serious student at the same time. I mean, after a football player ruins his knees, then it's the end of his career. Kevin has to be able to fall back on something to support himself at that point. He's not moving back home. I'm not planning to support him forever. Contrary to popular opinion, I do have a life of my own."

"It's not right when other people tell you how to live it, is it?"

"Exactly."

Kat finished her drink. Jonathan poured her another and set the bottle down as he gathered his thoughts.

"This next statement is long overdue. Kat, I really appreciate the excellent job you do directing the choir. I want to apologize for not telling you before in so many words, and I want to apologize for how you were railroaded into the position in the first place. I also—"

"I wasn't railroaded," she cut in. "I volunteered. Ruth said I was perfect for the job, and she was right. I have all the qualifications." Kat took another long sip of juice. "After all, how could I have turned Ruth down? She was my friend, and she was sick, and she needed my help."

"It's wonderful what you're doing with our choir. I just wanted you to know that I sincerely appreciate your hard work. You're a very special person, Kat. A very special person indeed." Jonathan touched her hand. "I think you realize now how special you are to me when we danced the other night and I—"

"Can I have little more sparkling grape juice? It isn't too bad for Californian."

He poured her the remainder of the bottle.

"Thanks. You're very, very welcome. About the choir directing, that is, but I don't need an anniversary present."

He quirked an eyebrow. "Anniversary present?"

Kat chewed her bite of food and shook her head. "Uh-huh. Darla told me you like to give little gifts on special occasions. A small box of chocolates would do it for me. I don't quite have Darla's appetite for sweets, thank goodness."

Jonathan nodded, at a total loss for words. "I see."

"I can't recall the exact date I did take over from Ruth. I

filled in off and on a bit before her . . . her illness took over. So you can't really mark a certain Sunday as my first time as choir director. I sort of blended into the position."

"Yes, you've blended in quite well." He smiled. "So well you could say I can't imagine anyone else standing in front of our choir loft ever again."

Kat put down her fork. She picked up her glass by its stem with two hands. "All I can imagine is that Ruth is still here with us, directing. She was so good at motivating people. I'm not. I just want them to do as I tell them to, no questions asked."

Jonathan could tell Kat had fallen into a reflective mood. "I understand. Sometimes people try your patience."

"That's where you're wrong," she snorted. "You have to have actual patience in order to try it. I was born with a half helping of patience and two helpings of arrogance. I want everyone to be perfect. Nobody's perfect. I know that. Well, nobody's perfect except Ruth, that is."

"What?" This wasn't where he wanted the conversation to go. He frowned. "Ruth was far from perfect. I should know. I lived with her for more than two decades. She was a redeemed sinful being just like the rest of us."

Kat drained her glass, then stood as if to clear her plate away. "Sure, in the everyday sort of sins you mean, but Ruth was practically perfect in every other way." She sighed. "I'll never be able to live up to her example. I'll always fall short. I've never been able to live up to anyone's expectations."

Live up to expectations?

Jonathan knew where Kat was coming from now. She was comparing herself to Ruth—or at least the public persona Ruth had led everyone to believe was the real her. It wasn't right to allow Kat to labor under such a false impression.

"Kat, you don't have to live up to anyone's expectations, least of all mine." He reached toward her hand again. "I love you exactly the way you are."

She stared at him for a full five seconds, then burst into tears.

Jonathan rose and pulled her into his arms.

"Don't you mean God loves me?" she sniffed.

"That, too," he soothed, rocking her against his chest. "I don't know why you think you're not lovable in your own right. You are."

"You really mean it?"

"If I say it, I mean it."

"Then the other night when we were dancing?" She stepped back from him and looked into his eyes. "You weren't just caught up in the moment?"

"I was — but I was more than captivated by you."

Jonathan gently tilted her chin up, lowering his lips to hers. Relaxing, Kat leaned into him and drew her arms up around his neck. Their kiss deepened. It was more than Jonathan could bear as the fireworks sparkled and sizzled between them. He wanted to make Kat his own, body and soul.

She stepped back. "Jonathan, I . . ."

"Hmm?" He kissed her forehead.

"The grape juice. I don't care for grapes too much. I'm afraid I'm going to be sick."

CHAPTER TEN

"What a wonderful dream," Kat murmured, half-asleep. She rolled over and flopped an arm across the warm, firm form lying in bed next to her. Her eyes instantly flew open.

"Jonathan! What are *you* doing here?"

"Good morning to you, too." Jonathan smiled and sat up, reaching toward the other nightstand for his glasses. "Don't you remember?"

Kat bit her lip and sank lower under the comforter. She remembered lasagna, talking about Kevin, and some awful red sparkling grape juice which didn't quite agree with her stomach, but she didn't remember asking Jonathan Rawlins to crawl into bed with her.

"I'm not sure," she admitted. "Did I . . ."

"Did you get sick? Yes, you did, but don't worry. We made it to the bathroom in time. I'm really sorry about the juice. Here I thought it was okay, and I didn't drink very much, but it caused you some kind of tummy upset."

What was he talking about? Tummy upset? Here they were in bed together, and she was in her favorite silk pajamas no less, and he was . . . all she could tell was that he was in one of Kevin's old football jerseys. She swallowed the bile building in her throat and clutched at her churning stomach. Would God strike her dead for seducing one of his homeboys? It felt like God was trying to strike her down.

"I suppose breakfast is out of the question at this point." Jonathan grinned at her. "Would you like a cup of tea instead?"

A low groan escaped her throat. "Tea would be lovely."

"Coming right up."

He flipped back the top cover to reveal he was fully clothed except for his shoes, and he'd been lying on top of the sheets rather than in between them. Kat scratched her head.

"You're still in your clothes," she thought out loud.

He paused at the doorway. "Of course. Where do you keep the tea?"

"On the shelf over the stove fan." She turned to her side. "You mean we didn't . . ."

He narrowed his eyes. "Didn't?"

"Uh, you know." She made a quick motion with her hands. "You know, what most men and women do whenever they get into a bed together."

"Sleep? Yes, you were out like a light after the last round of purging. You asked me to stay with you in case you needed help again, so I did. This bed is wide enough to sleep about four across. I hope I didn't do anything wrong."

Kat's eyebrows rose. "Wrong? No, you were the perfect gentleman. But . . . but—"

He tilted his head and observed her. "But what?"

"What will the neighbors think?" She sat up. "How do my neighbors know you didn't spend the night between the sheets with me in my silk pajamas—which, by the way, I don't recall putting on by myself last night? What will the gossips in town be spreading about the two of us come tomorrow?"

"Nothing. I'll tell Darla you were feeling under the weather last night, so I stopped by to check up on you. She'll straighten them out. I don't think we have anything to worry about."

"And my pajamas?"

Jonathan blushed. "You did have some help putting those on. You couldn't quite get your legs in without leaning on me, but Scout's honor I didn't see anything you don't show in a swimsuit." He turned. "Now let me go fix you some tea."

Kat crawled out of the covers and shakily stood. The alarm clock said seven. She grabbed her bathrobe and slippers, pulled a comb through her hair, and headed to the kitchen. She had to convince Jonathan of the seriousness of the situation. People would see his car in front of her home and link them together. Even an honorable man such as the Reverend Jonathan Rawlins could find his impeachable reputation tarnished by rubbing shoulders against a woman with a past like hers.

She froze at the entrance to the kitchen. Jonathan was whistling—really whistling—to himself as he filled the kettle with reverse osmosis water and placed it on the range. Had he been interested in her the first time Darla had pointed out his whistling behavior? The parts of their dinner conversation she could remember last night certainly indicated it was possible.

"Jonathan, about what you said last night, I—"

"You think you're up for some toast? I found the bread and the toaster."

"Yeah, I could manage it. Jonathan, I need to know if what you said was—"

"Jam? I see you've got jam here," he said, poking his head into the refrigerator.

"Jam's fine. Now, Jonathan, I—"

"I like it when you say my name." He grinned like a fool. "Sit down and let me get you a mug. They're over here by the plates, right? I saw them last night while I was putting the dishes away."

"You cleaned up?" Kat was impressed. A date who ate

her cooking and cleaned up after himself *and* didn't expect to jump on her bones? Good Lord! What on earth was wrong with'her? Was she scruffy-looking?

"Since you went to all the trouble to make supper, the least I could do is clean up," he explained. The kettle began to boil. He turned off the stove. "What kind of tea bag you want? This *cosmic peppermint* sounds like it might calm your jumpy stomach."

"It's more like my nerves," she said under her breath, before saying louder, "Yes, peppermint would be nice."

Jonathan fixed her a mug full of the fragrant tea and set it down beside her. "Toast will be ready momentarily."

Kat blew on the hot brew and sipped slowly. She did feel a little less addled. "Jonathan, about last night, I just wanted to know . . . I wanted to know . . ."

He smiled. "Why I didn't make mad, passionate love to you?"

"Uh, yes, that, too." She narrowed her eyes. "You did say you loved me, didn't you, or was my hearing adversely affected by food poisoning?"

The bread popped up in the toaster. Jonathan retrieved the pieces and slathered them with strawberry jam, then placed them on a plate in front of her.

"You heard right." He sat beside her and reached for her hand. "I love you, Kat."

"But you don't *love*-love me, right?"

His smile drooped. "What do you mean?"

"What I mean is—" Kat paused her explanation and chugged a fortifying sip of tea. How could she say this without hurting his feelings—or hers for that matter? "You don't find me attractive, do you?" she blurted.

"Whatever makes you say that?" He squeezed her hand. "Just because I don't believe in taking advantage of a beautiful woman with a belly ache doesn't mean I don't find her

159

attractive. On the contrary, I find you extremely attractive."

Her heart skipped a beat. "You do?"

"Yes, I do." He kissed her hand, then let it go. "Now eat your toast."

Kat did as she was told and chewed her breakfast. Still, the *why* of Jonathan's behavior worried her. Hadn't he been at least tempted to crawl between the sheets with her? Had her tarnished reputation preceded her? After all, a man of Jonathan's caliber probably wouldn't find her track record with the opposite sex appealing, but she knew her reaction to him was different. A man with a total lack of a score sheet . . . well, she didn't hold his inexperience against him.

"What if I hadn't been feeling poorly?" She raised an eyebrow. "You might have done something else?"

Jonathan pushed back from the table and retrieved a mug for himself from the shelf. "Kat, I don't think two people who have just expressed a romantic interest should hop into bed at the slightest provocation. God wants us to keep the marriage bed special. You understand where I'm coming from?"

She nodded. "Of course."

Kat continued eating her toast, but she couldn't bring herself to look Jonathan in the eye as she sat back down at the table. A warm feeling akin to embarrassment flooded her veins. Of course she knew where he was coming from. He was a minister, for Pete's sake. He couldn't let his libido run rampant. He had to keep his sexuality under tight control. He had to think about his reputation, his family, and his congregation.

On the other hand, she couldn't stop thinking she had been so long without a man in her life—or her bed. Kat nibbled her bread crusts. Could she honestly remain in a relationship for very long that didn't involve at least the occasional good old-fashioned roll in the hay?

"All done? You want me to fix you a couple more pieces of bread?" Jonathan asked.

"No, thank you." Kat rose from the table. "I've kept you long enough. I'm sure you've got better things to be doing with your Tuesday morning than babysitting a hungover music teacher."

"I do have to let Rolf out for his morning romp. He's been pent-up since six yesterday evening." He stood and pulled her into his arms and kissed her forehead. "Don't forget I have a piano lesson tonight."

Kat froze. A part of her wanted to melt further into his strong arms, but another part wanted to stay aloof, safe. "You're right. I'll see you about seven?"

"Seven it is."

She turned from him and ambled toward the bedroom.

"Kat, aren't you going to see me out?" he asked, a quavering tone in his voice she hadn't noticed before.

"I think you can do that yourself." She disappeared into her room and shut the door behind her.

Where did I go wrong?

The question haunted Jonathan as he took Rolf on a quick jaunt around the block. Bless his canine heart, Rolf only chewed on the newspaper on the kitchen floor and Jonathan's old shoes on the mud mat. Not bad considering Jonathan had left the pup inside for over twelve hours straight.

The question repeated itself again as he sat at his desk in the church office several hours later. God knew he wanted to make love to Kat, but something had prevented him from doing so—and it wasn't the fact that she was feeling ill or that his principles didn't allow it. Although he'd slept better with a feminine presence on the other side of the mattress last night than he had in many months, his dreams of Kat only seemed to intensify.

"Something is wrong with me," he muttered. He grabbed a pen out of his pencil cup and jotted down the names of the volunteers for the Oktoberfest celebrations so Darla could enter them into the bulletin program.

A busy afternoon of fielding questions from the VBS committee kept his mind occupied enough to keep his self-recriminations at bay. As four o'clock rolled around, the shrill ringing of the phone sent a tremor of dread pulsating through him.

"Pastor Jon, this is S-Sally," the nervous woman stammered. "I-I'm afraid I have some bad news. It's Aunt M-Mabel. Sh-she's fallen again. Gayle and I think she had a stroke. We got her to the h-hospital. She's in surgery now."

"Bless you, Sally. I'm glad you two have been checking up on her regularly. Have you contacted her daughter in San Antonio, yet?"

"N-no, Pastor. Could you do it?"

"Certainly. Let me get her number and some more information from you first."

Jonathan felt utterly drained. After a tense telephone conversation and a long visit with Sally and Gayle at the hospital, he briefly visited with Mabel's daughter, Eunice, at her mother's ICU bedside. Aunt Mabel was out of surgery but not out of the woods yet, according to her doctors. Time and prayer were the only things that could heal her now.

He drove home, downhearted and dejected. Aunt Mabel had always been such a support to him, particularly since Ruth's death. How could he bear to lose her?

He pulled into the driveway and shuffled into the house. It wasn't until after he'd let Rolf out to run around the backyard that he saw the message light flashing on the answering machine in his study.

"Hi, uh, it's Kat. It's seven-fifteen. You do remember you

have a piano lesson tonight, right?"

Jonathan flopped into his desk chair and rubbed his temples. "I hope Kat doesn't mind if I don't feel up to it tonight." As he picked up the phone to call her back, there came a knock at the front door.

"I heard the news about Aunt Mabel," Kat said, standing in the doorway. "Gayle called me right after I called you. Is she doing any better?"

Jonathan opened the door wider to let Kat inside. He led her into the family room where they both sat on the couch.

"She's stable after the surgery. They think they've dissolved the clot on her brain, but it's going to be touch and go for the next twenty-four hours."

"Poor, poor Aunt Mabel. She'd been getting around so good after her hip replacement, too. She said she was going to start coming to choir practice next week. Now this." Kat sniffed back a tear, her lip quivering. "She's going to pull through okay, isn't she?"

He tugged her into his arms. "She has a fighting chance. After all, look at all the people who are praying for her recovery."

"I mean the doctors. Gayle says they're saying—"

Jonathan hushed her with a finger to her lips. "Why put your faith in mere men? God is on our side. Miracles do happen."

Kat gazed at him through the glistening drops in her eyes. "You're right. Look at the two of us."

"What do you mean?"

"I mean, it's a miracle. Who'd ever think I would consider dating a man of the cloth, and even more miraculous, who'd ever think he would seriously consider dating me?"

He furrowed his brow. "Why wouldn't I want to date you?"

Kat shifted her weight away from him on the sofa. "I

know Jesus ate with the prostitutes and the tax collectors, but I doubt people of Germantown are going to be quite as open-minded when they see the two of us strolling down the street hand in hand."

"Don't be ridiculous," Jonathan said, shaking his head at her. An uneasy feeling grabbed at his heart. "People will be happy to see we're both happy."

"Will they?" Kat sighed. "I hope you're right."

"You seem to think we're doomed before we start. I don't see it that way at all. I see a long and beautiful future ahead of us."

"Together?"

Jonathan froze. What was the look in her eye which caused him to harbor some second thoughts himself?

"Of course I mean together. You're not out of sorts because of last night, are you?" he asked.

"Well, no . . . not really. I—"

"You don't think a man can have a real interest in a woman without expressing it in a more physical manner, do you?"

Kat shrugged. "It's never been that way in my experience. It's not to say I jumped in bed on the first date with every man I ever met, but I have to admit I've known you a lot longer already than I have most of my previous boyfriends, and we've not . . . uh, you know."

"Gone to bed together other than to sleep?"

"Exactly. I respect your position, though. Honestly, I do."

Jonathan didn't know whether to feel complimented or insulted. Here the woman he loved was sitting on his couch, patting his hand like he was the same age as one of her youngest pupils, saying she *respected his position* when it was obvious she didn't even agree with it.

"Kat, marriage is a serious matter. We can't just rush into—"

"Who said anything about running up the aisle?" She stood and paced around the room. "Jonathan, I don't think you're any more ready for marriage at this point in your life than I am, and I've been single for quite a bit longer than you."

"Then what are we talking about?"

"I'm just thinking aloud about how to define our *relationship*." She spun about on her heels, gesturing wildly with her hands. "For instance, if someone sees us eating out together some evening and asks us what we're doing spending time together, do we say we're friends or do we say we're boyfriend and girlfriend in the modern sense of the terms?"

Ah, it comes down to the image we project. Kat doesn't want people to think she's dating another loser.

Jonathan smiled. "Why can't we say we're friends who are getting to know each other better?" he suggested.

Kat halted in her tracks. "*Know* as in the biblical sense?"

The corners of his lips drooped. "*Know* as in we're learning more about what makes the other person tick, what dreams, hopes, and ambitions does the other person have and how do ours mesh with theirs."

"I see." She paced the room again. "What if one of us harbors the hope of sharing a more physical relationship without the benefit of a piece of paper from the courthouse?"

Jonathan rose and gathered Kat into his arms. "You're emphasizing the wrong thing here. The piece of paper isn't important. It's what the two profess in the eyes of God. You realize many of our ancestors never had more than an entry jotted in the front of the family Bible declaring them man and wife. They lived too far away from civilization and didn't have a clergyman or a judge to sign a legal document for them, but that didn't make them any less married in the eyes of God."

"So you're saying if a couple consummates their relationship they're married?"

He bit his lip and considered her statement for several moments before finally answering, "In a word, yes."

She averted her eyes and shook her head. "I have more husbands than the Samaritan woman Christ met at Jacob's well then."

Jonathan tilted her chin so he could see her face. Her lashes were wet with tears.

"I don't deserve someone like you to love me," she whispered.

He kissed her forehead. "I think you got that backward. I don't deserve someone like you to love me, but God sent you my way, and I'm not going to give you up without a fight."

Kat smiled. "Fight? I don't think so. You're the most peaceable man I know."

He harrumphed. "You've never seen me angry."

She gave him a thoughtful expression. "You know, you're right. I've never seen you angry — and you've never seen me angry. I guess we really do need to get to know about each other better."

"See? I knew you'd understand where I was coming from."

"You must be psychic."

He quirked an eyebrow. "What makes you say that?"

"I never said in so many words I loved you, but you seemed to know it already." She drew his lips closer to her own, sealing them with a long and lingering kiss.

"Hmm, I don't know," he murmured as he nibbled her earlobes a moment later. "Something in your behavior sort of put the idea in my head."

"You mean like this?" She drew him into another passionate embrace which could have lasted hours if the incessant ringing of the phone hadn't interrupted them.

"Hello," Jonathan croaked, disengaging himself from

Kat's enthusiastic hold. "Oh. They took her back in? I see. Shall I come now? No? Okay, please give me a call when she's back in ICU. Thanks, Eunice. Take care."

Kat frowned. "Something happen to Aunt Mabel?"

"Yes. She's suffered a bit of a setback. The doctors aren't sure they got everything, so they're taking her back into surgery. Her daughter and son-in-law are there and promise to keep me informed."

A tear trickled down his cheek as he ended the call. Kat wiped it away with a kiss. Jonathan pulled back.

"It's okay," she whispered. "I know how hard it is seeing Aunt Mabel in the hospital so ill like this so soon after Ruth's—"

"Yes, it's very difficult for me." He turned and headed toward his study, breaking down in full-fledged sobs halfway down the hall.

Kat led Jonathan to his bedroom and sat with him at the foot of his bed. She removed his glasses and gathered his head in her lap, tenderly stroking his tears.

"There, there. Let it all come out. There's no need to hold back. I'm waterproof. I won't shrink if I get wet."

"I'll try not to drown you." He sat up and paused as he looked into her eyes.

She had been weeping as well.

"Oh, Kat," he breathed. "You're such a comfort to me, and you need comforting, too."

Jonathan held her close. Then, something inside of him broke open and out flowed all his need to be held and to hold another in return. His mouth sought hers. Her lips parted, and his tongue met hers. Kat moaned and fell backward onto the bed. She coiled her arms around his neck, melding her body closer to his. He roved his hands freely across her curves, luxuriating in the softness of her skin, the warmth of her response. She groaned.

"Kat, Kat," he breathed against the sweet hollow of her neck. "Make love to me."

"Jonathan, I . . . I . . ."

"What?"

Kat sat up. "I can't."

CHAPTER ELEVEN

"We can't do this," she emphasized.

Jonathan stared at Kat, dazed by passion. "What do you mean?"

Kat had no idea why she'd reacted as she had. All she knew was she enjoyed Jonathan's touch. Did she ever enjoy it, but hadn't he convinced her just this morning they shouldn't hop into bed so soon in their relationship?

"This isn't the right time or the right place," Kat backtracked. "I mean, Mabel's daughter could call at any minute, asking you to come to the hospital."

Jonathan sat up and nodded in agreement.

Kat stood and smoothed her somewhat wrinkled cotton top and pants outfit. "I don't really think I can make love to you with so many pairs of eyes staring at me."

"Eyes?" His gaze wandered about the room. "Oh. The family photos are rather prevalent on the dresser tops, aren't they?"

Kat smiled. "No kidding."

"You're right. Here and now is neither the time nor the place." He stood and took her into his arms. "I believe you can take some solace in knowing I find you very attractive, Kat. Very."

"Likewise."

Their lips met in a confirmation of their words. Kat wanted to melt into his arms and never let go.

"I'd better get going now," she said breathlessly.

"Can I make up my piano lesson some other time?" he

asked.

She raised an eyebrow. "I suppose so, or do you want to change instruments? You play me well already."

He threw back his head and laughed. "You make my heart feel light even when it's hurting. How do you do it?"

"Magic, of course." She kissed him once more and turned to the door.

He reached out and grabbed her hand, pulling her back to his side. "I want you to promise me one thing."

"Anything."

"Promise me you'll never consider yourself unworthy of my love ever again. The past is in the past. It's forgiven and forgotten. Please forgive yourself and don't let your past relationships color how you see the two of us."

She nodded. "I won't."

"Good."

He led her to the front door. "I'll see you tomorrow then. Sweet dreams."

They sure will be.

"'Night, Jonathan. Sweet dreams to you, too."

"Mom, I don't know where you could have been last night, but I needed you."

Kat sighed and slumped into a kitchen chair. She'd had a premonition when her phone rang at precisely eight o'clock it wasn't going to be her idea of a good morning wake-up call.

"Calm down, Keely, and tell me what's bothering you, sweetie," Kat said in her calmest, most controlled mother's voice. "I can't help you if I don't know what the problem is."

"It's Nigel, of course," she wailed. "He says he wants out. He's had enough."

"Oh, baby. I'm so sorry." Kat did her best not to let the smile on her face show in her voice. "It's probably for the best, you know. Now you can concentrate on your studies and get ready for graduate school. Time will heal your pain."

"I don't want to go to graduate school. I don't want time to heal my pain. I just want Nigel."

Kat's heart felt like it could burst. If there was anything worse than the pain of a heartache, it was experiencing the same sting being suffered by someone you loved more than life itself. She knew how lucky she was now to have found Jonathan. One day Keely would find the right man, too. It just wouldn't be today. Keely had to finish her education and focus on her dream.

"Of course you want to go to graduate school. You've always wanted to go to graduate school. Remember what you told me in sixth grade? You want to come back from college and start up your own strings academy in Germantown, remember?"

"Not anymore." Keely's voice sounded flat, emotionless. "There are better people to teach than a bunch of hicks in the sticks whose parents only want private lessons for their brats so they can impress the neighbors with how much expendable income they have."

"Keely!" Kat cried. "Whatever makes you say such a mean thing?"

"It's true, Mom. Look at your own private pupils. Tell me, how many of them are on Food Stamps?"

Kat bit her lip, tapping her fingers against the table. "None."

"I thought so. Why do the rich kids get to enjoy all the perks? Why aren't poor kids allowed to have a little culture taught to them?"

"Why, of course all children should be exposed to music," Kat explained. "We can't always force it down their throats if they aren't serious about becoming more proficient practitioners. When parents put down good money for private lessons, you know they're serious—"

"Their mom and dad are serious, all right," Keely cut in abruptly, "but little Johnny or Suzy probably couldn't care less. I mean, how many five-year-olds would rather practice *Twinkle, Twinkle Little Star* on the keyboard over playing video games or hanging out with their friends?"

Kat shook her head and sighed. "You're not making any sense. You're just upset."

"Of course I'm upset. The love of my life walks out of my life, and you expect me not to be upset?" Keely's voice went up an octave. "I'm making plenty of sense, and you know it."

"So, what *are* you planning to do after graduation?" Kat asked, praying for wisdom.

"They need good teachers in the poorer school districts. I thought about applying for a job I heard about in a small town near El Paso."

"El Paso?" Kat clutched at her chest. "It's in a whole other time zone. Why not find a teaching job someplace closer, like maybe San Marcos?"

"As much as I love you, Mom, I don't want to live at home forever. I have my own life to lead, my own need to start a home for my own family."

An overwhelming sense of déjà vu shivered down Kat's spine. "Keely, are you telling me everything about this breakup with Nigel? Is there some other reason why you don't want to come back to teach in Germantown?"

"I've told you already, Mom. I don't want to be treated like a child anymore, particularly . . ." Her voice trailed away.

"Sweetie?" Kat pressed. "You can talk to me. Tell me what's really up with you."

"I've got to go now," Keely said in a hushed voice.

"Someone's here at the door. Love ya, Mom. Bye."

Kat put down her cell phone and rose from the table. "Some *sympathy* call. I need a shoulder to cry on."

She glanced up at the wall clock above the sink. Eight-twenty. Kevin wouldn't be back in the apartment from his early morning weight-lifting class until eleven. No one liked a snitch, but maybe it was time she found out a little more of what was happening between Keely and Nigel from a source closer to the action.

"She made it! She made it!" Darla exclaimed, skipping into the choir room. "The doctors are saying Aunt Mabel's chance of a complete recovery are very good."

"Hallelujah." Kat breathed out a sigh and leaned an elbow against the piano. "I've never been more relieved in my whole life. Are Gayle and Sally still with her?"

Darla plopped into her seat and picked up the folder beside her. "Gayle said she was fixin' to go home and grab her something to eat. She might be able to get here in about a half-hour. Sally? Well, you know how she is. She went home to take her meds and lie down and recuperate from the strain."

Kat sat at the keyboard and arranged her sheet music. "It's understandable. I didn't plan on practicing too many pieces tonight anyway. I think the choir has earned this Sunday off."

"You fixin' to sing a solo?"

"I hadn't planned to." She furrowed her brow. "You think I should?"

"The one you sang at Christmastime was lovely," Darla gushed. "Everyone thought so. Don't you know another, middle-of-the-year type of number?"

Kat shrugged. "Not one I can sing in a church. I suppose I

could look in the music files for something."

Brenna ambled in and took her seat. "Y'all hear the good news about Aunt Mabel? She squeezed her daughter's hand when Pastor Jon read her a verse from the Psalms."

"How did you know that?" Darla's smugness faltered a bit. "I just got off the phone with Gayle before I came over here, and she didn't tell me any such thing."

"I have a friend who's a nurse in ICU," Brenna explained. "I told her to tell me the minute Aunt Mabel got to feeling better. She's been texting me reports all day."

"She mustn't have a very difficult job if all she does is text with you all day long." A puzzled frown crossed Darla's features. "Hey, how did you get those texts? Weren't you working at the dairy today?"

Brenna grinned. "Yes, but I have a desk job now. I was promoted last week."

"Last week?" Darla's eyebrows rose. "How come I hadn't heard about this before now?"

Brenna shrugged. "Don't know. I see your Dillon in the office every morning. He's ever so nice. He always tells me good morning, too."

Darla crossed her arms over her wide chest and narrowed her eyes, staring hard at Brenna. "Is that a fact? What else has he been telling you?"

"Congratulations on the new position, Brenna," Kat interrupted, diverting her attention from marking her sheet music to save her from Darla's wrath. "It's great to hear your hard work has been rewarded at last."

"Am I early?" Matthias Ringleschmidt announced from the doorway. "I can come back later if I need to—"

"Get yourself in here, Matt," Darla commanded. "You're on time for once. It's the others who are late."

Kat knew Darla's bossy tone was caused by imagined slights but thought it best to stay out of the conversation.

"Yes, ma'am." He quickly took his seat. "Y'all hear the news about Aunt Mabel yet?"

"She's able to wiggle her toes on command," Brenna said, nodding. "It means she has good control of her motor functions, according to my friend."

"How come I didn't know about any of this?" Darla frowned. "Something must be seriously wrong with my news-gathering network. I'm always the first to know about things going on with our church members — *especially* major events."

The pencil lead in Kat's hand snapped as she pressed hard against the paper.

Have Darla's informants told her anything about Jonathan and me yet?

Kat took a deep breath, stood, and rapped three times on the piano top with her knuckles. She'd burn that bridge when she came to it. Now certainly wasn't the time.

"All right, people, let's settle down. I've got to play and hear you sing as well since Gayle and Neil are going to be late. Let's start on this very pretty rendition of *God Bless America* I want us to sing on the Fourth of July holiday weekend. If you notice these things, you'll see the sopranos sing a descant this time with the rest of us following along with a simple three-part harmony."

"I never thought it was possible, but it's a miracle how quickly this Oktoberfest is coming together, Matt." Jonathan followed the other council members from the church library to the parking lot after their weekly meeting. "Your wonderful speech in church last Sunday got everyone from seven to ninety-seven enthused about the plans for the new classroom building, too. Simply amazing. You should feel proud."

Matthias blushed. "I admit, it's going better than even I

thought it would. All we have to do now is collect the money so we can start raising the roof soon afterward."

"The polka band is booked?"

"Yes, the *Big Bad Boys of Polka* are ready, willing, and able. They have their own sound system, too, so we won't need to borrow any microphones from the sanctuary like we thought. It's just the lights we've got to arrange, and Charlie is working on those. We're talking the local radio station into loaning us their mobile outdoor spotlight."

"The big one they use for grand openings, right?"

"That's the one."

Matthias stopped at the driver's side door of his mud-splattered SUV. He looked down at his feet for several awkward moments. Jonathan sensed something was bothering his able congregation president, but Matt was having trouble articulating it.

"Is there anything else that you need help with that you didn't mention already?" Jonathan asked.

"Uh, no, there's just something personal I need to ask you, Pastor."

Jonathan had seen the look a thousand times before—eyes averted, hands in pockets, the slow rhythmic rocking on the heels and balls of the feet back and forth. Here he'd worked so hard to come across as being accessible, not judgmental with his parishioners. "You want to go inside and talk?" he asked, nodding toward the church.

"It's okay." Matthias paused, then added, "It's not about me."

Jonathan quirked an eyebrow "Oh?"

"It's about you."

"Me?" Jonathan's pulse raced.

Matthias kicked his toes on the dusty asphalt, then raised his gaze to meet Jonathan's. "I was wondering how you were coping with being on your own."

Jonathan's tensions eased. No one had put two and two together yet. No one knew about him and Kat.

"I'm doing as well as can be expected," he began, smiling. "I'm not quite the housekeeper I thought I was, but I manage. I wish I could get over to see Elizabeth and Josh more often, but they're busy with getting their place ready for the baby. I'm only in the way when I do visit, but that's going to change in a few months, I hope. Eli keeps in touch online, so it's not so bad."

"The puppy my father sold you — is he keeping you good company?"

Jonathan laughed. "Rolf is a master at keeping me company. Tell your father the next time you see him, will you? He must have given me the pick of the litter because old Rolfie is as intelligent and loving as he is hyperactive."

Matthias visibly relaxed. "I'll do that. Thanks, Pastor, for making my job a bit easier. I kept telling folks not to fret, you're doing okay as a widower, but they get to wondering and pestering me to check up on you."

Jonathan's curiosity was piqued now. "They want you to check up on *me*?"

"Sort of. They're just anxious to know you're doing all right. Darla says things about you whistling to yourself and wanting to take piano lessons. It gets people worried."

"Worried?" Jonathan narrowed his eyes. "About what?"

"You know how things get twisted around when they're passed down the grapevine. Darla says she thinks you've started seeing someone since she's not seen you look so upbeat since before Ruth got sick and all. Then other folks in town get to talking and, before too long, we have a regular rumor on our hands."

Jonathan frowned. "Rumor, as in a mud-slinging type of statement, is what you're saying?"

Matthias nodded. "Yep, unfortunately. I know for a fact

some ol' fool was saying he thought he saw your car parked in front of Kat Dubcek's house the other night and vice versa. He figured Kat was up to her old tricks again."

Jonathan took a step backward, hit by an unseen blow to the gut. "Her old tricks?"

The tall man furrowed his brow. "The implication was that Kat was *selling her wares*. I don't know where he came up with this foolishness. Everyone in town knows Kat has dated around, but she's never been formally charged with being a, you know, shady lady."

"I should think not."

Matthias shook his head. "People in a small town may say they forgive a person his or her past indiscretions, but they don't ever forget 'em, do they?"

"Yes, well, we all need to practice forgiving one another every day—particularly in a small town."

Jonathan glanced at his watch and backed away from the car. "I've got to get going now, Matt. Thank you for sharing your concerns with me. Thank you for not spreading idle gossip besmirching the good name of our choir director. Goodnight."

Jonathan half ran, half walked to his back door and let himself inside. Rolf attacked him with slobbery kisses.

"Down, boy, down!" he cried, removing the collie's paws from his once-clean shirt. "I'll walk you in a minute. Just let me change and make a quick phone call."

"Why all the cloak-and-dagger business?" Kat flipped on the porch light and opened her back screen door to let Jonathan and Rolf inside. "I almost didn't hear your knock, even though I knew you were on your way over. You can come to my front door, you know."

"I thought it would be easier this way. This way Rolf

doesn't have to come through your front hall and track in mud."

"Rolf's been rolling in the mud, has he?" Kat knelt to pet the playful pup on the head. "He looks pretty clean to me. Don't you, boy?"

Rolf replied with big wet kisses on Kat's cheeks.

"Oh, bad, bad boy!" She chuckled. "I wonder where Rolf has learned to be so affectionate."

Jonathan smiled. "Let's go inside and let the Casanova of the canine set stay out here and enjoy a rest."

Kat led Jonathan into the kitchen, switching on a few more lights as they went along the hallway. "I'm sorry it's so dark in here, but I was in the front room working on a solo number for this coming Sunday and — "

She stopped dead in her tracks when Jonathan turned off lights behind them.

"What are you doing? Trying to help conserve energy?"

His hand froze on the switch plate. "Something like that."

Kat quirked an eyebrow and leaned against the wall beside him. "You want to play nude tag in the dark?"

Jonathan laughed, a stilted sound, not his usual resonant, full-bodied guffaw. A sudden chill filled the air. She stood straighter and crossed her arms.

"What's up?" she asked.

"Nothing. Can't I just drop in and visit you from time to time?" He pulled her into his arms and kissed her once on the lips before letting go. He crinkled his nose. "You smell like Rolf."

Kat threw up her hands in exasperation and headed into the living room. "The thought of another man kissing me puts you off, am I right?"

"Another . . . man?"

"Rolf, the wonder dog, of course." Kat sat on the mended piano bench and frowned as a light bulb popped over her head. "So, that's why you're turning off the lights. You were thinking you'd catch someone before they left, huh?"

Jonathan lowered himself onto the edge of the bench. "Before who left?"

She stretched her fingers across the keyboard and played a slow, haunting blues melody. "Why, one of my other lovers, of course."

He swallowed hard. "Kat, I don't want to offend you, but have you been seeing anyone else besides me?"

Ow.

She stopped playing and turned to face him. "I told you a while back I'd given up on men forever, remember? Don't you believe me?"

"Of course I believe you." He stroked her cheek. "It's just that people in this town get to gossiping and—"

"They're telling you that I'm the type of woman who dates more than one guy at a time?"

Kat began to play again, soft and slow, dragging her left hand through the bass chords, heavy as lead. "Oh, I'm beginning to see what's going down here. It's my old friend the District Attorney spreading dirt on me just because I didn't go to bed with him the other night."

Jonathan paled. "Bradley T. Bradley asked you to go to bed with him?"

"Yeah. He thought I owed him one since he took me to the party shindig over at the Holbreicht's, but he's pretty much ruined his chances. He picked up some bimbo at the party right in front of me." The music faltered. "The nerve of the creep."

Jonathan leaned over and kissed Kat on the cheek. "He sounds like an idiot. How did he ever get elected?"

She shrugged. "Beats me. I voted for Chavez the last time myself."

They both laughed.

Jonathan smiled, apparently satisfied with her explanation, but Kat couldn't be certain. Who was gossiping about her in town lately? Darla hadn't come right out and accused her of anything scandalous at choir practice last night, but she had mentioned she had her sources. Why all the confusion in Jonathan's mind now?

"Are you jealous?" she asked, point-blank, picking up the melody again.

He started. "Jealous? Who me?"

"Of course, you. Does the idea my name could be linked romantically with any of a half-dozen well-connected men in the area bother you? Be honest. I have to know."

"The past is the past—"

"But the past affects the present which, in turn, affects the future, does it not?" She stopped playing and turned to study his expression. "Has it ever crossed your mind having your good name associated with a known *loose woman* could be detrimental to your job? Your position in the community? Your career?"

"No, it would never come to that," Jonathan insisted, shaking his head. "You're reading too much into it, Kat. People aren't talking about us at all. They don't even know we're seeing each other."

She nodded toward the dark hallway. "You want to keep it that way?"

"You mean my putting out the lights?"

Kat rose from the piano bench and crossed to the lamp nearest the front window and dimmed its glow. She pulled the drapes closed, excising the view of the outside world.

"There, no one can see us now. You didn't drive your car over like the other night, so there's no other way to connect your presence with my home unless Rolf gets to barking. It could be a little hard to explain to the neighbors since I've always been a cat person, but I could tell them I'm babysitting a friend's dog while he's out of town."

Jonathan stood. "You don't have to do this."

"You don't mind, do you?" She quirked an eyebrow, then hurried to the back porch. "I'll let Rolf inside so if he gets noisy the sound won't carry next door and—"

"Kat, I said you don't have to cover my tracks." He followed her into the kitchen. "We're adults. We don't have to go explaining our actions to anyone." He reached around her and shut the sliding door. "Leave Rolf be for now. He's sleeping comfortably enough."

The collie pup was snoring, curled up on an old beach towel Kat kept on the back stoop to use as a kneeling pad while gardening.

She smiled. "Poor fella looks tuckered out. You've been exercising him a lot?"

Jonathan chuckled. "I think it's the other way around. He's been exercising me." He put his arm around her shoulders and guided her toward the living room sofa.

"What a great exercise plan." Kat tried to keep her fears out of her voice. "I thought you looked like you were losing weight, but I didn't want to say anything in case you thought I was one of those women who wanted to stuff you full of their home-style cooking. After my frozen lasagna meal the other night, I think you know better."

They sat on the sofa together. Jonathan took her hand in his and kissed it.

"Can I borrow Rolf sometime?" Kat asked. "I could stand to shed a few pounds."

He pulled her closer. She wrapped her arms about his neck.

"Certainly," he said. "Rolf's got more than enough energy for two masters. Better yet, we could both go on the same diet."

"Instead of eating dessert, we have to find other ways to satisfy our sweet tooth, huh?" Kat grinned. "I could stick to a diet like that."

"I'm sold on it already," Jonathan murmured, sealing his promise with a deep and lingering kiss.

Are you sold on me?

Kat sighed contentedly despite her nagging fears.

Are you really sold on me, Jonathan Rawlins, or will you go off me like a bad diet when somebody points out I could jeopardize your social health?

CHAPTER TWELVE

"Daddy, whatever were you thinking?"

Jonathan flicked a fallen peanut shell off his khaki pants leg, frowning across the picnic table at his daughter who was eight and a half months pregnant with his first grandchild. Elizabeth was so like her mother in some ways, but in others? Well, at least she was consistent in her condemnation.

"I thought you said the Oktoberfest was a good idea to raise money?" he prompted her. "You seem to be enjoying your bratwurst, and Josh is —"

"Yes, I know Josh is enjoying himself," Elizabeth cut in, sulking. Her look sent daggers of disapproval across the dance tent to her spouse who was clogging on the wooden dance floor with several old high school chums — tipsy, male *and* female high school chums. It was rather cruel of his son-in-law to cavort so merrily while his wife was forced to sit still and watch from the sidelines. He patted her hand.

"Don't worry, honey. Just a few more weeks, and you'll be able to polka with the best of them."

"I don't want to polka. I just want to be able to see my toes again. You don't know how long it's been since I last saw my feet. They could have fallen off for all I know." She shifted her bulk in the lawn chair and lifted her long, auburn ponytail off her damp neck. "The box fans aren't doing the trick, either. I think it's why the Germans host these little get-togethers in October and not July and particularly not July in Texas."

He picked up a discarded flyer from beside his chair and fanned her. "I know it's not the most opportune time of the year, but we need to replace the Sunday School building as soon as possible. You've got to hand it to our church members—they've really worked fast to get this thing pulled together."

"I guess so." Elizabeth narrowed her eyes and stared at her father. Suspicion was her strong suit. "I hear tell you've been working closely with our choir director."

Jonathan swallowed half his can of Coke in one gulp and coughed. "Who . . . told you . . . that?"

Elizabeth smoothed her pale-green cotton maternity top over her swollen belly and pursed her lips. "A little bird told me."

"What did the little bird say?"

"She said Kat was teaching you to play piano. I find it hard to believe, Dad. You never were very musical. You can barely hold a tune."

"I'm a better singer than you think," Jonathan said, indignant at the thought that his own flesh and blood thought so little of his abilities. "I have a natural knack for the keyboard, I'm told. I have long fingers and a good reach."

Elizabeth snorted. "I hope that's all you're reaching for—keys on the piano. I don't want to hear you're reaching for anything else in Kat's house. She's got quite the reputation, you know."

Jonathan refused to dignify his daughter's remarks with a reply. He shifted his weight away from her and focused his attention on the stage. Elizabeth rested her head on a fist.

"You and Mom never did keep abreast of all the happenings going on at the middle school, did you? You both were such goody-two-shoes. You never would believe any of the bad stuff you heard about anyone. It's a wonder you survived all these years being so naïve."

"You know it's not naiveté to think only the best about others, Elizabeth," Jonathan said in a low tone. "Some preacher's daughter you turned out to be."

"I turned out pretty well." She sniffed. "Remember what happened to the Reverend Olson's daughter, Nell? Her wild behavior about split Community Baptist into two congregations."

Jonathan shot his daughter a disapproving stare.

"You ought to be glad Josh and I got the order right about marriage first, *then* children. Didn't she end up having a child by each of the defensive line of the high school football team?"

"The football team is here?" Josh plopped into his chair next to his wife. He caressed her stomach.

Elizabeth flashed her husband a pathetic look. "No, but the baby is hungry for some dessert. Can you get me one of those apple strudels, sweetheart?"

He sprang to his feet. "No problem, angel. Coming up."

"I could have gotten you some more to eat." Jonathan watched his exhausted son-in-law meander through the milling crowd to the food booths. "Josh looks like he could use a breather after the clogging."

"No, Dad, don't. I have to train Josh to wait on me hand and foot now so he'll know how to help out when the baby arrives."

"Now, honey, I don't think you should—"

"Pastor Jon, when are you going to take to the dance floor?" Caroline Zaye patted Jonathan on the back as she made her way toward the stage area. "If I can get my Charlie to cut a rug now and then, you should be able to do a little dancin', too."

Jonathan grinned at the dimpled-cheeked, silver-haired woman. "Why, Caroline, I thought you'd never ask."

"Woo-hoo, you are the sly one!"

Jonathan accepted Caroline's hand, following her to the floor. The band struck up *In Heaven There Is No Beer*. He needn't have worried about not knowing how to lead a polka as Caroline had no problem in doing so.

"Your Elizabeth looks like she's ready to domino any day now," Caroline remarked with a grin as they whirled around the dance floor. "Are you gettin' excited, Gramps?"

Jonathan laughed. "Oh dear. I'm about to be labeled *Gramps*. I hadn't realized the downside of having grandchildren, the growing old."

"It's not the only bad part, you know. There's the having to keep track of all their birthdays, confirmations, graduations, and other sundry anniversaries and Christmas presents. Lord Almighty, if it ain't a drain on the bank account."

"I'll never get out of debt, huh?"

"No, you won't. You've heard that my youngest boy and his wife are fixin' to have their second bundle of joy and my sixteenth grandkid this coming month." Caroline sighed. "I realize now I should have told ol' Charlie to holster his dang pistol after number five came along."

Jonathan's cheeks reddened at her frankness. "You're such a card, Caroline. I know for a fact you adore each and every child and grandchild whose photo decorates your mantelpiece."

She winked. "True enough."

The music drew to a close, punctuated with a loud burst of clapping and cheers. Jonathan led Caroline back to her seat beside her husband, turned to check on how Elizabeth and Josh were fairing, then headed toward the bottled water booth.

"P-Pastor Jon," Sally called out behind him as he crossed the parking lot. "Look who's here."

"Aunt Mabel." Jonathan knelt beside the wheelchair and squeezed her frail hand. The tiny woman in the chair beamed a crooked wisp of a smile up at him. "You're look-ing wonderful, Mabel. Getting stronger every day, I hear."

"She is, she is," Sally said for her friend. "The doctor says she should get a little sunshine, so I volunteered to push her around today."

"That's great." Jonathan stood. "Now, if both you ladies will excuse me, I'm in need of some water. The polka takes a lot out of a grandfather-to-be."

Mabel's gray eyes flashed bright. Somehow Jonathan knew exactly what she was trying to communicate without words.

"Yes, my grandchild-to-be is seated over in the tent," he said, directing them toward his former seat. "Go on over and visit with Elizabeth a spell, you two. She'll appreciate the company."

Wiping the back of his hand across his damp brow, Jona-than left them to join the long line in front of the bottled wa-ter stand. Whoever came up with the idea of sticking reverse osmosis tap water into a plastic container and slapping a fancy price tag on it could have never imagined how popu-lar the stuff would turn out to be.

"Your dancing is improving faster than your piano play-ing," Kat said quietly behind him a few moments later.

He turned and smiled at her. She looked beautiful in her mock lederhosen hot pants and Alpine peasant blouse outfit complete with hiking boots, mountaineer's hat, and fake braided pigtails.

"I have my moments. You fixin' to teach me how to play your portable piano next?" he asked, leaning close.

Kat pulled away and shook her head. "Remember, we're in public," she whispered. Stepping back, she raised her voice a notch, "I don't give accordion lessons. At least not yet. I've got to remember how to play it better myself before I can go about inflicting the knowledge on others."

"You play fine. Didn't the crowd go crazy after that little ditty you did about a half hour ago?"

"No, they went crazy because my pretend lederhosen strap sort of snapped and those hormonally challenged teens in the mosh pit thought maybe my shorts were fixin' to fall down." Kat's cheeks colored. "I guess if you can't entertain your audience one way, try a striptease."

Jonathan chuckled. He wanted so badly to reach out and draw her close to him and kiss her he could taste it. They had decided now was not quite the time, and this was not quite the place to announce their budding relationship to the congregation.

"Too bad I was sitting so far away. I missed the *strap action* bit," he murmured for her ears only.

"Why, Pastor Jon, are you coming on to me?" Kat said breathlessly, wrinkling her nose at him.

"Not in public, remember?" He quirked an eyebrow. "Is there any reason we can't polka at least once or twice or ten times?"

She bit her lip. "Hmm, I don't see how once or twice could hurt but first I've got to get a water and a sit down to rest a while. I'm sweating in these boots, and I've got an awful feeling I'm fixin' to lose one of my braids."

Finding himself next in line, Jonathan purchased them both an icy bottle of water before leading Kat to his table in the main tent.

"Hello, Elizabeth," Kat said, taking a seat beside Jonathan. "Baby due any day now?"

"Hello, Kat." Elizabeth nodded, scoping out Kat's costume. "I've got about three weeks officially, but one never knows."

"You're right. One never really knows. My twins came early."

"I bet they did."

Jonathan sensed a subtle contempt for their table guest in his daughter's voice and manner. He leaned across and patted her hand. "Did Josh get you a strudel, honey? If not we can—"

"That was quite a rousing number you performed during the band's break," Elizabeth cut in, pulling her hand away. "I never knew you were such an accomplished accordion player."

"I'm not." Kat chuckled, then took a swig of water.

Elizabeth leaned forward. "So, where did you get your accordion? Who taught you?"

"I inherited it from my late uncle. I'm self-taught. The music is easy enough, but the hand coordination and pumping really takes some learning to do properly. It's practically an aerobic workout just to pick up the thing."

"It does look rather heavy. It is why you keep it parked on stage?"

"Right. Plus, I don't want the kids to go banging willy-nilly on the buttons and keys. It's old, and I want it to last a while longer so I can pass it on to Keely."

Kat bent over to loosen her bootlaces. Jonathan's gaze involuntarily dipped to Kat's plunging neckline, then rose to meet his daughter's glare. Jonathan could tell his fascination with the choir mistress' cleavage wasn't lost on his daughter.

"There, much better." Kat sighed, falling back into the chair. "These boots are murder."

"But they make the outfit," Elizabeth purred, "especially those braids. However did you grow your hair out so fast?"

Kat grinned. "Fake hair. My friend Hannah MacDonald works for a beauty supply company, and she found some false hair matching mine and put these together. I think I'll use them for dress-up day in October at school, too."

"Not with those clothes." Elizabeth shook her head and rolled her eyes. "It would never do."

"Really? They sort of all go together. I can't wear the Swiss Miss braids without the lederhosen and the blouse." Kat turned to Jonathan beside her. "What do you think?"

Jonathan nodded as he put down his water bottle. "I think it's a very nice ensemble."

Elizabeth gave a droll laugh. "Always the diplomat, aren't you, Dad? You'd say the same about a pig in a petticoat, wouldn't you?" She turned her attention back to Kat. "You know, you really have to take everything my father says with a grain of salt."

Kat furrowed her brow. "I don't know. Your father has always been straight-up with me. He's the most honest man I've ever met."

"Yes, he probably is, isn't he?"

Elizabeth's snide tone could not be denied. Jonathan cast a disproving glance at his firstborn and her innuendos. He stood and lifted Kat by an elbow to her feet.

"Shall we dance?" he asked.

Kat blinked. "Shouldn't we drink our water and visit a while longer?"

"No, I think Elizabeth needs a little time alone. Let's go."

Jonathan led Kat to the edge of the dance floor mid-song. They held their breaths and plunged into the boisterous crowd of merry-makers waltzing around and around in front of the small stage.

"You can't be afraid of tight places in a polka tent," Kat shouted above the roar. "It's body to body in here."

Just then a rather hefty couple bumped into Jonathan's back, throwing him closer against Kat. A warm jolt of awareness surged throughout his frame when his lips tickled her cheek. He drew an unsteady breath.

"You okay?" Kat asked, winded.

"I'm fine. I'm just glad most folks in here took a bath before they came."

She laughed a throaty chuckle. "How can you say that? It smells like a barnyard in this tent."

"Nothing wrong with it." He pulled away from her as the crowding eased up. "Sorry to squeeze you so tight there for a moment."

"I'm not." She slid closer to him. "I kind of like it. No wonder some churches are against dancing. It's downright decadent. It makes me want to hold you closer and never let go."

She was right. Kat felt so good in his arms. Smiling, Jonathan whirled her about faster and faster in time with the music.

After they'd made uncountable circuits of the dance floor, the song drew to a close. They clapped for the band and caught their breaths for a brief second before the musicians struck up *The Beer Barrel Polka*.

Jonathan quirked an eyebrow. "One more time?"

Kat's eyes sparkled like liquid jewels. She licked her lips and wrapped her hands about his shoulders.

"Why not. That was only half a song. You owe me another."

So entranced were they in each other's embrace, their second dance lasted until the end of the set a half hour later.

"We're off to rustle up some grub," the bandleader announced, "We'll be back in ten."

"I forgot!" Kat cried. "I'm up next. Help me get to the stage, would you, please?"

"Coming through," Jonathan said in his most authoritative voice, clearing a path through the crowd for Kat to follow like Moses dividing the Red Sea. "Make way for the intermission talent."

"Thanks." Kat grinned. Jonathan placed a hand on her backside and boosted her up to the stage. "Go and sit down now. Your poor feet are probably aching."

He touched the center of his chest. "Funny, I don't feel a thing anywhere but here."

"Heartburn, Pastor?" Darla asked as he made his way back to his seat. "That's what you get for eating too many brats and dancing so hard. You and Kat reminded folks of Ginger Rogers and Fred Astaire out there. Quite a pair."

Jonathan's mind jumped a gear. If others noticed how he and Kat seemed to complete each other, then maybe they really were meant to be together. Perhaps there was no real reason for them not to make their relationship public.

"We reminded you of Ginger and Fred, did we?"

"Yep. You're kind of tall and lanky like Fred, and she's got the platinum blonde, fake hair sort of like Ginger's." Darla placed her food plate on the table across from Elizabeth and sat beside him. "All you need is the top hat and tails."

"A top hat and tails?" Jonathan chuckled. He glanced over to the stage area and smiled.

Kat started her musical set for a handful of dancers.

Darla shoveled German potato salad into her gaping mouth and half swallowed. "Hmm-hmm, good. Y'all sample any of the goodies yet?" she asked Elizabeth.

"I shared one of Sally's apple strudels with Josh. It was okay," Elizabeth said, shrugging. She turned toward her father and cast an icy glare at him. "Speaking of men who run about all afternoon dancing while leaving a poor pregnant woman to sit all alone, you ought to be famished after burning so many calories on the dance floor."

Jonathan tore his gaze from Kat on stage and picked up his water bottle. He took a long swig, then replaced the cap. "No, actually I feel pretty good. I need to watch my food intake and burn calories anyway."

"How's your exercise program with Rolf going?" Darla asked, still chewing her cud.

"It's coming along great. I do weights every other day, and Rolf walks me at least an hour or more every night. I can even fit into some of my old jeans now."

Darla clapped her approval. "Bravo. Aren't you proud of your daddy, Beth?"

Elizabeth gritted her teeth into a smile. Jonathan knew how much his oldest child hated her name being abbreviated in any way, shape, or form.

"Of course I'm proud of him, *Dar*. He's looking more svelte than he has in years."

"He's dressing so nice, too," Darla added, winking. "He's become Germantown's most eligible bachelor according to the weekly society column."

Elizabeth's eyebrows rose a foot. "He is?"

"I am?" Jonathan was incredulous at the thought. "Who put me up for that particular honor?"

Darla giggled. "Why, no one. People just notice how upbeat you've been acting lately, and they get to talking. They're thinking you've come out of your mourning period."

"It's only been seven months since Mom passed away," Elizabeth gasped. The color drained from her cheeks.

Jonathan crossed to his daughter's side. "Are you all right? Can I get you something?"

"One of those strudels will do the trick," Darla advised. She put down her fork and stood, clearly oblivious to how her comments had affected everyone else at the table. "I'm fixin' to go get a strudel or two myself. You want me to pick you up one?"

"Thank you," Jonathan replied automatically.

"Comin' up."

"Tell me you're not seeing anyone, Daddy," Elizabeth blurted as soon as Darla was out of earshot. "I mean, it's simply unthinkable for a widower of your age to be seeing another woman so soon after his wife has been laid to rest. It's monstrous, it's—"

"It's not that soon after your mother's funeral," he cut in. "I'm not old, Elizabeth. I'm only going on fifty."

"Still, it's disgusting to think you'd even consider replacing Mom in your life without as much as a pause."

An ache welled in his heart. Jonathan sighed. How could he convince his daughter just because he loved Kat didn't mean he never loved Ruth?

He took Elizabeth's hand in his and caressed it. "Now, honey, you know that I will always love your mother—and I always will love you and Eli and Josh and the baby on the way—but you've got to realize that I'm a man who needs more than just memories and photos on the walls to keep me warm at night—"

"Oh, no! Don't tell me you're seeing someone." She grabbed an empty paper plate and madly fanned herself. "I'll have a stroke on the spot if you say you are seeing someone."

Jonathan swallowed hard. He had to be extra-careful choosing his words. Both his daughter's and his unborn grandchild's health could be at stake.

"No, I'm not seeing anyone," he said flatly, patting Elizabeth's hand in slow motion.

The pain stabbed at Jonathan's heart again. The whole world seemed to be shrinking into a dark tunnel of numbness around him.

He stood. "Let me get you another bottle of water."

Marching directly to the water booth without so much as a glance to his right or left, Jonathan collided into Matthias Ringleschmidt's broad chest.

"Sorry to run into you like that, Pastor," Matt said, dusting himself off. "You ready to make the announcement on how much we've raised so far?"

"Announcement?" Jonathan's mind was miles away. He blinked once, twice, then came crashing back to reality. "Oh yeah, the announcement about how the fund-raising is going. Sure, we can do it in a moment. I need to get Elizabeth some water. She needs to stay seated as much as possible."

Matthias smiled. "Any day now, I hear. Okay, I'll meet you then up at the stage area with the numbers right after Kat is finished."

Kat is finished. Kat is finished.

He nodded. "All right, Matt."

The water line was mercifully short. Jonathan returned to the table just as Darla came back balancing four dessert plates in her arms.

"I couldn't decide between the apple strudel and the Black Forest cake, so I got two of both!" She plopped the paper plates onto the table surface. "After all, the money *is* all going to help put up a new Sunday School building. Which one do you want, Beth?"

The pregnant woman rolled her eyes and snatched the water bottle from Jonathan's hands. "No, thanks, *Dar*. I'll wait until later."

Darla shrugged and picked up her fork to dig into the healthy-sized piece of cake. "Suit yourself then."

Jonathan lowered himself into his chair and forced his gaze toward the stage. Kat's accordion performance was in full swing, and the polka diehards were dancing and clogging away with merry abandonment.

What could he say? How could he explain his actions? All Jonathan could think of was *not now*. Now was neither the time nor place to discuss this matter. Besides, Elizabeth and Josh would be leaving for home after church tomorrow sometime. He and Kat could talk over their relationship then.

Their relationship.

It sounded so clinical, so unromantic, so unloving. So

over.

"That was Kat Dubcek on the accordion," Matthias announced over the PA system. "Everyone give her a big round of applause."

At the sound of clapping, Jonathan broke from his trance. The music had stopped. It must be his turn to head to the microphone. He stood and walked robot-like to the stage.

"I see our very own Pastor Jon is heading this way to help me make this next announcement. Let him come on through, all y'all."

Bodies on the dance floor stepped back faster than a rattler could strike. Jonathan accepted a hand up from Matthias at the front of the stage. The band members took their places behind him. Kat stood several steps to their left, playing a lively tune as Jonathan positioned himself at the microphone.

"Thank you for all the hard work you've taken on as congregation president, Matt." Jonathan forced a smile onto his face, breaking his heart all the more. "You and the council and all the volunteers from St. Luke's have been working night and day to get this Oktoberfest together, and all your efforts have paid off well. Am I right, folks?"

A roar of approval rose from the crowd.

"Now we want to hear the numbers. How much have we raised to build our new St. Luke Youth Education Annex?"

"Drum roll, please." Matt nodded at the musicians behind him. He grinned as the suspense mounted.

Jonathan cleared his throat dramatically. "The amount raised as of six o'clock this evening is a whopping fifty-six thousand, five hundred twenty-one dollars and seventeen cents!"

The tuba and accordions joined in with the cymbals in a musical flourish as the crowd cheered. Jonathan handed the microphone back over to Matthias.

"Can you believe it?" he asked the crowd.

The masses whistled their approval.

"The party isn't over until ten," Matthias reminded them. "So please, keep eating and dancing and playing carnival games. We'll be able to afford some new furniture for the kids if we can raise more. Now once again, here for your enjoyment and dancing pleasure are the Big Bad Boys of Polka."

Jonathan followed Matt down the side steps and out into the relative quiet of the game booths area in the side parking lot.

"I thought you said we could raise enough to complete the project without borrowing a dime, Matt?"

"We will. We have a few hours to go, and I haven't counted all the concession monies yet. Have faith, Pastor."

Jonathan smiled and relaxed. "You're right. Besides, we're more than three-quarters there if you count all the free donations of building materials we've been promised."

"Don't forget our *sweat equity* either," Matthias said. "We've got plenty of talented carpenters in this congregation. We'll save a bundle on labor costs."

"What's all this about sweating?" Kat teased as she approached the two men.

Jonathan took an involuntary step backward.

"I thought only musicians in leather shorts were suffering unduly from the heat."

"It's the price you pay for authenticity." Matthias chuckled, pointing a finger at her. "We really owe you one for recommending the band. They're excellent."

"You're welcome. Anything to keep some former music students of mine gainfully employed."

She looked from Matthias to Jonathan. "If you get a chance, Pastor, you ought to talk to the tuba player, Tubby. He's fixin' to become engaged and mentioned to me he'd really like to get married in a church even if his girlfriend wasn't so hot on the idea."

"All right. I'll be sure to talk to him." Jonathan's voice was monotone.

Kat flashed a perplexed expression at Jonathan's lackluster response. "Good." She backed away. "I'm going to go help out Brenna with the bottle toss now. I'll let y'all get back to whatever you were discussing when I so rudely interrupted."

Matthias nodded politely. "Thanks for all your help, Kat."

Jonathan sighed, watching Kat stride away without a backward glance.

"Pastor?" Matt waved his hand in front of Jonathan's face. "You still with us?"

"Uh, I'm still here. I'm sorry. I'm feeling a bit ... distracted."

"Those shorts do it to me, too, but I know my wife's lurking around here somewhere, so my eyes better stay glued to Kat's pigtails." The tall man paused and thoughtfully considered Jonathan for a moment. "You've got a thing for Kat, don't you?"

Blood rushed to Jonathan's face. "What?"

"Don't say I blame you. She's the right age, goes to the right church, and she definitely fills out a pair of lederhosen like no other woman can."

Jonathan furrowed his brow. "I thought you warned me that I should stay away from Kat, people were talking already like we were—"

"Yeah, I know, but people are going to talk anyhow. If you really like her, you oughta think of asking her out sometime."

Should he tell Matt that he and Kat had gone on a date or two already? Should he tell him Elizabeth's comments had scared him into seriously considering not pursuing the woman he loved?

"Date? Me? I'm too old, Matt," Jonathan said, forcing a laugh for effect. "Besides, I have my family to think about. The grandbaby's due any day now, and with Eli serving in the armed forces, I never know from one day to the next what he might be up to and—"

"Matthias Ringleschmidt!" a shrill female voice shrieked. "Where have you been? They're having trouble with the smoker, and you're lollygaggin' around without a care in the world."

Matt's shoulders slumped. "I'm afraid my darling wife summons me. I'll see you in a couple of hours then, Pastor, to update the total."

Jonathan patted his friend on the back and smiled. "Take it easy, Matt. You're doing a fine job."

"Thanks. Remember, don't let others dictate how you live every second of your life." He looked toward his wife gesturing at him, a permanent frown tattooed on her lips. "Or else you could wind up regretting large portions of it."

Jonathan considered Matt's words as he went to check on Elizabeth. Yes, he would regret his life if he and Kat weren't able to be together. There had to be some way he could convince Elizabeth it was proper for him to seek another companion in life. It was wrong for a man to live the remainder of his years alone.

"You'll never guess who arrived," Elizabeth sing-songed, quirking an eyebrow as her father approached the table.

"Who?" Jonathan looked around and spied his son-in-law sitting two tables over chatting with several old schoolmates.

"Kat Dubcek's daughter, Keely. I believe the tall, dark, and handsome guy with the dreadlocks following her is her boyfriend. At least, I sure hope he is."

"How nice."

She lowered her voice. "You're not catching my drift,

Dad. It's obvious Keely's in a *condition*."

Jonathan frowned. "Condition? Is she sick?"

"From about six to eight most mornings, give or take an hour."

"Elizabeth, exactly what are you implying?"

"Nothing." She leaned back with a satisfied, smug expression plastered across her pretty features. "Just don't be surprised if you hear a big commotion over near the games in the next few minutes. I pointed them in the direction to where Kat was helping out."

"Hi, Brenna. How's the bottle toss doing?"

Keely Dubcek stood hand in hand with her lover, smiling with satisfaction as it became obvious to others that it wasn't an excess of junk food and pizza which caused her formerly flat stomach to poke out from under her belly top.

"Hi, Keely. Long time no see. Who's your young man?"

"The name's Nigel." He flashed a bright smile at the shy woman and leaned closer to shake her hand. "So, pretty lady, this party is called an Oktoberfest. You tell me, how come it's not in October?"

Brenna blushed under his gaze. "I don't know. I guess 'cause the roof on the Sunday School building won't last much longer, that's why."

"Where's Mom at, Bren?" Keely asked.

"Your mom went over to the cashiers to dump our tickets and get some more soda pop bottles." She swallowed, glancing about nervously. "Where's your brother, Keely? How's school going?"

"Kevin's around here somewhere, chatting and drinking with his old football buddies. School? I'll be finishing up my classes by this spring if all goes according to plan. I may not quite make it to the graduation ceremony, though."

Brenna nodded in understanding. "Oh."

"Keely?" Kat called out. "Keely, is that you?"

Kat wound her way through the milling throng with several liter bottles stashed under both arms, heading straight toward her daughter's all-too-familiar back. "You told me that you and Kevin weren't able to come and—"

Keely turned around, patting her roundish midriff in an obvious attempt to call attention to it.

Kat froze in place. "Help me, Lord," she whispered.

CHAPTER THIRTEEN

"Hi, Mom." Keely leaned her head toward her companion. "Aren't you going to say hello to Nigel?"

"Hello, Nigel," Kat managed at last. "You two drive over together?"

"We all came in Kevin's car," Nigel said, baring his brilliantly white teeth as usual. "He's around here somewhere."

Kat didn't want to feel bitter, but she did. She crossed to behind the booth and deposited the bottles of soda pop at Brenna's feet.

"Any business since I left?" she asked.

Brenna sighed. "None too much. Things is fixin' to wind down for the night. It's almost the little ones' bedtime, I reckon."

"Can I toss a few hoops then?" Nigel asked.

"Sure," Brenna replied, "but you need to purchase some tickets first." She pointed to a table across the parking lot. "Right over there. Five tickets for a dollar or twenty-five cents apiece."

"I think we can afford that." He gave Keely a quick buss on the cheek. "I'll be right back."

Kat placed her hands on her hips and shook her head as Nigel strolled away. She turned to her daughter and lowered her voice.

"I see now why you were wearing the big, bulky sweatshirt the last time I visited Austin. I had my doubts over *the air conditioner is too cold for me* story."

"It's true. I'm easily chilled these days." Frowning, Keely

crossed her arms. "Let's not discuss things here in public, Mom."

"So, when and where *are* we supposed to discuss *things*?" Kat's voice soared up the scale in both pitch and volume. "In the hospital, right after you deliver?"

"Don't act so melodramatic," Keely muttered. She pivoted on her heels and ambled away at a good clip.

Kat followed her.

"Don't worry. I can handle the booth by myself again," Brenna shouted after them.

"Keely?" Kat called out, breathless. "Baby, wait up."

A few dozen yards away, Keely plopped down on her faded jean-covered bottom under the low branches of a tree. Kat did likewise, realizing it was going to be difficult getting up again gracefully while wearing stiff leather lederhosen.

"Oh, honey." Kat reached to clasp her daughter's hand. "What's going to become of you?"

"Me? I'm fine, and the doctor says the baby's fine. You're freaking out for no reason."

"Keely, you're having a baby, and you're not married and —"

"Mom, it's no big deal these days," she cut in, pulling her hand away. "I'm not due until late February anyhow. I'll be finished with my student teaching after fall term, and I'll on-ly have a few self-paced studies to finish in the spring, so it's going to work out just fine. I'll get my degree."

Kat sighed. "What about graduate school? I thought we were planning on going to graduate school?"

Keely rolled her eyes. "You got that one right — *we* were planning on it, but *I* wasn't always that keen on it, at least not going right away. You know, there's nothing wrong with waiting a few years or attending grad school part-time."

Kat furrowed her brow. "It's Nigel again, isn't it? I mean, beyond his obvious role in this crisis situation, he's talked you out of your dream of opening a school for strings."

"No, I talked myself out of it, Mom. A long time ago." Keely averted her eyes and picked at a lonely tuft of grass on the ground beside her. "After I started college, I realized there was a lot more to the world than life in boring old Germantown, Texas. There are lots of places to teach music and lots more worthy students who need the education."

"So Nigel has talked you into moving back to Jamaica with him?"

"No, he hasn't. In fact, he wants to stay longer in the US. He's got a really good chance of making the pros if he continues kicking as well as he does."

"I see it all now." Kat hugged her middle. She felt sick to her stomach. "People will say he's only marrying you to keep his green card. He hopes they won't deport him if he's married to a citizen."

Keely stared hard at her mother. "Whoever said anything about us getting married?"

Kat's jaw dropped. "What? He doesn't want to marry you?"

"No, it's the other way around. I don't want to marry him, or, at least, not right away. How do I know he isn't marrying me because he feels responsible for the baby?"

"He ought to feel responsible for the baby," Kat said louder than she'd planned.

Curious heads rotated to look in their direction.

She rolled to her knees and leaned nearer her daughter's ear. "He loves you, doesn't he?"

"He says he does. I believe him, and I love him, too, but it doesn't change anything."

"It changes everything, sweetheart. You two really ought to—"

"How does he know I'm not marrying him for his money?" Keely interjected. "After all, if he goes pro after next year he could be making millions in football."

"Really?" Kat tried hard not to let her eyes pop out of her head. "He's got a good chance of going pro, you think?"

Keely frowned. "I knew you'd see him that way—the ultimate meal ticket. I'm not marrying Nigel—or any man for that matter—just for his money or to slap a last name on my child." She placed a comforting arm around Kat's shoulder. "Times have changed, Mom. You don't have to do like you did and marry the guy who knocked you up and suffer like you did."

"Who said I didn't want to marry your father?" Tears glistened on Kat's cheek, unchecked. "Things weren't all that bad. Don't think about your dad like that, Keely. I want you to remember the good times."

"I remember some of the not-so-good-times, and my friends long ago filled me in on what really happened to him. Kevin may have bought the story, but I never believed Dad was a bullfighter, you know."

Kat sniffed loudly and wiped her wet lashes with the back of her hand. "No, I don't suppose you did. You were always smarter than me."

Keely smiled and gave Kat's shoulders a squeeze. "Only because you taught me so much." She stood and dusted her seat off, then took Kat's hand and helped her to her feet. "We can discuss this later at home, Mom. Right now, I can see Nigel is winning coke bottles hand over fist. Poor Brenna could really use your help."

The sound of electric table saws and other building equipment was music to his ears. Grinning, Jonathan pulled into the parking lot and switched off his engine. He enjoyed watching the enthusiastic construction workers as they laughed and sang while framing the walls of the new annex.

It was coming along beautifully. The Oktoberfest had been a great financial success and, along with donations of building supplies and plenty of volunteer labor, the congregation was assured it would not fall deep into debt.

"God is really smiling upon St. Luke's," many townspeople had said to Jonathan recently. "Otherwise last week's hail storm wouldn't have taken out the old structure's roof so completely, making it easier to demolish."

Best of all, Jonathan concluded, the congregation had unanimously approved a name for the new building as beautiful as the structure would be itself — The Ruth Rawlins Memorial Education Annex. A plaque with Ruth's name and a small engraved likeness would hang beside the front door upon completion. He had found it nearly impossible to hold back his tears as he had turned over the first spade full of dirt at the groundbreaking ceremony. Ruth, who had been an advocate for developing their Sunday School programs, would have been proud.

Jonathan gave Old Man Ringleschmidt and the other workers a wave, whistling as he strolled toward the church office entrance. Odd, he hadn't felt like whistling in a long while. Not since the Oktoberfest, in fact. It probably had something to do with how concerned he had been with Elizabeth's well-being for the last three weeks, he supposed. When she finally went into labor at two o'clock in the morning three days ago, Jonathan could scarcely believe he was about to become a grandfather. Upon cradling little Jeremiah Joshua in his arms, kissing the softness of his downy head and hearing his indignant newborn protests against the noisy, cold, cruel world, Jonathan's cares and concerns vanished in a puff of smoke.

"Mornin', Pastor." Darla's attention never left the computer screen as she typed prayer requests into the bulletin template. "You over at Beth and Josh's place last night again?"

Jonathan picked up the mail from the bin on the corner of her desk and yawned. "Yes, I was. How did you know?"

Grinning, she looked at him sideways. "The bags under your eyes, of course, and the fact Kat Dubcek left a message tacked on your corkboard about this Sunday's hymn selections instead of calling you at home."

Jonathan grimaced. He hadn't called Kat to cancel his piano lessons for this past week, and he'd stood her up the week before, too. Kat would understand that his undivided attention was needed elsewhere right now.

Jonathan had to admit Kat had been acting rather preoccupied herself lately. She had even gone so far as not to return his call two days ago suggesting they go for a jog in the park. Were they drifting apart?

"Any other important calls or messages I need to know about, Darla?" he asked, trying to get his thoughts back on track for the day.

"Not at the moment." She swiveled in her office chair and scanned the calendar blotter on her desk. "Don't forget we're the host congregation for the district-wide taskforce on Christian education on the thirtieth."

"How could I forget? The good thing is, Matt says we should have the exterior of the annex finished by then and at least some of the classrooms ready to show our visitors."

"The dedication plaque should be ready by then, too." Darla heaved an audible sigh. "I sure wish Ruth could be here to see everything—the new baby, the new building, everything."

Jonathan gave his secretary's shoulders a squeeze. "I do, too, but it's okay. She knows about everything already."

Darla sniffed. "You really think she does?"

"I know she does."

Jonathan shared a coffee and a few minutes of meaningful

conversation with Darla before settling behind his desk to ready his sermon text for the coming Sunday.

Kat's note distracted him, however. An hour later, he picked up the small slip of paper, unfolded it, and reread it for a third time. It wasn't the contents of the note he found disturbing since it was simply a listing of the hymns she'd chosen for this Sunday's service. It was the manner in which she related her request which chilled him to the bone. The note possessed the cold, efficient tone of a complete stranger.

Here are the hymn selections for August 9. Note we are using the second tune for the last hymn as the first one boasts too broad a range for the average member to sing with any confidence.

"Has it been too long since we danced, Kat?" Jonathan muttered, resting a weary chin against his propped-up fist. He carefully folded the paper once more and slipped it into his service book, returning to his sermon outline.

He tried to make excuses for their apparent drifting apart. They both had been busy these last three weeks. His thoughts had been thoroughly occupied with Elizabeth and the baby. Kat, he knew for a fact, was busy getting ready to start teaching school again in a couple of weeks.

Jonathan put down his pen a moment later with a sigh. He couldn't deny it any longer. He had been doing the most avoiding lately. He'd been working so hard not to mention Kat around Elizabeth to avoid distressing her again that he'd almost stopped thinking about Kat altogether—or at least thinking about her in his waking thoughts. In his dreams Kat's warm, womanly curves pressed close to him continued to entice and excite him in a way no other woman ever had or could.

"What can I do, Lord? How can I make amends to the woman I desire and not upset the daughter I love?"

"Mail call," Darla announced, marching into his office.

She placed a square, flat package in front on him and looked around suspiciously. "Who were you just now talking to when I came in?"

"Talking to?" He feigned innocence. "I've been as quiet as a church mouse all morning. Maybe I was reading some of my sermon text aloud. It does help me phrase things better sometimes."

"Oh." She spun on her heels and went the way she came, hesitating at the door.

Jonathan quirked an eyebrow. "Yes?"

"Who do you know in Memphis, Tennessee?"

"No one I can think of. Why do you ask?"

Darla shrugged. "I don't know. It's where that package came from, though. Just curious."

Jonathan's brow furrowed. He picked up the lightweight package and glanced at the return address. Daryl's Music Emporium. Swift as a lightning bolt, it came to him—God had heard his plea on how to make amends to Kat and had answered his prayer in seconds flat.

"I remember what this is now," he said, mostly to himself. "This is some music I ordered off the Internet. I thought we might be able to use it for the education taskforce meeting and I was going to run it by Kat's this afternoon for her approval. I'm glad it arrived in time."

"Well, you've got plenty of time to preview it yourself. Kat left for Austin yesterday."

"She did?" Jonathan swallowed a jagged lump in his throat. "She didn't say anything to me in her note about not being here Sunday."

"Kat is fixin' to be back by Saturday night. Something about not being able to sleep on the twin's couch with their loud neighbors blaring rock-and-roll all night long on weekends. She wanted to be there today to accompany Keely to her doctor's appointment." Darla lowered her voice and leaned toward him. "You did know Keely was pregnant, didn't you?"

"Not officially, no," Jonathan admitted.

Darla rolled her eyes. "I forget how blind men can be sometimes. My own Dilly didn't think Keely looked any different, either, at the Oktoberfest." She shook her head and chuckled. "How can you mistake the *with child* look on a tall, skinny gal like Keely when she's wearing a belly top? I mean, it was blatantly obvious to all the mothers there at the festival she was advertising the fact."

"She can't be far along, can she?"

"She's into her second trimester, I'd say. Kat hasn't said much about it to me yet. I think it's all too new for her and has sort of put her life into a tailspin. She's been acting like a zombie at choir practice lately."

A flood of guilty feelings washed over Jonathan, threatening to drown him in remorse. Here when Kat needed his support and encouragement the most, he'd been off in his own little world. What must she think of him?

"Finding out that your daughter is pregnant is rather stressful on a parent. I should know." It was a trite statement, but he was at a loss as to what else to say.

Darla certainly didn't need any more fuel to rocket off on a gossip tangent. "No kidding. There's been no hint of any wedding between Keely and her beau, either. I hate to say it, but folks around town are all saying *like mother, like daughter*."

Jonathan frowned and stared at her. "What's that supposed to mean?"

Darla fidgeted in place, clearly uncomfortable with the icy glare Jonathan sent her way. "You know how it is sometimes, Pastor. Not every woman who wears a white wedding dress is entitled to wear one, but Kat's my friend, and she's a good gal at heart. I've never held her slightly less-than-shining past regarding members of the opposite sex against her."

"Nice to know she has a supporter in you." He cleared his throat, turning his attention to the papers in front of him. "Now, if you'll excuse me?"

"Sure thing. It's back to the salt mines for me." Darla put a finger to her lips with a *shush* and closed the door behind her.

Jonathan picked up the package and pried open a corner to check on its contents. "*101 Rare Polka Waltzes*. Yep, that's what I ordered, all right."

He gently slid the collector's LP back into its mailing container and looked at the clock on the wall. It would be at least thirty-six hours before Kat returned from Austin. He really wanted to give her the present this weekend, but it was going to be hard finding the right time and the right place to present it to her. Harder still would be finding the best way to phrase his apology for ignoring her for so long.

"Twins. Dear Lord, why? Why twins?"

Kat muttered the question to herself over and over again as she drove along the dark, winding Hill Country back roads. It was all just sheer, dumb luck, she guessed, and a possible genetic predisposition, the doctor had said. She bit her lip in frustration until the pain faded to numbness and then nothingness. Why had she ever agreed to accompany Keely to her ultrasound? Ignorance was bliss.

From around a bend in the road came a fuzzy brown blur about wheel-well high, bounding directly in front of her car's path. A deer? Kat slammed on the brakes and cursed.

She jerked forward and rocked back into her seat. The car screeched to a halt and stalled out. She flipped on her high beams and looked down the road. It must have gotten away in one piece. It would live another day, or at least until deer-hunting season got underway — lucky critter.

"Why, oh, why can't some hunter shoot me and stuff my head and stick me on their living room wall and put me out of my misery?"

Sighing, she threw the car into park and ground the starter. After a few weak protests, the engine spluttered back to life and agreed to putter on down the ranch road toward town. She realized how fortunate it was she and the deer hadn't suffered a head-on collision. Her little sedan would have never survived the encounter. She hated to admit it, but unlike a few natives of the Hill Country area, she wasn't much into road kill.

"BB wouldn't mind nibblin' on a little bit of venison, though," Kat recollected, trying to stay awake. It was almost midnight, and she had to be up early to direct the choir in the morning. "He'd have barbecued it over some mesquite briquettes and thrown some jalapeños on top. Hmm-hmm, good. Gosh, I haven't had any decent barbecue since, since . . ."

Since that party-faithful gala at Judge Holbreicht's spread. You remember the little get-together, don't you? You were thinking of crawling between the sheets to enjoy some horizontal tango with Mr. Bradley T. Bradley that night. Fool you are, you chickened out.

"I did not chicken out," she chided herself, rolling down her window to let some fresh air slap across her face. She had to do something to keep from losing her concentration. Talking to herself seemed the best alternative to falling asleep at the wheel.

Only twelve miles to go . . . she was practically within walking distance. She didn't need to run her car off the road so close to Germantown and meet up with some of Bradley's buddies from the highway patrol. She needed to stay focused, alert, but her imagination would have none of it.

You could have enjoyed a good, predictable roll in the hay with dear ol' BB, you idiot. Jonathan would have been none the wiser. Instead, you're just a frustrated old has-been with a pregnant daughter and a football jock son about to flunk out of English class and —

"All right, that's enough." Kat gritted her teeth, slapping the steering wheel to make her point. "I am *not* frustrated because I didn't make whoopee with Jonathan or BB or the entire offensive line of the *Cowboys* or anybody else for that matter. I'm frustrated because I'm always working so hard to get everything right in my life — and my children's lives — and nothing ever works out right no matter how hard I try."

Tears rolled freely down Kat's cheeks. She dabbed at them with the corner of her sleeve.

"Lord, help me. I am just too tired, and I don't want to go it alone anymore. Please, Lord, help me."

As soon as the words flew from her lips, Kat felt the heavy burden she'd been carrying all these years lifting from her shoulders. Her heart reveled in an unfamiliar lightness, unfettered from the lie which had chained her to the past.

"I'm not alone, am I?" she whispered. "Jonathan's there. He can help me get Keely and Nigel to act like responsible adults and do the right thing. Yes, why didn't I think of that before?"

Maybe because the man's been out of contact for almost three weeks now? Because he's got much better things to do with his precious time than deal with your unwed pregnant daughter? He's got his own married daughter and a grandbaby to be concerned about now. So don't be a wimp and don't waste his time. You've managed okay on your own in the past. You can do so again.

She sniffed, then glanced in the rearview mirror. With mascara running in rivulets down her cheeks, she looked like so many miles of bad road without a prayer in the world the pothole patrol would ever arrive.

"Jonathan's not a selfish man. It's his job to help people.

I'm people. He can help me even if he can't bear the sight of me."

That's right, the nagging devil on her shoulder prompted her. *He acted like you had the Black Death or something at the Oktoberfest when you came over to him and Matthias while they were chatting. He's canceled all his piano lessons since then. Didn't Elizabeth practically give you the cold shoulder herself that night? Like daughter, like father?*

Kat bit a nail. "Keely did mention something about seeing Elizabeth staring daggers at my back. It's so hard to believe she's Ruth's child. Ruth would have never treated anyone so rudely."

Ruth. Where is a friend like Ruth when you need her?

The glare of oncoming headlights startled Kat, shaking her out of her reverie. She sat up straighter and made sure she hadn't drifted over the center line on the two-lane winding road.

She sighed. Kat knew there was no comparison between her and Ruth. Ruth had been a wonderful human being. She didn't raise children who got into trouble, and she didn't go running around whining all the time. Ruth had bravely kept her cancer to herself until the pain had become so obvious even she couldn't keep her illness a secret any longer. Ruth Rawlins was a role model. Kat should act more like Ruth.

After all, hadn't Jonathan dearly loved Ruth?

"That's it!" Kat cried. "The answer to all my problems."

The three-mile marker outside of town flashed by. Kat pressed the accelerator to the floor. Time to get home and stop belly-aching about what could have been, should have been. There was nothing she could do about becoming a grandmother. There was nothing she could do to make Kevin understand the nuances of the English language well enough to pass his class. There was nothing she could do to make Jonathan care for her as much as she cared for him except to . . .

It seemed so obvious now. She didn't know why she didn't think of it before. She would do it. She would become another role model, another Ruth. She sighed. It wasn't going to be easy.

"Good sermon, Pastor." Charlie Zaye congratulated Jonathan with a brisk shake of his arm at the narthex door after church. "I see you've discovered becoming a granddaddy can be quite inspirational."

Jonathan chuckled, glancing over at Jeremiah dressed in white sleeping soundly in his mother's arms as Elizabeth chatted with Caroline. "It is, Charlie. Indeed, it is. We've got the most perfect example of how we all need *to hunger and thirst after spiritual milk* each and every time the little eating machine over there opens his mouth."

"You'd be amazed how much Jerry likes to nurse," proud papa Josh added to the conversation. "Elizabeth runs around the house practically topless most days with her bra flaps turned down and—"

"Hush your mouth." Elizabeth looked daggers at her husband. "What are you trying to do? Make me sound like some kind of brazen hussy?"

Josh gave her a quick peck on the cheek. "Never, sweetheart. In a million years, no one would ever call you *brazen* anything."

Charlie winked and patted him on the back. "Good recovery there, son." He turned back to Jonathan. "Your boy in the service coming home anytime soon?"

"Eli says he's coming home for the holidays. I tried to talk him into coming home for his nephew's baptism, but he says his country needs him and now's not a good time to leave his post."

"What a patriot. I know you miss him, but I know you're

mighty proud of him, too."

"That I am, Charlie. That I am."

Jonathan smiled, nodded, and continued shaking hands with visitors and members as they filed out the back of the sanctuary. He tried not to seem overly obvious as he scanned the crowd for signs of Kat, but all too soon he was forced to give up. He swallowed his remaining pride and humbly asked the source of all knowledge how Kat could have slipped out of the church without him knowing it.

"She left right before the benediction, Pastor," Darla informed him. "She told the choir before the service she had quite a few things she needed to attend to since she was gone to Austin and didn't get home until after midnight last night. She tiptoed on down the back stairs to the music room when Gayle started in on the last hymn."

"I see." He did his best to hide his disappointment. "By the way, nice dress you're wearing today, Darla. Germantown High School colors, right?"

His secretary beamed, twirling about in her finery. "Yes, it is. I bought it a few years ago for our twenty-year reunion. Everybody always compliments me on how well it suits me."

"Yes, it does," Elizabeth said drolly, shifting the sleeping baby onto her shoulder. "I can't think of anybody else who can carry off wearing bright red and neon yellow polka dots the size of dinner plates like you can, Dar."

"Why, thank you, Beth."

Jonathan observed his daughter's reaction as Darla and her family exited. He found it difficult to determine whether Elizabeth was being complimentary or plain cruel just now. Only Ruth had been able to discern the true intentions of their daughter's heart.

"Ready for Sunday dinner?" Elizabeth asked. "We only have a couple of hours before Jeremiah wakes up. I'm starving."

"So am I," Josh agreed. "Surviving on less than three or four uninterrupted hours of sleep a night makes me hungry."

Jonathan squeezed his son-in-law's shoulders and stroked the baby's cheek with a finger. "How those days seem only like yesterday to me. Let me change out of my robe and I'll meet y'all next door in five minutes, okay?"

They turned to go. "Don't keep us waiting, Dad," Elizabeth gently scolded. "All I have to do is reheat the casserole I brought and toss the salad."

Jonathan exited the sanctuary, nodding to Matthias and some of the other trustees as they closed the front doors and switched off the lights and ceiling fans. Upon reaching his office, his gaze wandered to the package on his desk.

"Elizabeth, Josh, and the baby will stay until six, tops," he said to himself, removing his liturgical garments and hanging them in the small cabinet opposite his desk. "Then Rolf and I can take our evening stroll over to Kat's after they've gone home."

With his plan to reconcile himself and Kat set in motion, Jonathan placed the record under his arm and headed toward the parsonage.

"Let's see. Carry the two and add these three things together and that's the result."

Sighing, Kat put her pencil on the kitchen table and rubbed her bleary eyes. She'd been working on this budget for over six hours now. It was far from perfect, but it was manageable. With her salary and health benefits from the school district, plus her private lessons income, she could support Keely and the twins for a year if necessary, provided everyone agreed to live within the confines of the budget, there were no unforeseen medical or car expenses, and Kevin agreed not to move back home so they could use his bedroom as a nursery.

It was a lot of *ifs*. Kat bit her lip. The largest *if* of all depended on her son. If Kevin couldn't graduate this spring and find a paying job, and he landed homeless and hungry on her doorstep, she didn't know what she would do. She didn't want to force Keely out into the work-a-day world before she felt physically and emotionally ready to leave the twins, but it might become necessary.

Kat picked up the pencil and wrote a note reminding herself to ask Superintendent Grayson if she foresaw any possible openings in the music department for a strings instructor next fall. She felt very pleased with herself. She was handling this crisis with as much calm and stiff-upper-lippedness as Ruth Rawlins would have done.

"Thank heaven I never got around to replacing Mr. Friskies. One less mouth to feed and one less body to shelter." Kat rubbed at the sore muscles in her lower back, exhausted from her extended afternoon of decision-making and bedroom furniture rearranging. "I do miss the little fella running in and out of his kitty flap now and then. He was such a good listener for a cat. I never felt crazy talking to myself like I do now."

A low, scratching sound at the back door startled her. She gulped. It happened again.

"M-Mister Friskies?"

Dropping her pencil, Kat sprang to her feet. She tiptoed over to the sink window to catch a glimpse outside. Rolf was stretching his paws against her screen door.

"Oh, it's you two," Kat said, opening the door wide. Jonathan could mistake the tiredness in her tone for disappointment she realized, but she didn't have the energy to sound otherwise. She crouched and petted the friendly puppy behind the ears. "I thought Mr. Friskies had come back from the dead for a moment."

Jonathan shifted his weight back and forth on his heels. He slipped a rectangular package in his free hand back under his arm. "If now's inconvenient, we can visit another time—"

"No, it's fine. Please come on in. I could use the company. I've been by myself too long today."

Jonathan commanded Rolf to lie down on the back porch and rest, then followed Kat into the kitchen.

"Would you like some coffee?" she asked, reaching for the can on the shelf near the coffee maker. "I was about to make myself some."

"Thank you."

He's acting rather wooden, like he's feeling uncomfortable around me.

Kat couldn't help but pick up on the tenseness in Jonathan's posture as he sat at the table and placed the rectangular package beside his chair. It had been over three weeks since they'd last been anywhere near each other. It appeared the physical separation had caused a partition in their emotional relationship as well.

There's no need to mourn.

Things always worked out for the best if they were a part of God's will. Ending their close association was the kind of sacrifice a woman like Ruth would have made.

Nervous, she began to make small talk as she filled the coffee maker with water and added grounds to the filter. "Elizabeth and the baby looked very pretty today. It was a lovely ceremony."

"Yes, it was, but they all are lovely, aren't they? This one just happened to be extra special to me because Jeremiah's my grandson."

Kat pulled two mugs down from the cabinet. "Are they fixin' to give the baby a nickname someday? I can't imagine him starting school and having to learn to spell Jeremiah right off that bat."

"Josh is already calling him Jerry, but you know how Elizabeth is about nicknames." Jonathan shrugged. "We tried calling her Beth when she was little, but she never liked it, and she'll have none of it nowadays."

"Yes, she's definitely an Elizabeth. She's not a Beth, Liz, Liza, Eliza, Lisa or Lizzie for that matter."

Kat placed the mugs on the table along with the sugar bowl and sat opposite her guest. "On the other hand, I actually think she married a Josh if there ever was one."

Jonathan furrowed his brow. "What makes you say that?"

"Well, because Josh has always been such a laid-back person." Kat shook her head, chuckling at the memory. "I remember Josh so well from my seventh-grade general music class. He was always smiling, always handing in his assignments late—if ever—and always acting as if nothing in the world ever bothered him. It's just amazing how two such opposite personalities attracted each other in the first place."

"They're more alike than you might guess just from looking at the surface."

"How's that?"

Jonathan sat straighter and angled himself more toward Kat. "They share similar values. They have a common history. A lot of shared experiences growing up around here."

"Oh?"

"Yes, I really believe God brought them together the day Josh kicked his football over the back fence into our yard, and he had to come over to retrieve it, and Elizabeth answered the door. He and Elizabeth were both fifteen and ready for Cupid's arrow, you could say."

"I could see how that would help," Kat admitted with a sigh, "knowing all about the other person and their past. People aren't really attracted to people they know they wouldn't want to marry and grow old with."

He raised an eyebrow. "So, you're saying we should always trust our gut instincts when it comes to love?"

Kat looked away. A tearing sensation burned in the corners of her eyes. "Not necessarily."

Jonathan reached over and captured one of her hands in his, forcing her to look him in the eye. "What if our heart and head agree? Isn't that a sign it's a good relationship?"

She shook her head. "The head should always be the final arbiter. If it says the relationship doesn't bode well in the long run, then it's better to call it quits before anyone gets hurt."

He squeezed her hand and brought it to his lips in a penitent kiss. "I'm so sorry, Kat, about being absent so much these past few weeks. What with Elizabeth and the baby and all I—"

"No need to apologize," she cut in, pulling her hand away. "Your actions are understandable and commendable in the situation. One must include family members as well when considering the merits of continuing a relationship. There's always more to bear in mind than the personal feelings of the couple involved."

Jonathan seemed to sink into his chair. "I don't think we're hurting any of our family members, Kat," he said after regaining his composure. "In fact, I think now is the right time for us to come out and announce to everyone that we are—"

She placed a hand to his lips. "No, don't say it. Now *is* the right time for an announcement, but not that one. It's time we come to terms with what's best for all parties before we embarrass or involve anyone else. We both have grandchildren to think of now. We have to do what's best for the next generation."

He swallowed hard. "You're saying it's better if we parted now so nobody suffers in the long run because of our . . . attraction?"

"Yes, that's right." She dropped her chin to her chest. She couldn't bear to watch his hurt expression any further. "We both know what's expected of a preacher's wife, Jonathan. We both know very well I will never meet the criteria. I have two grandchildren on the way. Keely's expecting twins. There aren't any wedding bells ringing in the near future for them, either. Lord knows I've tried to talk them into it."

"I know you're hurting," he said, "but it's their lives. It doesn't have anything to do with the two of us. It's completely — "

She silenced him with a wave of her hand. "Yes, it does have something to do with us. I should know — I've tried for years to live down my own past in this town. It's difficult, if not outright impossible, to make people forget when you've led a rather colorful life like I have."

She took a deep breath and continued. "I'm not sure Germantown is ready for a man of the cloth to be associated with one of its more notorious citizens — a woman with a past like myself. I don't think I could live with myself knowing I destroyed your family's good name. Think about little Jeremiah and Elizabeth and Josh and Eli and . . ."

Kat was about to say *and Ruth* but then thought better of it. It was the memory of her dear friend which gave her the strength to go on, to get the words out that Jonathan desperately needed to hear and understand.

"Just think seriously about what I said, please." She rose to check on the coffee. "You want some coffee?"

Jonathan shook his head. "No thanks." He glanced down at his hands, then placed them on the table and pushed himself to his feet. "I'd better take Rolf on his walk now if you don't mind. Some other time, perhaps?"

"Sure. Go right ahead."

She followed him to the covered porch and watched as he attached Rolf's lead and guided the pup toward the exit.

"We'll talk again," he said mechanically.

Kat nodded. "Yes, we will." She pushed open the screen door and smiled. "Have a nice walk. The weather's been pleasant for mid-August, don't you think? I know the kids are going to hate being cooped up inside the school starting next Wednesday."

"Yes, those first weeks are always the hardest adjusting to a new routine." Jonathan looked at Rolf and pulled on his lead.

Rolf whimpered.

"Come along now, boy."

Kat waved them goodbye. Rolf stopped and cast a sad expression toward her, his usually spastic tail now wagging slowly. A sharp ache sliced through her heart. Both she and the poor animal assumed he'd never visit Kat's back porch again.

CHAPTER FOURTEEN

"Night, Dad. E-mail is efficient, but it's always good to hear your voice."

"It's good to hear your voice, too. Take care, son. I'm looking forward to meeting your Gillian in person. She sounds like a very special lady. We'll see y'all at the holidays then. Goodnight."

Jonathan smiled and clicked off the phone, placing it on the nightstand beside his head. Even if his own love life wasn't the greatest lately, it was nice to know Eli's was blossoming. Could two military careerists really hope for a happy, stress-free relationship? It was a question which begged asking, but Jonathan told himself he wasn't going to interfere. He'd let love—and Eli's innate intelligence and sound decision-making skills—take their course.

Jonathan rolled to his side and picked up the book he was reading, only to lay it aside a moment later. It was hard to concentrate. It was harder still to sleep these past few weeks since he and Kat had last spoken at any length. He realized now that she'd been right all along. Their respective family situations at the present were more than enough for each of them to handle. They really didn't have the time or energy to work at developing a strong relationship. Kat had Keely and her developing pregnancy to worry about, and he had Elizabeth and the baby—and now Eli's approaching engagement—to consider. They both led very full lives.

The following Tuesday after Jonathan and Kat had come to their *understanding*, Kat suggested he find another piano teacher. Jonathan had been reluctant at first, as Kat's gentle instruction had motivated Jonathan to explore his innate musicality in ways he'd never thought possible, but now he saw the wisdom of her suggestion. Gayle wasn't the most inspired of instructors, but she did the job, and she was willing to work with him for a half hour at the church before choir practice most weeks. He'd be able to competently play a simplified version of *O Holy Night* by the time Eli and his soon-to-be fiancé arrived for the holidays.

He'd felt awkward at times dealing with Kat at church these past few weeks, but somehow he had managed. Meanwhile, Kat handled her musical duties with her usual professionalism, choosing to leave notes on his corkboard rather than discussing musical selections with him in person.

The true test of the finality of their break-up was how no one seemed to notice any difference in the manner in which they regarded each other. Everything and everyone were as before. This included Darla, Jonathan's self-proclaimed confidant and protector.

"Pastor Jon," Darla said late one afternoon while they both sat in the front office folding a special insert for Sunday's bulletin, "you ever feel lonely living in that big ol' empty house of yours?"

"Not particularly." He thought of Elizabeth and company's last visit just two days ago. "Why do you ask?"

"Just curious. You seem well-adjusted and all, but you know it's been a year now since . . . since . . ."

"I know what you mean." Last year this time was when Ruth had revealed her terminal cancer prognosis to the congregation.

"I was just thinking, maybe . . ." She stopped folding papers and twirled her hair around a pudgy finger.

"Thinking?" he asked, somehow intuiting what was coming next before Darla could open her mouth.

"I was wondering if you'd ever considered accompanying a lady to a social function."

A momentary twinge of regret hit him as memories of dancing with Kat flooded his mind. He pushed the images away. "What kind of a social function?" he asked.

"Oh, any kind," Darla began innocently enough. "Like to a dinner-dance sort of event—like the one my mom-in-law has an invite to next Saturday."

"Your mother-in-law?" Jonathan's eyes bulged. Clearing his throat, he tried hard not sound overly harsh. "Dillon's mother is about seventy-five, isn't she? She lives in the Alzheimer's unit at The Golden Rule Nursing Home as I recall."

"I know that, Pastor, but she does have a social life. Just because she doesn't always remember who her kids are and what year it is and what her own name is doesn't mean she can't go out on a date from time to time."

"No, of course not." Jonathan felt awful. He knew how sensitive Darla and her family were about their loved one's condition. It was admirable Darla cared enough to make sure Mrs. Dierdorf's existence was an enjoyable one. What could it hurt to accompany the old lady to a nursing home party?

"I'd love to accompany your mother-in-law to the dinner-dance next Saturday," he said, grinning through gritted teeth. "It would be my pleasure."

Darla winked. "Why, thanks for asking her, Pastor. I'll tell her tonight when we go by to visit, but I don't want you to get your hopes up too high. She may turn your offer down cold."

"Turn me down?"

"Yes, she was married to the former CEO of the dairy after all, and she does have her standards. She may think you're not quite boyfriend material, if you get my drift."

Jonathan squelched his laughter. The whole idea had

seemed ridiculous to begin with, but the relief he felt two days later when Darla passed on the sad news of Mrs. Dierdorf's rejection of his offer was genuine. What a relief it was, knowing he wasn't considered decent *boyfriend material* after all.

So why couldn't he get his heart to agree with his brain?

Jonathan glanced over at the alarm clock. Eleven PM.

"All things work to the good of those who love Him," he repeated.

It had been Ruth's favorite Bible passage. Ruth, who could always see the good in every terrible situation—including her death. Ruth, the icon of the perfect pastor's wife, who Kat confided was her own model of how a woman in crisis should act. Ruth, whose image stared down at him from the walls of his home and told him life waits for no one . . . life is to be lived *now* and to the fullest and with no regrets.

Sighing, Jonathan picked up his book and absentmindedly flipped the pages with his thumb.

"Who am I trying to kid?" he admitted to himself. "I miss Ruth, but I miss Kat more. I miss her a lot. Kat's real and she's now, and I wish she was here lying beside me, but she's got her own life to live, and I respect that. I have no right to force my life with its own problems and worries onto her. I have to love her enough to let her live her life on her own terms, the way she thinks is best."

Jonathan put the book on the nightstand and switched off the light, only to find himself staring up at the ceiling in the darkness. Even with Rolf sawing logs at the foot of his bed, he found these early autumn nights unusually cold.

"Ms. Dubcek! Ms. Dubcek!" The high-pitched eighth grader's squeal reverberated down the hallway for the millionth time this week. "When are you fixin' to listen to my band?"

"Can we talk about this after class, Isabella?" Kat said as calmly as she could manage. The child was a regular nuisance. So needy, so whiny — so much like herself lately.

"But you promised two weeks ago you'd listen to us and tell us what you think about our sound." Isabella Lemp's freckled face crumpled into a pout. "We wanna get on that battle of the bands show in Austin, but we ain't throwin' our money away on the entry fee if it ain't worth it."

"Isn't worth it," Kat said, correcting the girl's English. "You're right. I did say I'd listen to you before you spent your money entering the contest." She bit her lip, glancing at her watch. "I have about half an hour today after school before I have to teach a private music lesson. Will that work?"

"Yep, that's great. We've got our guitars and amps stashed at Regan's house just across the street. We'll grab them after last period and come right back to the choir room. Okay?"

"Fine, dear. I'll see you, girls, then."

Kat sighed. What had she gotten herself into now?

Kat made her way upstream against the crush of adolescent humanity toward the teacher's lounge. This was her one and only free period of the day, and she wanted to make the most of it.

"If it isn't our beleaguered choir teacher," Ryan Weiss, the brass instructor, teased Kat as she collapsed into an old overstuffed chair beside the coke machine. With a pot belly, a perpetually sunburned nose, and blond hair rapidly fading to white, Ryan resembled a Texas version of Santa Claus. "How's the world of vocal music treating you these days?"

"Wonderful, simply wonderful," Kat murmured, searching her pockets for some change so she could purchase a can of her afternoon caffeine fix. "Rats. I'm out of quarters."

"Here." Ryan inserted several coins into the slot. "My treat. I can tell a teacher who could use a break a mile off."

"Thanks." Kat smiled, accepting the cold pop can from her colleague. "You're a life saver. I owe you one."

"Yep, and you will owe me one after I get through telling you this bit of news." The band teacher crouched close to her chair and lowered his voice. "I hear tell on the grapevine the school district may be looking for an elementary orchestra instructor next year. Isn't your Keely working toward certification in teaching fourth through eighth?"

"Yes, she is. She wanted to teach only secondary, but I told her to go ahead and get certified for teaching all grades. She's top of her class. When will they list the posting?"

"They may not list it. Essentially, they're just putting out feelers to see what kind of response there'll be from the elementary parents. I caught wind of this program from Mr. Spellman up at the high school, since he knew I taught strings before I came here."

"Are you interested in the position yourself?" Kat asked, praying Ryan's answer would be no.

"Not really. I enjoy teaching brass better than strings. Less time wasted helping the kids get their instruments in tune. And the younger set needs a lot more hands-on attention compared to the middle schoolers. I don't need any more frustration in my life."

Kat breathed a sigh of relief. "I understand."

"If anyone says anything to you, Kat, remember, you never heard about this from me."

"Promise. But how can I float Keely's name to the bigwigs without seeming too obvious?"

He shrugged. "I don't know yet, but I'll work on it. She is fixin' to graduate this spring, right?"

Kat forced a grin. "Of course she is. Everything's on track

academic-wise."

Ryan stood and nodded to another teacher as she approached the beverage machine. "Good. Tell Keely to get her resume and transcripts together, and I'll let you know when she should send them in. Deal?"

"Deal." Kat stood and shook his hand. "Thanks, Ryan. You don't know how much better I feel knowing there's a chance Keely will be gainfully employed next year after the . . . well, you know."

He winked. "Don't mention it, Granny."

Kat sunk into the chair and wearily closed her eyes. "Don't worry, I won't—Santa."

Forty minutes later, the bell alerted Kat her planning time was over.

"Some good use of time that was," she mumbled to herself, heading back to the classroom. She realized she was tired and under a lot of stress and not sleeping well, but she didn't think she'd drop off so quickly and sleep so soundly in a noisy lounge. Ryan's news about the job opening had given her some hope and a feeling of relief. Her worries about Keely's and the twin's future may soon well be over. She couldn't wait to give Keely a quick call and tell her the good news.

One more general music class and she could call it a day. Kat deposited herself behind her desk and smiled. She handed the chapter test on the classical composers to the kids one by one as they came straggling in. She worked on her paperwork while her students worked quietly until the period ended.

At the peeling of the bell, Kat gathered up her things and headed for the door. "I'm out of here."

"Where are you going, Ms. Dubcek?" Isabella Lemp shouted at Kat who was rounding the corner of the hallway leading to the teacher's parking lot.

She stopped in her tracks and bit her lip. "Home?"

"What about our band?" The carrot-topped girl lifted a red, electric guitar. "You promised to listen to us after school, remember?"

"Oh, it was today, wasn't it?" Kat scratched her head and tried hard to appear senile, not selfish. She turned around and followed Isabella back to the classroom. "Can y'all be quick about it? I really have to make an important phone call."

"Sure. We've only got the one song down any good at this point. It's all we need to win the prize anyhow. That, and look good in our makeup."

Kat pulled out her key and unlocked the door. "Makeup?"

"Yeah, we're going to paint our entire bodies with flowers and peace signs and colorful squiggles. Hippie-like."

"Your clothes?" Kat asked, switching on the light.

The other band members, two eighth graders and Isabella's sister in sixth grade, filed in silently behind them.

"The makeup *is* our clothes," Isabella said, grinning. "My brother says it's the only way we'll win, and we're not going to take any chances."

Kat blanched at the thought. "Now, girls, you can't perform in public wearing nothing but body art and a smile. It's—it's just not done." She sat in the first row and motioned for the girls to set up their guitars and small electronic drum set. "We'll talk more about your outfits and presentation another day. Right now, let me just hear what you've been working on musically, okay?"

"Okay," the pre-teens mumbled.

After a few minutes, three student-sized electric guitars were plugged into their portable amps, and the drummer, Isabella's pint-sized sister, nodded she was ready to begin.

"All right, this is an original song written by all of us in the band—the Evil Weasels, that is," Isabella announced. "We call our song, *Suicidal Squirrels*."

Gritting her teeth into a smile, Kat sat and listened to the original composition for a full three minutes. About the only section of the lyric she understood involved rhyming the word *squirrel* with *girl* and *road* with *mowed* repeatedly. She vowed never to complain about professionally produced popular music ever again.

"Whatcha think?" Isabella asked, eyes shining. The band members crowded around Kat and pleaded for her honest opinion. "Is our sound, like, really different or what?"

"Different is a very accurate term to describe your sound," Kat began gently. "So, how long have you all been studying guitar and drums?"

Isabella's younger sister piped up, "I've been watching MTV since I was about four."

"Me, too," came the others' responses.

Kat sighed. "The MTV music learning method. I see."

How in the world was she going to get out of this alive without crushing these obviously motivated girls' musical dreams? This was the one thing she hated above all else in her career, the part where she had to tell people to give bowling a try instead of music.

"So, should we enter the band contest, Ms. Dubcek?" Isabella asked bluntly. "Or do we totally suck."

"Well, not totally." Kat cringed at the slip of her tongue and the crestfallen looks on their innocent faces. "I mean, I think y'all should wait out the contest this year, practice some more, take some regular guitar lessons, and then try again next year when you've got a larger repertoire. You know, you've got to know at least one other song so you can perform an encore. You can't disappoint your audience by not playing an encore."

The girls mumbled among themselves and indicated the

affirmative.

"Yeah, you're right," Isabella spoke on behalf of the group. "We really haven't had enough time to practice and learn a bunch of songs. Thanks for telling us not to waste our money on the contest this year, Ms. Dubcek."

"You're welcome." Kat stood and heaved a long sigh. "Now, let's get our things packed up and clear on out of here."

With Kat's help, the band members untangled their cords and unplugged their electronics and carried them out into the hall.

"You know, girls, I was wondering about your band's name," Kat began. "*Evil Weasels* sounds a bit sinister, don't you think? Y'all are such sweet girls. Why not choose a more upbeat sounding name like, say, The Bluebonnets?

A collective moan erupted from the group. Kat shrugged, then offered to help tote their equipment to the front steps of the school.

"What's all this about squirrels committing suicide?" she delved further. "I've never heard about any such thing in my life."

"They do." Isabella winked at her friends. "You should see them at our cousin's house in St. Louis. The squirrels run right out in front of cars all the time there. They're pretty stupid. Besides, we couldn't think of a rhyme that went with *prairie dogs* other than *hairy hogs*. We all agreed that we didn't want to sing about pigs."

Kat rolled her eyes. "Thank goodness. Good luck, girls." She gave each child a quick hug and then waved the future rock stars off toward home before making a beeline to her vehicle.

"Squirrels committing suicide," she muttered, pulling out of the parking lot. "What's the world coming to if killing yourself isn't something set aside only for humans?"

Once home, Kat called Keely. "I've got good news," she cried as soon as her daughter picked up.

"Really? Me, too, Mom!" Keely shouted. "In fact, I was fixin' to call you tonight and tell you about it. Nigel proposed!"

Kat slumped against the kitchen wall, emotionally drained but happy. Her grandbabies would have more than one provider. She didn't have to feed two more mouths in six months' time all by herself. "What finally made y'all change your minds?"

"His parents."

Kat grinned. "I love them already."

"Nigel told them about the twins, and now they want us to come live with them in Kingston after he graduates."

Kat's heart jumped and took up residency in her throat. She pulled out a chair and sat at the table, leaning her shaking elbows on its surface for support. "What? You're going to take my grandbabies away from me?" she asked.

"Well, no, Mom, not forever. I mean, it's not a sure thing Nigel can get on a professional football team as a kicker. You made your doubts about how high the odds were of becoming a pro player quite clear the last time you were here."

"Yes, but . . ." Kat's voice faded into nothingness.

"So, it's back to Plan B as Nigel says. He's going to finish his degree in recreational therapy and then he can work for his dad at the resort. Can you imagine living near the surf and sun year-round? They said family members could stay free at their hotel during the off-season, too. Isn't that fantastic?" Keely paused, then, "Mom? You still there?"

"B-but what about you—*your* career plans?" Kat managed after a moment. "I-I found out about the perfect job for you today."

"How nice," Keely replied, "and I may take you up on it. You know, Nigel has at least a year's worth of classes to take and pass before he graduates. He still may try out and make a professional football team."

"So, you two aren't moving to Jamaica right away?"

"No, we're not. It's why we're getting married during winter break. Nigel's parents said they won't support us financially if we're living *in sin*. They insist their grandchildren have a proper last name."

Kat breathed out a sigh of relief and smiled. "I really love them now. They're flying here?"

"Yes, in late December. I told them they may need to pack a sweater or two, and they said *what's a sweater*?" Keely laughed. "Don't they sound sweet?"

"They certainly do."

Kat quietly chuckled as Keely went on and on about her future in-laws and their eccentric habits. Then it struck her — were the kids planning on getting married at St. Luke's? In the next couple of months, would she have to spend more than just a few moments in a public place each Sunday in the presence of Jonathan?

"Of course, Mom," Keely replied. "I'd love Pastor Jon to marry us. He will do it, won't he?"

"I'm sure he will, but you'll have to ask him yourself. You're an adult member of the congregation after all."

"Sure. Can you give me the church number? I'll call him as soon as you hang up. I don't want him to rent out the church or fellowship hall on the date we've picked out. Nigel's parents are buying their plane tickets as we speak. If Pastor Jon can't marry us, we'll have to ask Judge Holbreicht to do a civil ceremony instead."

"No!" Kat shouted, without thinking. "I-I mean, no, don't worry about it. I'm sure Pastor Jon will be happy to perform your wedding. I want you to have a nice, traditional wedding. I'll even go to the church music files and dig out some nice pieces. Maybe you could ask some of your high school orchestra friends to play in a string quartet at the reception?"

"Yeah, that's a great idea. Emily told me she'd play violin at my wedding if I did at hers, so now's a good time to take her up on the offer. You're the greatest, Mom."

Tears welled in Kat's eyes. "Thanks, baby."

After some brief discussion on instrumentalists and where to look for a maternity bridal gown and how Kevin could walk her down the aisle, Keely hung up. A knock at the front door a few minutes later reminded Kat she had to teach a piano lesson.

Later, after the adrenaline of Keely and Nigel's good news wore off and fatigue set in, Kat found herself collapsed on the sofa in front of the TV, staring blankly into space. Her baby girl was getting married. Her baby was also going to be a mother by spring. Her other baby also had informed her he'd passed his English course with the help of his former high school teacher. There was a chance Keely would get the job at the elementary school, and she and Nigel and the babies would live nearby, at least for a while. There was a chance Nigel the kicker would join the Cowboys and make her the most popular music teacher in the whole Texas Hill Country. Kat heaved a contented sigh. Her life didn't seem to be so crazy, awful, and out-of-control after all.

So why did she tremble at the possibility of interacting with Jonathan in the near future?

Kat stood and paced. He hadn't called her in weeks. He hadn't pressed his suit when she'd told him it was for the best they separated on friendly terms. He had treated her with the same respect and kindness he always did with all his congregation members. He had treated her pretty much the way she had wanted him to treat her — and she hated it! What could she do?

"The only way I can draw Jonathan's attention is to act more like myself than I have lately," Kat concluded. "If I continue to let him think I don't need him—I don't *want* him—then he's going to think I don't care about him, and I do. I really do."

Kat crossed to the front window and stared out into the blackness of the night, confronting the darkness of her inner demons. "Oh, Jonathan," she whispered. "How do I make you understand I love you, but I'm not strong enough to be a Ruth?"

"About time." Elizabeth snorted and turned from the sink where she stood scraping off dishes in the disposal before depositing them in the dishwasher. "I doubt Keely's going to find a dress that fits her at this point. Maybe she ought to check out a tent-maker?"

"So cool her fiancé is a field goal kicker for the Longhorns." Josh closed his eyes and settled back against the sofa in the Rawlins's family room. "What I wouldn't have given to have a chance to play football at that level—to have a chance of making it to the pros."

"You wouldn't enjoy being a professional football player, Josh." Jonathan smiled, watching his grandson happily bat at his play-gym objects suspended overhead. "You'd be on the road so much that you wouldn't get to see much of little Jeremiah. You wouldn't want to miss out on this very short, but very important part of his life now, would you?"

Josh opened his eyes and lowered himself to the floor to lie on the opposite side of the baby quilt. "Of course not. How could I even think of not being around to watch my Jerry grow up?" He kissed the baby on the forehead and then blew on his kicking feet. "Don't you worry. Daddy's never gonna leave his widdle Jerry-werry."

"His name is Jeremiah. That's Jer-e-mi-ah, not Jerry," Elizabeth growled. She threw down the dish towel and crossed to the action. "How many times do I have to tell y'all that my son's birth certificate does not have the word Jerry on it? He's not a slang term for Germans."

Josh popped up on an elbow. "Why not? I'm part German and so are you. Isn't everyone around this town at least part German, Dad?"

"Probably." Jonathan chuckled. "I think that's where it gets its name, too."

Elizabeth glared at the two men. "Y'all know I hate nick-names. They're so . . . so . . ."

"Stupid?" Josh suggested.

"Common?" Jonathan volunteered.

"Yes, that's it. Common." She knelt and scooped her son up to her shoulder. "My son may have a wet diaper, but he's far from common."

"I agree, sweetie." Josh rose and followed his wife to the bedroom where they kept the diaper changing items.

Jonathan pulled himself up to the sofa, trying hard not to eavesdrop on their conversation. The sounds of a husband-wife interaction were, on one hand, music to his ears. On the other, they were heart-wrenching. Would he enjoy a friendly argument with a woman who'd share his life ever again?

"There, there, snoogums, all nice and dry and clean for Granddaddy." Elizabeth sat and placed the baby in Jona-than's arms. She gave her father's shoulders a quick squeeze. "You acted like you could use a hug there for a moment. Missing Mom?"

"No, not really." Jonathan looked down at his grandson and smiled. "He does have her eyes a bit, doesn't he? I guess they're really your eyes, though."

"He's got my eye shape, but Josh's coloring. Sometimes he reminds me of Eli as a baby. It's the double chins, I guess."

"Your brother does not have a double anything on his

body these days," Jonathan gently scolded her. "The Marines will make any body into a lean, mean fighting machine." He sighed. "I'm ever so grateful they also train people like Eli to recruit other people. I don't like to think of the possibility of Eli being sent anywhere dangerous on active duty."

"Me, neither."

"What's Josh up to?" Jonathan asked a moment later.

Elizabeth slipped booties onto Jeremiah's feet. "He's checking out your fitness gym in the garage. You ever use it?"

"A little. Rolf has about worn me out lately. I don't have enough energy to bend the weights after a good long jog with Super Dog."

"I'm glad you're getting in shape, Dad. I'm extra glad you agreed to keep the shaggy beast outside on Sundays when we visit, but don't you think you're overdoing the fitness thing a bit?"

Jonathan slanted his eyes at her. "What do you mean?"

"I mean that you've lost quite a bit of weight. I know you want to look good in your new clothes, but it's ridiculous at your age to slim down to a toothpick. I want you to have enough meat on your bones so, when a good dust storm blows over, you don't get picked off your feet and blow away like a tumbleweed. Mom's not here to feed you properly, so it's up to me to say something before you dwindle away to nothing."

"That good, huh?" Jonathan reached under the baby with a hand and patted his rock-hard abs. "I haven't felt this slim in years. It's wonderful."

"You look nice, but remember, you don't have to dress like a fashion model, you know. You're a minister."

"Meaning?"

Elizabeth shifted, removing her arm from the back of the

sofa. She stood, turning away from him. "I don't think ministers have to give the impression that they're cover models. You're getting too . . . too . . ."

"Attractive?" Jonathan filled in.

"Well, yes, in a middle-aged father sort of way. I guess you could say you've got one hot bod, but I don't want that comment to go to your head and—"

"Why not?" Jonathan challenged her. "Are you afraid the female members will throw themselves at my feet?"

"Exactly. That's it." She turned and reached for the baby.

Jonathan held on tight to his now sleeping grandson.

"Leave Jerry alone a moment, Elizabeth. He's happy in his Granddaddy's arms. I want you to tell me more about why I'm not allowed to attract women."

"Dad," she whined, "not now. There's a child in the room, for pity's sake."

"The child doesn't understand a word we're saying even when he's wide awake." Jonathan sat up and lifted his chin high. "Why is it that you don't want your father to have a serious relationship with a woman? Is it because you feel I'm betraying your mother's memory?"

Elizabeth stormed out of the room, heading toward the kitchen. "You can do whatever you like, Dad. I mean, haven't you already? I saw how you were looking at Kat Dubcek at the Oktoberfest. Everyone in town saw how you were looking at her there. Everyone in town saw you two dancing the night away together. Everyone saw her daughter with her pregnant belly hanging out over the top of her raggedy jeans and—"

"So, you're simply afraid of what people will think, what people will say about your father if he's seen with a woman in a social situation?" Jonathan laughed and shook his head. "Here all this time I was worried I might actually break your heart if I started dated again, but that isn't it at all, is it?"

She spun around, hands on hips. "Yes, it is."

"No, it isn't. Honey, you're not really against me dating—you're just afraid of what others in this little town think of you and your family. Elizabeth, you and Josh don't even live here anymore. You don't have to worry about hearing gossip about your old man in the big city. No one there will care or even know."

"*I'll* know." Elizabeth's eyes filled with liquid emotion. "Eli and Josh will know. Don't you care what Mom's friends will be saying behind your back? Crazy Jonathan Rawlins at St. Luke's is fooling around with his own harlot of a choir mistress—"

"That's enough!" Jonathan cried. He scrambled to his feet and handed the sleeping child back to his mother. "I will not have you casting aspersions at Kat or any of her family members. Kat's behavior toward me has always been above reproach, which is more than I can say about some of my own toward her at times."

"Oh, Dad, how could you . . ."

He lowered his voice, trying to calm her. "I want you and Josh to collect Jerry's things and go on home. I won't allow you to return to this house again until you're ready to apologize to both me and Kat."

Jonathan grabbed the diaper bag from the coffee table and headed to the front door. He slipped the bag strap onto Elizabeth's shoulder and kissed her on the cheek.

"Go on home now."

She began to cry. "I'm sorry, Dad. I didn't mean to say those ugly things. Please forgive me."

He pulled her close and kissed her forehead. "I forgive you, baby. I realize you're under a lot of stress from losing your mom and having a baby a short while ago, but you're going to have to watch your tongue. You're setting a bad example for my grandson here, and I won't have it."

She sniffed and nodded. "You're right. Mom would have been shocked to hear my mouthing off lately."

Jonathan softened his tone as he led Elizabeth out the door and across the driveway to their car. "You put Jerry in his car seat before he wakes up. I'll tell Josh y'all are tired and need to go home now and take a little nap. Next weekend when you come to visit you are going to apologize to Kat for the unkind things you said about her and Keely."

"How will I do that?"

"At Sunday dinner. I'm inviting Kat over."

Josh peeked out from around the open garage door. "We're going?"

Jonathan swung open the side door and readied the baby seat. "Elizabeth is feeling tired, and the baby's asleep. I think it's time y'all went home and rested some."

Josh nodded as he approached the car. "We'll see you next Sunday then?"

"Of course." Jonathan paused, catching sight of Elizabeth's ashen complexion. His heart skipped a beat. "What's wrong?"

"The baby . . . his color seems off," she whispered. "His lips look blue."

Grim faced, Josh rushed over to his wife's side. "Get in. We're heading straight to the hospital."

CHAPTER FIFTEEN

K at opened her front door and froze in place, shocked at
the sight that greeted her.

"It's awful, simply awful!" Darla wailed, blue mascara
running down her cheeks, pooling in the cleft above her
smeared pink lipstick. "Can I come in?"

"Please do." Kat stood aside and ushered the crying
woman to the closest chair in the living room. "What's
wrong? It isn't your mother-in-law, is it?"

"No, no. She's as healthy as a horse—except for her
memory, that is. No, it's Pastor Jon." She took a long, shud-
dering breath. "I was over at the county hospital this afternoon with my niece, the candy striper, for a Ladies Guild
function. Just about the time I was fixin' to leave I saw them
outside the ER. It's awful, just awful . . ."

Kat slid into the chair opposite. She swallowed hard and
clenched her hands into fists. She had to know.

"Was he . . . was Pastor Jon in an accident?"

"Oh no, he's fine. It's little Jeremiah. He's sick, very sick.
Pastor talked to me briefly and told me the doctors think the
baby might have a congenital heart defect. They put him and
Elizabeth in an ambulance and rushed him right over to
Austin to see a children's surgeon, and Josh and Jonathan
followed behind. It's probably something they can fix in a
single operation they tell me, but I was so upset after I heard
the news that I dropped my niece off down the street. I
couldn't stop crying. So, I came over here to call Dilly to tell
him I'd be a little late getting home. Is that okay?"

The knot in Kat's stomach relaxed. Jonathan was all right, but his grandson was hurting, so Jonathan was hurting, too.

"It's fine, Darla. You stay put and let me get you some water."

"That would be great." Darla sniffed back a tear and hiccupped. "Thanks, Kat. You're a true pal."

Kat retrieved a glass of water and handed it and a box of tissues to her guest, then sat back down and listened carefully, making mental note of the location of the hospital Jeremiah was being taken to in Austin.

"Dilly says he'll be over right after the game is finished in a few minutes to pick me up. I must look a wreck." Darla loudly blew her nose on a tissue, then pocketed it. "You'd think being a church secretary I'd be used to hearing news like this—I'd be able to handle the pressure better. At times stuff like this really gets to me."

Kat reached over to pat Darla's hand. "Don't be so hard on yourself. Crying in this sort of situation is understandable. You're a mother, and you know how scary it is to have a sick child. Plus, you've been a good friend to the Rawlins family for a long time, and it's been a very stressful year for them."

"You're not kidding. I thought I was going to die this past January when the cancer took Ruth. She was such a rock. She wouldn't be reduced to tears at a time like this, you know. Oh no. She'd be prayin' and busy fixin' stuff to make things easier on everyone else."

"I know." Kat sighed, nodding at the memories. "I'll never be able to fill that woman's shoes. She was a living saint."

"Amen to that." Darla hiccupped once more, observing Kat through narrowed eyes. "Now, tell me why would you want to fill Ruth's shoes?"

Kat started. "No reason. I mean, I . . ." She bit her lip.

Darla continued to regard Kat with open curiosity.

Kat had to say something, but what? "I just meant that every congregation seems to have a Ruth at some time or the other, and our pastor just happened to be married to her," Kat babbled on. "I wonder if we'll ever be able to replace her. I mean, I wonder if he'll ever be able to find another woman who could replace her in his heart."

"Probably not. Ruth is irreplaceable. She was definitely one-of-a-kind. I think it's good we cherish our memories of her and use her as an example to live up to." Darla wiped away a straggling tear and smiled. "You gotta admit, though, you've made Pastor's heart these past few months feel a bit lighter. It's something you can take pride in, Kat."

The tempo of Kat's heart quickened. Darla had known about her and Jonathan all along? What should she do? Should she lie? Should she be brave and admit the truth? Should she leave town and book a one-way passage on a slow boat to the Arctic?

"What are you saying?" Kat said at last.

"I'm saying, I finally figured out why Pastor Jon was whistling all the time, and why he wanted you to teach him the piano, and why he ordered a polka album for you off the Internet. It wasn't for him, for sure." Darla pointed at a rectangular parcel sitting forgotten beside the piano. "I may not be the sharpest tack in the bin, but I am observant at times."

Kat followed the line of Darla's pointer finger and remembered the package Jonathan had left behind the last time he and Rolf had visited. She had been meaning to drop it by the church office. Somehow, she had never gotten around to it.

"So, that's what that is." Kat rushed over to the piano and tore off the cardboard protective wrapping. "*101 Rare Polka Waltzes*. I've always wanted a recording like this." She hugged the LP close to her heart. "You say he got it for me?"

"I don't know who else it could be for." At the sound of a

car horn outside, Darla rose and peeked out the front window. "There's my darlin' Dilly. I'm feeling a bit calmer now. I'll just follow him on home in the car."

Kat escorted the church secretary to the door. "You won't go around telling folks about Pastor Jon giving me this record, will you?"

Darla planted her feet wide apart and placed her hands on her hips. "What do I look like, Kat Dubcek—your common, every day, busybody, gossip-monger? Nothin' could be further from the truth. I tell ya, y'all's secret is safe with me—for the moment. I'll be awaiting to hear more about what you and Pastor are up to soon, however. My patience does have its limits. Fair enough warning?"

Kat grinned. "Fair enough."

Waving goodbye, Kat watched the Dierdorfs drive away in their respective vehicles before racing to the back door to slip on her shoes and grab her purse and car keys. With any luck, and very little weekend highway patrolling, she'd be by Jonathan's side in less than an hour.

The information desk clerk at the front entrance confirmed Jeremiah had been taken into surgery soon upon arrival. Friends and family members could wait in the designated waiting area or in the cafeteria or chapel. Kat followed the signs leading to the surgical floor.

"Jonathan?"

"Kat?"

Jonathan jumped up from the sofa where he had been sitting with his Bible open in his lap. They had the waiting room all to themselves.

"Kat, how did you know I'd be here?"

"Darla came by and told me about the baby." She sat beside him on the couch as he took his seat. "Is Jeremiah doing okay?"

"Yes, he just got out of surgery and is in the recovery area. Elizabeth and Josh were allowed to put on scrubs and go in to be near him. They say it was a rather simple, straightforward procedure to close a little hole in the wall of his heart he was born with. He'll be perfectly fine from now on, the doctor assures us."

Kat placed a comforting hand on his shoulder. "I'm relieved to hear it."

Jonathan covered her hand with one of his. "I'm glad you came."

"I'm glad to be here." She smiled.

He raised an eyebrow. "Are you?"

"Yes, I am." She sat straighter and cleared her throat. "Jonathan, I want to apologize for what I said to you the other day. I—"

He leaned over, silencing her with a kiss. "Apology accepted." He pulled her close, and she rested her head on his chest. "I'd like to apologize to you, too."

"For what?" she asked.

"For giving you the impression I don't care about you and the stress you're under, what with Keely being in her condition and all. I care, I do."

"I know you do." Kat sat up and brushed her lips against his once and then again, slower, and with more passion this time. "Apology accepted," she purred.

A low chuckle escaped his throat. "This has got to be the most fun I've ever had in a hospital waiting room."

Kat kissed him on the nose. "Let's hope PDA's are allowed in here, and they don't kick us out."

"PDA's? Portable Display Units?"

"No, public displays of affection. It's a schoolteacher code word for kissing and holding hands."

"I like holding your hand, Kat." Jonathan gave her hand a

squeeze. "You give me such strength. I don't think you realize how much strength you possess sometimes, or how God uses your strength to help others as well as yourself."

Kat widened her eyes. Was he really saying her character traits came anywhere close to Ruth's?

"You think so?" she asked. "I always thought I was the type who fell to pieces and ran whining to others to help bail me out of my difficulties."

"There's nothing wrong with asking for help. It means you're strong enough to admit you can't go it alone." He sighed and shook his head. "I talked to Keely on the phone the other day. She tells me you were convinced you'd have to go it alone when it came to supporting your grandchildren."

Kat shrugged. "I guess so. How did I know that Nigel and Keely were going to make the right decision to get married and Nigel's parents were independently wealthy types who don't mind helping the kids out? I only heard they worked in a hotel before—I wasn't told they actually *owned* the hotel until recently. I rest easier at night knowing my retirement savings are once again secure."

"You know, two incomes can make your retirement even more secure," he murmured close to her ear.

Kat raised an eyebrow. "Two incomes?"

Jonathan lifted her chin and lowered his lips, lingering in a long, fervent kiss, pulling away slowly.

"I have an excellent retirement plan from the church, you know," he said. "I have a nice house to live in rent free as well."

"You're trying to dazzle me with your wealth and charm, aren't you?" She grinned, then sighed. "We've got a few more hurdles to jump than rent payments, don't you think?"

She nodded toward the end of the corridor where Elizabeth and Josh had emerged from the surgical suite. Jonathan and Kat scooted apart and sat up straighter in their seats.

"Daddy, he looks so pink now. He's doing really well the recovery nurses all say." Elizabeth dabbed at the tears collecting in the corner of her eyes.

Josh remained unusually silent, but Kat sensed that the young man's somewhat blank facial expression spelled relief.

"You two sit down and rest a minute," Jonathan advised them.

The couple sat in the small loveseat opposite the couch. Almost simultaneously they realized who was sitting next to Jonathan.

"Hi, Kat." Josh looked first at Kat, then his father-in-law. He grinned the same grin he had flashed at them whenever he had spied them dancing at the Oktoberfest. "Thanks for keeping Dad company."

"Why, hello there," Elizabeth said quietly. "I forget sometimes how fast news spreads in Germantown. Where's the rest of the St. Luke's contingent?"

"They're on their way. Darla told me the news first, so I got a head start on the rest."

"Thanks for the warning." Elizabeth settled farther into the seat. Her red-rimmed eyes and her normally coiffed hair unwinding from her ponytail spoke of how the strain of the day had taken its toll. "It might be a while before we can make it back for a visit, so it'll be nice to see our friends here in the city for a change."

Elizabeth leaned her head against her husband's shoulder. "Sorry we probably won't be able to join you and Dad for Sunday dinner this coming week. Maybe some other time?"

Kat glanced at Jonathan out of the corner of her eye. "Sunday dinner?"

"Yes, we were fixin' to invite you to join us—me, the kids

here, and little Jerry," Jonathan explained, winking at his daughter. "It was all Elizabeth's idea."

"What a lovely thought." Kat tried hard not to sound incredulous. She smiled and nodded instead. "Thank you for the invitation. We'll have to do it some other time when everything settles down a bit."

"Yes, it would be better." Elizabeth covered her mouth with a hand and yawned. "I never did take my nap today, did I?"

"No, you didn't," her husband agreed. "I suppose we could lean back and get a little shut-eye here. Doctor Reyes said she'd meet us here in a short while to tell us how long Jerry is going to have to stay in the hospital."

Jonathan stood. "Good idea. Kat and I will go for a little walk and give you some peace and quiet and be back in a moment."

Kat rose and followed Jonathan out into the corridor. Hand in hand, they strolled to the elevators, got out on the ground floor, and made their way out the front entrance to the privacy of a waiting park bench.

"Elizabeth really wants me to come to Sunday dinner?" Kat asked as she sat beside Jonathan on the bench.

"Yes, she did. We enjoyed a little discussion about it, and it seems I may have taken her too literally before. She doesn't dislike you. She's just not sure she can see me with another woman besides her mother. Don't worry—she'll get used to it in time."

"How can you be so certain?"

"I'm not, but I trust that the Lord will soften her heart and make her see how much I need you beside me."

He lifted her hand to his lips and pressed a kiss of promise to her palm. "You're my rock. I feel lost and lonely when you're not with me."

Kat wanted to scream and dance about in delight but contained herself since a hospital wasn't the right place to make a scene. She couldn't deny the happiness radiating throughout every inch of her being. Jonathan needed her. He felt he could trust her, depend on her. She wasn't just someone to keep him company on a walk or keep his bed warm at night.

She caressed his cheek. "I feel the same way about you."

"Then why should we wait?" Jonathan winked. "I don't think it's necessary to have a long engagement period at our time of life, do you?"

"Engagement period?"

"You know, the time before the wedding."

Kat frowned. "Wedding? Whose wedding are we talking about here?"

"Ours of course." He furrowed his brow. "You do want to get married, don't you?"

Wasn't this what she had been waiting for all this time? Now that Jonathan had actually said the M word out loud, Kat found herself thinking she wasn't so sure. She had Keely and Nigel's nuptials to deal with first, then the arrival of her grandchildren and then she had to get Kevin through his last semester and into a robe and mortarboard and hopefully into a job and—

"I . . . I don't know," she managed at last.

His face paled. "I thought you wanted us to . . . wanted us to be . . . you know, *close*."

"You mean do I want to go to bed with you?" The words came out wrong. Kat hardly recognized this part of herself, but she found once she started she couldn't stop. "I'd be lying if I didn't say yes, but if that's all you think marriage is about, Jonathan, then you've got another thing coming."

Kat stood and marched toward the parking lot. Jonathan sprang to his feet and followed her along with the eyes of several bystanders who couldn't help but hear Kat's loudly spoken declaration.

"Wait up, please," Jonathan called out. "I didn't mean I wanted us to get married right away simply because I want to get you in bed. I love you, Kat."

She halted and whirled about to face him. "I love you, too, but I've managed to keep my raging hormones in check quite admirably these past few months, if I do say so myself, considering my past." She lowered her voice and continued, "So don't say you want to rush me to the altar simply because you're afraid I'll jump your bones if we hold off any longer. Because I won't."

He flinched. "I'm not saying you can't wait. Honestly, I'm not."

"Then what *are* you saying?" Kat looked him straight in the eye. "I think I know what you mean better than you do, Jonathan. You want to go rush out and tell everyone we're engaged, effectively pre-empting their ability to make comments about us being seen in public together so your name isn't dragged through the mud. That's it, isn't it?"

Jonathan raised his hands and dropped his chin to his chest. "All right—you've got me. Yes, I admit that I do want to keep the small-town gossip about us to a minimum. If we make a public declaration and we are serious in our commitment to each other, then it does alleviate some of the idle speculations. I'm not thinking only of myself. I'm thinking of you, too."

"Thanks." Kat turned and started walking away again.

Jonathan followed close on her heels.

"My reputation can't get much worse in Germantown than it is already. In fact, I can only gain a few points on the gossips' reputation meter by having it linked with yours." She stopped in front of her car and sighed. "I hate to leave you like this, Jonathan, but I thought since I was in the area I'd go on over and check up on Keely and Kevin before heading home. I have school tomorrow."

"I understand." He pulled her into his arms and kissed her on the lips and forehead. "Kat, I want you to know I'm not trying to force you into marriage. If you don't feel like discussing it now, when you've got Keely and her pregnancy on your mind, that's okay. I'll be ready whenever you're ready."

Kat blinked away the tears coalescing in the corners of her eyes. How could she be so heartless to the man she loved? But something deep down inside was warning her to take it slow, to not jump headlong into marriage again. After all, she had been madly in love with Dirk and had run off and gotten married in a hurry. He hadn't turned out to be a very good choice now, had he? She couldn't forget how history tended to repeat itself regarding herself and men.

She climbed into her car and started the engine. Jonathan leaned an arm on the driver's side window and pointed to the package in the passenger seat. Kat lowered the glass.

"Are you enjoying the polka music?" he asked.

She shrugged. "The cover looks wonderful, but I haven't had the chance to listen to it yet. Thank you so much—I didn't realize the package you left behind was for me until today. You should have told me about it sooner."

"And take away the surprise?" He flashed a purposeful grin. "I knew you'd get around to listening to the record eventually, like I know with certainty you'll be ready to listen to my marriage proposal again someday soon."

Kat squirmed under Jonathan's intense gaze. "How can you be so sure?"

"Because I have faith in you, Kat Dubcek," he replied solemnly. "Once I start preaching, I keep on preaching until I've made my point."

Kat clapped as her young pupil brought the piano piece to a

satisfying close.

"Very good, Adam. Everything you've played today was first-rate. You've been practicing those thirty minutes a day like I told you to, haven't you?"

"Yes, ma'am. My mom made up a new house rule. I can't play video games until I've worked on my piano. I've been doing a lot of piano practicing lately."

"It's paid off. You sound great. Aren't you proud of yourself?"

Adam scrunched up his nose and shrugged. "I guess so. You know, some days I get so much into playing piano I actually forget to play video games. My friends all think I'm weird."

"Don't pay them any mind. They're just jealous." Kat gave the future lady-killer a quick hair tousle of support. "Now, I want you to promise me you'll keep practicing like you're doing. I see good things happening in your future if you do."

Adam collected his music from the music stand. "You mean I'll grow up and play football for the *Longhorns* like Kevin does some day?"

"Not exactly," Kat replied, chuckling, "but you might be the drum major in the band."

"Knock, knock," Hannah MacDonald announced, peeking around the edge of the front door. "Can I come in?"

"Come right on in. We're wrapping things up now."

"Hey, Mom, Ms. Dubcek says I could be a *Longhorn* someday."

"She did now, did she?" Hannah winked at Kat as she handed her son his jacket. "Kevin is doing some mighty amazing things according to the paper — that interception in the game against the *Sooners* for example."

Kat nodded with a sigh. Everyone in town talked about her son's football prowess night and day, it seemed. "He's doing some amazing things according to his recent grades, too. Who knows? Maybe he'll get picked in the pro-draft after all. Either him or my soon-to-be son-in-law."

"Wow, then you'd know two professional football players!" Adam cried. "I can say I take piano lessons from their mom."

"I guess you could." Kat scratched her chin in thought. "I wonder if I advertised my football connections I could raise my rates?"

"If you do, please remember those of us who knew you when." Hannah laughed. "I'm not sure we could afford lessons otherwise."

Kat patted her friend on the back. "Don't worry. I'll never forget my early supporters."

"Thanks." Hannah motioned Kat away from the piano area while Adam tugged on his coat. "The word on the street today is that you and Pastor Rawlins are a couple," she murmured behind a hand.

Kat rolled her eyes. "Gee whiz, the gossip mills are really slowing down around Germantown. Darla's known about the two of us for at least a week. Must be football season getting in the way."

Hannah winked. "Probably. So, tell me more about you and the stylishly dressed church man. Any hot dates yet?"

"No, not really," Kat said with a nonchalant tilt of her chin, "unless you count the time I almost threw up on his shoes."

Hannah's eyes widened. She took a step backward. "No kidding? You got sick? What happened next?"

"He put me to bed, of course." Kat strolled to the door and held it open for her guests to exit. "Feel free to pass that choice tidbit around town just in case it hasn't gotten out yet."

"I would never go around spreading gossip about you,

Kat." Hannah's hurt was evidenced in both her voice and features. "I hope you realize that."

Guilt washed over Kat like she'd been baptized in a Hill Country spring flood. She gave her friend a hug.

"Forgive me. I know you wouldn't do any such thing. I'm a bit touchy today. It's hard enough sharing the spotlight with my son and soon-to-be son-in-law as celebrity football players. I'm not comfortable with being a hot topic these days. Lord knows it shouldn't bother me after all these years, but somehow it does."

"Of course it does. You're only human."

Hannah took her son by the hand and nodded to her SUV in the driveway. "Go get in the car now, sweetie, and look at the surprise I got you in the bag."

"Is it the RT plane I asked for my birthday?"

"Close. It takes batteries."

Adam raced out to the car, flung open the back door, and hopped inside.

"I hope he isn't disappointed when he finds out it's only a flashlight." Hannah smiled. "I know you've weathered a few tough storms over the years in this town, Kat, but it doesn't make them any less stressful to deal with. You've always been my heroine, you know."

"Your heroine?" Kat blinked in disbelief. "Why? We've got so many outstanding citizens in these here parts. Surely you could come up with a better person to look up to than me."

Hannah put her hands on her hips and pointed a finger at her. "Stop with the putdowns. I don't think you realize you set a better example than you think. You see, you've put up with the stupid talk and the lies and the nasty chitchat forever, but you've never let it scare you away. You stood your ground and kept on doing what you're good at doing and never repaid any of the ugliness in return. It makes you a small-town hero in my book any day."

"Hey, Mom!" Adam shouted, head hanging out the window. "There's nothing in here except a bunch of toilet paper, a flashlight, and some package marked *feminine protection at its best*. What's that supposed to mean?"

Hannah blushed and slapped her forehead in embarrassment. "We'll talk about that later, son." She touched Kat lightly on the arm. "See you around, Ms. Role Model."

"Sure thing." Smiling, Kat stepped out onto the front stoop and waved them off. "Remember to keep practicing, Adam. Good things are going to happen to you some day. I guarantee it."

Upon reentering the house, Kat approached the stereo in a corner of the living room and picked up *101 Rare Polka Waltzes*. Turning the cover over, she skimmed the back-liner notes.

"Hmm . . . I guess I shouldn't be too hard on Adam. Even when good things happen to me, I still somehow don't believe they're true, do I?"

She slipped the record from its sleeve and gently laid it on her turntable. Thank goodness she hadn't let Kevin drag her antique stereo off to college like he'd wanted to. After a scratchy start, the percussive sound of accordions, clarinets, and tubas issued forth from the speakers, rushing over her in a welcoming flood of warm and happy feelings.

"One, two, three. One, two, three . . ." she counted off over and over again. She twirled about, reliving the magic once again of being held in Jonathan's arms as they waltzed across the dance floor. "One, two, three. One, two, three . . ."

Exhausted, she collapsed pell-mell on the sofa. The song came to a close. A minute later, the doorbell alerted her to her next student's arrival.

"No rest for us wicked role models, I guess," she murmured, rising to answer the door.

"What did Kat think about the record?" Darla tossed the daily mail onto Jonathan's desk.

"What record?" he answered without looking up. He had been spending a lot of time with Elizabeth and Josh at the hospital watching Jerry get stronger each day. So much time he had forgotten until this morning he had to finish the quarterly district report and mail it back by this afternoon.

His secretary stood at the door and tapped her foot.

"Oh, you mean the polka waltzes." Sighing, Jonathan put down his pen and rubbed his burning eyes. "She didn't mention that she'd gotten around to listening to it as of yesterday when I talked to her on the phone. I'm trying not to act too pushy. We've both been a bit busy lately."

"No kidding. It's certainly no way to keep a relationship going with only phone conversations and the occasional present."

Jonathan frowned. "It isn't?"

Darla crossed her arms. "No, it just doesn't cut it with today's woman. She's gotta know you care. She's gotta feel assured that you think of her every single minute of every single day."

Jonathan furrowed his brow, returning his attention back to the paperwork. "I don't believe Kat is all that insecure about our relationship. If she was, she would have agreed to get married right away."

Darla's eyes widened. "You asked her to marry you already?"

"Sort of." He put down his pen again. "It was a bit precipitous of me. I realize it now."

"I would say so." The church secretary snorted her disapproval. "You've barely begun to date, and you've already asked her to sign on for life." She shook her head. "Tsk, tsk,

tsk. Maybe *you're* the one who's feeling a bit insecure."

Jonathan frowned. Is that how people saw him? Insecure? He straightened in his chair. "It's not insecurity to want to start spending the rest of your life with someone right away—it's commitment."

"Commitment to an insane asylum, you mean." Darla threw back her head and laughed. She stopped her guffawing a few moments later when she realized Jonathan wasn't joining in on the joke. She shrugged. "Well, I thought what I said was funny."

"Ha, ha," Jonathan deadpanned.

Softening her tone, Darla leaned closer. "I mean, don't y'all want to get to know each other better before signing on the dotted line for life?"

"*Know*, know, or know as in the biblical sense of the word?"

"Why, Pastor!" she cried, her pale face turning beet red. "How can you say such a thing?"

"I'm not the one who mentioned it first. Besides, everyone in this town seems to think we've already had . . . had . . ." He leaned back and folded his arms across his chest, clearing his throat as Darla's expression egged him on. "Everyone assumes we've gotten to *know* each other better already, and nothing could be further from the truth."

"You mean y'all haven't?" Her jaw dropped in disbelief.

Jonathan cringed. What was wrong with him? Why did the members of his flock doubt his sincerity? Why did he feel the overwhelming need to continually defend his and Kat's reputations in the first place?

"Of course not." He picked up the form in front of him, scavenging his desk for the return envelope. "Now, if you'll excuse me, I've got to get this thing mailed back to the district office as soon as possible."

"I'll take it in when I go check our PO box."

Standing, he sealed the manila envelope closed and pressed on the return address label. "No, thanks. I'm leaving for the day anyway. Go ahead and set up the answering machine to forward the calls to my voice mail if you please, Darla. Thanks."

Jonathan snatched his jacket off the coat tree and headed for the door. "See you tomorrow."

Darla slunk slowly to her desk chair. "'Bye, Pastor."

A sudden wave of remorse overcame Jonathan as he walked next door and got into his car. He wasn't normally so snippy with Darla, but he just couldn't let her go on thinking that he and Kat were . . . well, *intimate*. If he cut off the rumor mill at its source, then the flood of wisecracks and cute looks he'd encountered everywhere he went in town lately would dry up. If he had to hurt Darla's feelings temporarily, to save Kat's reputation in the long run, then so be it.

After dropping the letter at the main post office, Jonathan found himself driving on automatic pilot toward Kat's house. She wasn't expecting him, but then again, maybe a little surprise was just what she needed about now.

Jonathan paused outside Kat's front door. Was that polka music he heard playing inside?

"One, two, three. One, two, three . . ."

He hated to knock and interrupt her count, but soon the song came to a close. It was now or never. He rang the doorbell.

"Why, howdy stranger." Kat's grin was infectious. "This is a nice surprise. I thought you were my four-thirty lesson."

"I'm sorry. I'll come back if it's inconvenient—"

"Don't you dare." She grabbed him by the elbow and pulled him inside. "Besides, they're almost fifteen minutes late, so that means they've canceled. I'm out some money."

He followed her into the living room. "I hope it doesn't

261

happen very often."

"It happens occasionally. A lot of my pupils are in more after-school activities than their parents can humanly keep up with, and they get their schedules crossed. More than likely I'll be getting a call in the next half hour explaining the absence. Here." She stopped him in the middle of the room. "Don't move."

Racing over to the turntable, Kat scooted the needle onto the second groove, then returned to Jonathan's side.

"Ready?" she said, her eyes sparkling.

He took her hand in his and pulled her close. "Ready, willing, and able."

The next couple of waltzes were lively numbers, full of tuba flourishes and clarinet solos. Jonathan laughed as he and Kat hopped, skipped, and bumped around and around the room, knocking a floor lamp over in the process.

"Sorry." Breathing heavily, he bent to straighten up the light fixture. "It looks intact. Shall I turn it on and check it out?"

"No, don't bother. I like it dark in here."

In the fading sunlight of a fall day, long shadows caused by the bright neon tube light perched over the top of the piano's music stand fell across Kat's face. She changed the music to a big band ballroom dance recording. Grinning, she welcomed him back into her arms for a slower dance.

"It's been a while since we've danced," she said, sighing. "I'd almost forgotten what it felt like."

"I haven't forgotten." Jonathan stroked her cheek and gazed deeply into her eyes. "I'm just sorry that our respective families possess such a knack for distracting us."

"It's not on purpose. Your little grandson can't help it if he has a heart condition. How is Jerry doing anyway?"

"He's as fit as a fiddle and ready to go home. The doctors are going to release him within the next few days. He's past the tricky part. They just want to observe him and monitor his growth a bit longer."

"That's great news." Kat laid her cheek on his shoulder and closed her eyes.

"How are your grandchildren-to-be doing?" he asked.

"I'm just hoping the bride makes it to the ceremony. Twins are often born prematurely. Kevin and Keely arrived two weeks early."

Jonathan raised an eyebrow. "Shall we move the wedding date up a few weeks then? There are several Saturdays not spoken for in November yet."

Kat raised her head. "I think they'd love to have it earlier, but the groom's parents can't make it until later. I'll keep praying for the babies to make it to term. It's better for them anyhow."

"Of course." He rubbed his cheek against hers. "Those Saturdays are still open on the schedule, though."

"Meaning?"

"Meaning it doesn't have to be Keely and Nigel's wedding penciled in then . . ."

The song ended. Kat crossed to the turntable and switched off the stereo.

"I don't know, Jonathan. I just don't feel it's fair to the kids if we preempt their happy day with our own nuptials."

He frowned. "What do you mean it's not fair? Just because Keely's mother gets married a few weeks before she does? Our wedding doesn't necessarily take away from the joy of Keely and Nigel's own special day. We don't have to make ours an elaborate event—just a small service for our family members."

"That's exactly what Keely and Nigel are planning—a simple ceremony with just family and close friends." Kat turned on her heels and headed into the kitchen. "She's wearing a street-length dress, albeit a maternity one."

"Really?" Jonathan followed close behind. "Keely told me she was wearing white. I thought that meant she was wearing the traditional long dress and veil."

"We looked, but we'd have to order a gown special made to fit her at seven months gone, and it may not have been ready in time. We decided to go with what the bridal store had in stock."

"I see." He sat at the table as she headed to the stove area. "There's nothing wrong with more relaxed attire at a wedding. Personally, I think Elizabeth went a bit overboard with her bridal gown. She had to have the top-of-the-line, designer-original kind of dress. I'm still paying for it."

Kat beamed a crooked grin. "So like a daddy—indulging his daughter's whims." She opened the pantry. "So, what do you want for dinner? I've got several boxes of macaroni and several cans of tuna fish . . ."

"Please, no more mac-cheese for me. It's all I can really cook and I'm a bit tired of it." He reached out and pulled her, laughing, into his lap, sealing her lips with a kiss. "Why don't we have dessert first? Do you mind?"

"Not at all," she purred.

Kat returned his kiss with equal enthusiasm. Jonathan's hands caressed her shoulders. Nothing else in the world mattered except the two of them at this moment in time. Nothing. There was no beginning or ending to their love for each other. There was no right or wrong way to express it . . .

She stiffened. "I'd better start dinner now."

"Why? Aren't you cooking yet?" he teased, nibbling at her earlobes.

"Definitely. I'm practically ready to boil over."

"Then let's skip dinner and get down to the good stuff." He moved his hand down to her thigh.

CHAPTER SIXTEEN

K at pulled away. "Jonathan! Hold your horses. You really surprise me at times."

He furrowed his brow. "How is that? Aren't you pleased I find you desirable?"

"Of course I am, but it's just . . ." Kat extricated herself from Jonathan's embrace and crossed back to the stove. "It's just I respect your position on keeping the marriage bed undefiled. It's not a principle that I've always managed to keep well myself in the past, but I'm trying here. I'm really trying."

"I can tell, and I appreciate your effort. But I have also come to the conclusion you're a very beautiful woman who deserves to be made love to — regularly. If you aren't ready to march down the aisle yet, then perhaps we can reach a compromise."

"Compromise?" She wrung her hands. "You not saying that you're willing to . . . before we're . . ." Her voice dropped to a whisper as her eyes widened. "Are you?"

Jonathan stood, tugging Kat into his arms. "Yes, if it means you don't have to *boil over* and I don't have to spend any more sleepless nights in a cold shower, then, yes, I'm willing."

"Did aliens happen to capture and replace the Jonathan Rawlins I know — and love?" Kat tipped her chin back and considered him closely. "You don't have to do this, you know."

"Do what?"

"Compromise your principles for my sake. I'm not worth it."

"But you are." He kissed her on the forehead. "I love you, Kat, and I don't want to lose you simply because you're not quite ready to make a commitment."

A lone tear graced her cheek. "A commitment? You think I'm afraid of making a commitment?"

"Yes, isn't that it?" he said, kissing away the silent river of emotion. "I know your first marriage wasn't exactly ideal and it made you gun-shy. I'm not going to force you into making a decision against your will."

She sniffed. "I appreciate your patience in not forcing me into anything I'm not ready for, Jonathan, but I love you for who you are, not the man I'm changing you into."

Kat detached herself from his embrace and headed to the front door. He followed close behind.

"You're not changing me," he insisted. "I'm the same man inside. It's our relationship that's changing. That's all."

She leaned against the open door. "Not all change is for the better. I should know. I tried to change myself—make myself more like Ruth so you would respect me. I see now it backfired. You—and everyone else in this town—will never see Kat Dubcek as anything but some kind of good time gal. Well, I'm not."

Jonathan reached for her hand, but Kat moved it away.

"I thought . . ." He dropped his chin to his chest in defeat. "You're right. Change isn't always for the better. I won't force my affection on you or ask you to marry me again until you say you're ready."

He exited in silence.

"What are you doing to yourself?" Jonathan chided himself on the short drive home. "And what are you trying to do to Kat?"

"Mom? You seem awfully quiet. Is everything all right?"

Kat turned in her seat and smiled at her daughter. Keely was weaving strands of ribbons and silk flowers into hair wreaths for her flower girls and maid of honor. In the soft glow of the lamp, Kat had never seen her baby girl look more composed, more beautiful than she did tonight, the night before her wedding ceremony.

"Yes, everything's fine, honey," Kat said, folding another place setting card in half. Thank goodness for a first-rate color printer in the teacher's lounge and some leftover cardstock from the art department. "I trust Nigel's family wasn't too put out with their accommodations at the Dew Drop Inn. I can imagine what they must be thinking about a Depression-era motel."

"They found it charming. Very authentic, I believe are the exact words Nigel's dad said at the check-in desk. Don't worry about it."

"I'm not. It's just that I feel like such a poor hostess. Of course, the bride's family is supposed to foot the brunt of the wedding costs, and it's all I can do to pay for your dress and cake and the small reception we're having. I just feel so . . . so . . ."

"Overwhelmed?"

"Yes, that, too, but what I was fixin' to say was that I feel so *cheap*."

"Mom!" Keely put down the wreath in her hand. "Don't say things like that. You've done more than enough for us. Besides, you need to think about saving your money to spend on your grandchildren."

Kat chuckled. "That's certainly one way of putting things into perspective."

Keely smiled. "You see? Where would you be without me?"

Tears threatened to burst the dam on Kat's emotions. "What *will* I do without you? My baby girl is growing up and leaving home for good. I'm about to become a grandmother in a few months' time . . ." She sniffed. "I'm growing so old these days. It's like my life is almost over."

"There, there." Keely hugged her mother, rocking her back and forth. "You're not losing a daughter—you're gaining a son-in-law. You're not really losing your son anytime soon, unless Kevin can get his act together and graduate this spring. Don't go all mushy on me. You're far too young to worry about being old, too. Just forget about all this *my life is over* stuff."

A rush of brisk late autumn air swept through the cozy living room as the front door burst open on the idyllic scene.

"Hey, Mom, guess who I just ran into down at the grocery store." Kevin dropped his bag of soft drinks and junk food on the piano bench as he shrugged out of his jacket.

"It wouldn't be a pro-football agent looking to draft you, would it?" Keely replied with a sarcastic glint in her eyes.

Kevin's widened. "Is there an agent in town? How come no one told me?"

"Get the bottles off my piano bench." Irritated, Kat shooed her overgrown eating machine into the kitchen. "Now tell me, who did you run into down at the store?"

Kevin placed his sack on the table and extricated a soft drink bottle. "Eli. Eli Rawlins. You know, Pastor Jon's son. He's in town for a couple of weeks to celebrate the holidays. Get this—he's officially engaged."

"How nice. Someone he met in the Marines, I take it?"

"Yep. She's good-looking for a soldier, too, let me tell ya. He said they met last summer during a war game exercise and . . ."

As Kat sighed, Kevin's voice faded away. Everyone was getting married it seemed but her. She had no one to blame but herself. She had been the one to say no to Jonathan's proposals. She had been the one to keep him at arm's length, for the most part, these past few weeks, too. She reasoned it was for her own good—and his as well. Whenever she was in Jonathan's arms it was just too tempting to take him up on his offer of a *compromise*. Why was it when she was acting so strong, so much like her heroine, Ruth, she felt so weak?

" . . . And then Eli proposed to her. Can you imagine that? In army fatigues and green face paint?"

At the sound of Kevin's laughter, Kat shook herself from her reverie. Somewhere in the middle of his story, Keely had entered the kitchen and gotten in on the conversation.

"I don't think I'll consider how Nigel and I met unromantic ever again," she said, grinning.

Kat's eyes narrowed. "How did you two meet exactly? You said something about meeting Nigel at one of Kevin's jock parties, but I don't think you ever told me the specifics."

"I went to one of Kevin's jock parties because I was bored out of my skull one Friday night, and in walks this snappily dressed guy with dreadlocks and the brightest smile I'd ever seen. I probably would have never talked to Nigel if it hadn't been for that beer can splattering all over my shirt."

Kat crossed her arms and looked sideways at her children. "Beer can?"

Keely giggled. "Yes, one of Kevin's jock friends shook up a can and exploded it all over the room. I ran into the bathroom to blot the foul stench out of my good shirt when I bumped into Nigel at the sink. It seems the beer had sort of drenched his dreadlocks."

Kat crossed her eyes and playfully stuck out her tongue. "Ugh! You mean you met Nigel cleaning up in the bathroom?"

Keely shook her head.

"It almost tops army war games for romantic first meetings. He didn't ask you out on a date while toweling his hair dry, did he?"

Keely smiled. "You guessed it."

"Hey, not everybody meets the love of their life at a Mexican bullfight." Kevin placed an arm around his mother's neck and gave her a quick squeeze. "Huh, Mom?"

Keely rolled her eyes as she strolled toward the living room. "For sure."

Kat pulled away from her son to sort through the contents of the junk food bag. "Kevin, I never told you this about your father, but ..." She hesitated. What purpose did it serve to repudiate her son's hazy memories of his father?

"Told me what?"

Now she was on the hook. She bit her lip and furrowed her brow in thought. "I ... I never told you, we didn't actually meet at the bullfight. We met at a party after the bullfight."

He nodded slowly. "And?"

"It really wasn't much more romantic than Keely's story, I'm afraid."

"It's okay. You're doing much better this time around. I can tell."

Kevin headed to the refrigerator and gathered the ingredients for his after-dinner snack. "You want a turkey and cornbread stuffing sandwich?"

"No, not right now, honey."

Kat turned to go back to the living room to finish place card folding when Kevin's comment struck home. She halted in her tracks.

"What did you mean when you said I'm doing better this time around?" she asked him, point-blank.

Kevin emptied his arms of turkey, salad dressing, leftover cornbread stuffing, and cranberry sauce onto the counter and began to assemble his culinary work-of-art. "What I meant was that you and Pastor Jon act more romantic than you and Dad ever did. All I can remember really is you two fighting all the time."

She hugged him. "I'm sorry, baby."

"It's okay, Mom, but whenever I see Pastor Jon look at you—like today at the rehearsal dinner—I can tell he's not the yelling type. I can tell he's madly in love with you. He's not one of those jerks like the stupid lawyer guy you used to date."

"You mean Bradley? You pegged him all right. He's a first-rate jerk."

Kat took a step back, observing her son as he sat down with his late-night snack. "You know, I never realized how much you noticed about my dates before now. You and Keely never said much to me about them at the time."

Kevin took a bite of his sandwich. "What could we say?" he said, his mouth half-full. "You're an adult. You go on a date whether we like it or not. I'm just glad you fell for someone with class like Eli's dad. He's great husband material."

Husband? Kat's heart raced. She sat at the table beside her son. "What makes you say that?"

Kevin shrugged. "I dunno. Maybe 'cause he's a great dad to Eli and Elizabeth and he and Mrs. Rawlins never yelled at each other in public. Plus, Darla told me that he's already asked you. What did you tell him?"

Kat couldn't believe she was having this conversation with her *son* of all people, a young man with nothing but football on his mind most of the time. Even Keely had remained mute about her and Jonathan's relationship, although Keely had smiled at her when they sat side by side at the rehearsal dinner.

"I told him . . . I told him I wasn't marriage material," Kat confessed. "I just didn't think now was the right time for me to get married what with Keely and Nigel getting married and the babies coming and all."

"You're still worried about me not having a job after I graduate, aren't you?" He reached out and grabbed his mother's hand, tenderly patting it. *"No problemo, mi madre. Yo tengo un trabajo con mi Coach despues de collegio si lo quiero."* He took another bite of his sandwich.

Kat's jaw seemed to scrape the floor. "Your coach has asked you to work with him after you graduate?" She blinked several times to break her stare. "Hey — you actually said that in Spanish. You've been studying, haven't you?"

"Sí, es verdad." He raised an eyebrow. "I have a new study tutor, too. Her name is Alejandra, and she comes from Barcelona."

"I see." Kat sighed. "We have another long-distance love affair in the family."

"No, Alejandra lives only about three blocks from me. She's a junior. If I stay on as an equipment manager for the team next season, I'll be able to see a lot more of her."

"Yes, I'm sure you will," Kat muttered with a shake of her head.

"So, are you going to accept Pastor Jon's proposal?" Kevin asked.

She halted at the doorway and turned back around. "I don't know. I'm not sure I'm the right woman for the job."

"Job?" Kevin raised an eyebrow. "You mean being a preacher's wife?"

Kat nodded glumly. "You got it. Just think of whose shoes I'd be trying to fill. It's unthinkable."

"Whose shoes do you have to fill? Mrs. Rawlins' shoes?" He put down the remainder of his sandwich. "Nah, just be yourself. People love you just the way you are. I can tell Pastor Jon does."

"You can?" Kat widened her eyes. Her son was becoming

more and more amazing by the minute. "How can you tell?"

"I just can. I guess it's how he looks at you. I noticed his face goes all excited just like Coach's does whenever we make a two-point conversion."

Kat chuckled. "Wow. I'm as exciting as football."

"You are," Kevin agreed, returning his interest to his snack.

Kat shuffled back to the bride-to-be in the living room. "You need any more help with the silk flowers, sweetheart?"

Keely shook her head, laying the wreath aside and picking up a heart-shaped, ivory, lace-covered pillow from the coffee table. "No, I'm just about done. I'm going to double-check the sewing on the rings on the ring bearer's pillow just in case. I don't want Darla's youngest pulling them off thinking they're his Cracker Jack prize or something."

"Good idea." Kat plopped back down on the sofa and began folding place cards once more.

They sat quietly working for a few minutes before Keely put down the pillow she was holding and turned in her seat.

"Be sure to place your card next to Pastor's at the guests-of-honor's table tomorrow," Keely reminded her mother.

Kat put down the card she was folding. "I don't understand. You keep telling me that, but the real guests of honor are you and Nigel and your wedding attendants—Kevin and your cousin Emma. Extended families usually sit at a table nearby."

"Mom—"

"As it is, I'm afraid I'm going to make Nigel's family hate me forever for having to share a table with your Grandparents Kajinkski." Kat sighed. "You know, they've been known to cause heartburn even when they're in the best of moods."

"So you say, but you know it isn't true. Grandma and Grandpa K. are just a bit on the quiet side. They're not grimacing at people all the time like you think they are— they're just concentrating and trying to keep up with the conversation." Keely smiled. "You know, you act a bit over-sensitive at times. It's been how long since you saw them?"

"It's been a while," Kat admitted. "Why should they come out here all this way unless something big is happening with you or Kevin? I'm not that important to them in the scheme of things."

"I think you're more important to them than you think you are. To a lot of people, you're very important."

Keely stood and rubbed her hands together. "Almost ten o'clock. I think I'll call it a night so I can get my beauty sleep. I don't want my hair and dress to be perfect yet have bags the size of dinner plates under my eyes in all the photos."

"Good girl." Kat stood and gave her daughter a big hug. "I'm proud of my big girl. She's all grown up."

"And out," Keely added with a wink. "You get some rest, too. You look worn out, Mom."

"I am a little. I'll be off to bed soon."

Keely headed to her room, Kevin entered the living room and grabbed his jacket.

"Where are you off to again?" Kat asked, stepping in front of her son as he headed toward the front door.

"To the Lone Star. It's Nigel's bachelor party, remember? This is the last night on earth this man has to go crazy before he's chained down to my sister for the rest of his life."

"I thought Nigel was spending the evening quietly with his parents?" she asked.

Kevin grinned sheepishly. "It's the cover story. They're probably fast asleep now. It's why we said we'd meet him at ten."

Kat raised an eyebrow. "We?"

"The football team, of course. You can't have a decent bachelor party without your teammates. Oh, and I invited

Eli, too."

"Eli Rawlins?"

He bent and kissed her on the cheek. "Don't stay up too late, Mom. You look tired."

"So I've been told." She sighed. "Be careful, and don't stay out too late or drink too much. Both you and the groom have to look and act halfway decent tomorrow morning."

"Hey, don't worry. I'm the designated driver. The groom is on his own."

"Wonderful."

Kat shook her head, watching her son peel out of the driveway and shift gears, careening on down the road. She let the curtains drop and headed toward her room. An odd thought jumped into her mind, but she dismissed it. It was absurd. Jonathan would never attend a bachelor party. No, not in a million years.

"I don't think she suspects a thing," Kevin announced, pulling up a chair at the table upon his arrival at the Lone Star Bar and Grill. "I don't think Keely has let on anything, either, amazingly enough."

Nigel leaned back and smiled at his future brother-in-law. "Good. You've kept up your end of things. How goes it from your end, Josh?"

Josh took a swig of his root beer and put down the mug with a gasp. "All set. Elizabeth had Darla call the district office and the Reverend Keller has agreed to perform the ceremony."

"I've got the rings," Eli Rawlins added, pulling a jeweler's box from his jacket pocket. "When Dad saw it, I told him it was Gillian's engagement ring box. Luckily he didn't think to ask why I was still carrying the box around since she's wearing the ring."

"Perfect," Nigel said. "Then it's definitely time to celebrate, gentlemen."

Kevin nodded toward the door as the first of the team members filed in. "Your dad said he'd drop by for a while, didn't he, Eli?"

Eli shrugged. "He did, but don't be surprised if he stays only fifteen minutes or so. He's not much into parties."

"Fair enough," Kevin conceded with a wink. "I think it's only fitting he at least makes an appearance at his own joint bachelor celebration — don't you?"

"Bob! It's great to see you." Jonathan rose and shook hands with the slightly balding, stout older gentleman entering the church office. "What are you doing here?"

"I'm here to perform a wedding." The Reverend Bob Keller laid a fleshy finger aside his nose, then lowered himself into a chair opposite Jonathan's desk. "One which happens to involve a dear old friend of mine."

Jonathan narrowed his eyes and sat back down. "I have no idea what you're talking about, Bob. The wedding fixin' to go on here today involves two young people, one of whom is fairly far along in her pregnancy."

"She would be your intended's daughter, correct?"

"Yes, she's Kat's —" Jonathan did a double-take. "Did you say *my* intended?"

"You have proposed to Katrina Dubcek on several occasions. I have witnesses who will attest to that fact."

Jonathan furrowed his brow. "Well, yes, I have, but she's refused to set a wedding date so far."

"Then today's your lucky day." Bob Keller leaned closer to the desk and lowered his voice. "I have it on the highest authority she can't refuse your proposal today, especially when you have a ring and all."

"I don't have a ring. Eli's the only one who has a ring in our family, and he's already given it to his fiancée, Gillian. You're not making any sense."

"Yes, I am," Bob said with a wink. "Jonathan, you don't realize how lucky you are. You have a family who cares about you very much. They want to see you happy, and they want to see you and Kat happily married. I can't think of a more beautiful early Christmas present."

Jonathan blinked. "But, Bob, I just can't propose to Kat during Keely and Nigel's wedding service and make it a double ceremony. It isn't done. I don't want to take away anything from their special day."

"You'll only add to it. They want to share their happy day with you and Kat." The older man's eyes crinkled in amusement. "They've pretty much told me so themselves."

"They did?" Jonathan scratched his head and shrugged. "I shouldn't be surprised when it comes to young people these days. But what will Kat think? What if she refuses to go along with it?"

"Then you'll be no worse off than you are now." He stood and brushed donut crumbs off his suit jacket. "I've got to fetch the papers from my car. I'll be right back."

Jonathan rose and walked with his guest to the exit. "I-I don't know about this . . ."

Bob paused and patted him on the back. "Have faith, Jonathan. Have faith."

Jonathan stood and stared at the back of Bob Keller as he waddled from the office. He did have faith — but what about Kat? Did she still have faith in him?

"Mom, stop your fussing, or you'll mess up my hair," Keely whined, coughing to clear her lungs. "I'm wearing enough hairspray to cover the heads of the entire choir — including the males."

"It'll help keep your veil in place, sweetheart," Kat replied, putting the can down on the bathroom counter. "There." She sniffed and stepped back and surveyed the results. "You're simply beautiful."

Keely handed her mother another tissue. "Thanks. Now don't go streaking your mascara. I don't want to be seen with a woman with two watery black lines down her face."

"Sorry." Kat blew her nose. "I can't help it. It's hard to believe I'll be a mother-in-law in a few minutes' time. You ready to go out to the foyer?"

"Yes, I think so." She hesitated.

Kat put an arm around her daughter. "It's okay to be nervous. All brides get the jitters."

"It's . . . it's not the jitters, Mom."

Kat raised an eyebrow and smiled. "It isn't?"

"No, it's more of an attack of the guilts. There's something I'm not supposed to tell you, but I really think I should."

"What's that?" Kat frowned.

The bathroom door flung open. Darla stood with hands on her hips, a human stop sign in a scarlet chiffon dress.

"Y'all fixin' to come on out, or should we shoehorn the congregation in here? Gayle's about finished her pre-wedding repertoire, and Matthias is too hoarse to sing another solo."

Grinning, Kat escorted Keely to the door and followed Darla up the stairs to the sanctuary.

"Mom," Keely whispered. "There's something important you should know. Have you talked with Pastor Jon yet this morning?"

"No, I haven't had the time, but we talked yesterday at the rehearsal luncheon."

"You love him, right?"

Kat froze as she reached the top step. She turned to face

her daughter. "Well, of course I love him. What's that got to do with your wedding?"

"You want to marry him, right?"

Caressing Keely's cheek, Kat looked deep into her eyes. "Yes, I do want to marry him, but I'm afraid I've told him no one too many times." She sighed loud and long. "Never mind all that now. Today's my girl's big day, and I won't dwell on my past mistakes, numerous though they may be."

Wagner's wedding march began. Kat smiled and lowered her daughter's veil. "We'd better hurry. They're playing your song."

Kat dabbed at her eyes as Keely and Nigel repeated their vows and exchanged rings.

Such a simple yet lovely ceremony. I can almost picture Jonathan and myself standing here . . .

She was never so glad to be sitting in the front pew than today, so she could enjoy it all and still have access to her stash of emergency tissues handy. Darla had been so kind to provide a box for her and her parents, whose normally stoic expressions wavered today between tears and smiles. Weddings certainly had a way of affecting every member of the family.

Her gaze roamed to the lectern side of the altar area and the rather stout gentleman sitting there. Odd, Jonathan had never mentioned that the Reverend Keller was to be in town today and wanted to co-officiate the ceremony by reading the lessons. Kat had been surprised Keely, a stickler for details, had readily given this change of plans her blessing. If it hadn't been for a brief introduction to the jovial Reverend Keller upon their arrival at the church, Kat would have never known about the additional clergyman until after she had escorted Keely up the aisle and taken her seat.

"Before we continue with the message, we have a special

presentation," Bob Keller announced from the center of the top step.

Keely and Nigel stood to one side and allowed Jonathan to cross from the chancel down the steps to the front pew where Kat sat.

Jonathan knelt in front of her and pulled a ring box from his jacket pocket. He opened the box and removed a sparkling diamond solitaire. Taking Kat's hand in his, he slipped the ring on her finger.

"Will you marry me, Kat?" he asked.

The world stood still. Kat forgot how to breathe. Jonathan's face grew flush.

"M-marry *me*?" she squeaked.

He smiled. "Yes, will you marry me?"

"Yes. Oh, yes, yes, I want to marry you, Jonathan," Kat cried, throwing her arms around his neck.

Jonathan hung on to her. "How about right now then?"

She pulled away, remembering where she was. "You mean right now? Here?"

He chuckled. "Well, we're in a church . . . and the Revered Keller is agreeable if you are."

Kat looked up and caught Kevin's wink and Keely's nod and Nigel's beaming smile. They had planned this all along, and she had been moping around so much she hadn't been sharp enough to catch the signs.

She smiled. "If my daughter and her new husband are agreeable, and the reverend is agreeable, then I'm agreeable."

Jonathan pulled Kat to her feet and escorted her to stand beside her son, daughter, and new son-in-law. Eli, Elizabeth, and Josh took their places beside Jonathan. Jonathan and Kat clasped hands and turned to face each other.

The Reverend Keller cleared his voice and began, "With your children as witnesses, do you Katrina Mary take Jonathan Edward to be your lawfully wedded husband? For richer or for poorer, in sickness and in health, to have and to hold from this day forth so help you God?"

Kat blinked back a tear and smiled. "I do."

"And do you Jonathan Edward take Katrina Mary to be your lawfully wedded wife? For richer or for poorer, in sickness and in health, to have and to hold from this day forth so help you God?"

Jonathan smiled, squeezing her hands. "I do."

"May I have the rings?"

Eli handed two simple bands of gold to the minister. Jonathan and Kat exchanged rings and received a blessing.

"Now by the power given to me by the state of Texas, I now pronounce both these couples man and wife."

He took a step back and announced, "Gentlemen—you may now kiss your brides."

Nigel drew Keely into a passionate embrace. Kat hesitated, struck by the gravity of their circumstances.

"What's wrong?" Jonathan whispered.

Kat glanced at the congregation from the corner of her eye. "Is it proper for a preacher's wife to be seen kissing the preacher in church?" she whispered back.

"On this occasion, it most certainly is," Jonathan assured her. He pulled her into his arms and kissed her firmly before letting her go. "After all, Bob's the one preachin' to the choir today."

EPILOGUE

"Merry Christmas, Aunt Mabel." Jonathan stepped down from the red and white poinsettia-covered altar area and approached the front pew to shake hands with his dear friend and cheerleader. He turned to Kat as she approached from the pew opposite and winked. "You've met my wife before, haven't you?"

"Don't be so silly." Kat playfully pushed her new husband to one side. She knelt and took the older woman's hand in hers. "We're anxiously awaiting your return to choir practice, Mabel. The alto section just isn't the same without you."

"'Bout time," the older woman said from one corner of her mouth. "'Bout time."

"It's about time you rejoined the choir?" Kat asked.

Sally slid over in the pew to interpret for her stroke-injured friend. "Sh-she means it was about time you two got married, I think."

"Really?" Jonathan raised his eyebrows. "You've been cheering for us for some time, eh, Aunt Mabel?"

Mabel nodded slightly and looked straight at Jonathan. "Saw the light. Kat—the one for you."

"The light? The one?" Kat wondered. "Whatever does she mean, Sally?"

Sally shrugged. "I-I don't know exactly. She sort of told me the other day how she had noticed how Pastor Jon had been gazing at our choir director and that it was only a matter of time before you two . . . well, you know."

Jonathan smiled. Did Mabel see the heavenly light ascend over Kat, too? No, it wasn't possible. She hadn't even attended church that Sunday. In fact, she had been absent from church quite a bit this past year due to illness. She had been at home recuperating from her hip operation first and then she had almost died on the operating table after her stroke. When could she have seen the light? Unless . . .

"I'm glad you made it back to tell us, Aunt Mabel." Jonathan kissed Kat on the cheek and squeezed the dear old lady's hand once more. "Get well so you can start singing with the choir again soon. I know I don't have to tell you how much I've always enjoyed preachin' to the choir."

ABOUT THE AUTHOR

The daughter of a minister and granddaughter of missionaries, Cynthianna grew up watching *Star Trek* and reading the science fiction classics, along with Harlequin romances by the bushel. Somewhere along the line she figured it was just as fun to write stories as it was to read them. She has published both contemporary and fantasy romantic-comedies (the *Loving Who* series) and writes SF/paranormal erotic-romance under the pen name of Celine Chatillon. The BloodDark series (co-written as Cindy A. Matthews with her husband, Adrian J. Matthews) is her latest Y.A. science fiction series.

Cindy and Adrian are frequent guests at science fiction cons where they serve as panelists on writing/publishing and *Doctor Who* topics. They enjoy chatting with friendly folk. Feel free to email or meet up with Cindy at an author's chat. You can find her online at the following websites:

Her author website: http://www.cynthianna.com

Her blog: http://www.cindyamatthews.com

Facebook: https://www.facebook.com/Cynthianna.CelineChatillon

Twitter: http://twitter.com/cynthianna3

Goodreads: http://www.goodreads.com/celinechatillon_cynthianna

Pinterest: http://pinterest.com/cindyamatthews